Cousin Jack

By

K.McKechnie

To Mike & Barbara

RB

REDGATE BOOKS

First published in Great Britain in 2019
by Redgate Books
Redgate House, Eastington
Devon EX17 6ND
www.redgatebooks.co.uk

A CIP catalogue record of this book is available
from the British Library

ISBN 978-0-9955686-2-4

Printed and bound in the UK
by Short Run Press, Exeter

DEDICATION

This novel is dedicated to the Cornish Jacks, their families and their descendents who abandoning their homeland, took their mining skills and their culture across the world.

GLOSSARY

ADIT – a level tunnel (usually driven into a hillside) in order to give access to a mine, and used for drainage or the hauling of broken ore.

AVENTURERS – usual term for mine investors in the 19thC.

ATTLE – waste rock.

BAL – a mine (from Cornish '*pal*' a shovel, and hence a digging').

BAL MAIDEN – a woman or girl employed at surface on a mine, generally in the dressing of ore.

BANKSMAN – a miner stationed at the top of the shaft responsible for dumping ore raised from underground

BEAM ENGINE – a type of steam-engine much favoured in Cornwall for use in pumping and winding on Cornish mines. The power from a large cylinder set vertically in an engine-house was transferred via a massive rocking beam or bob to the pumps in the shaft outside.

BLENDE – zinc sulphide.

BOB PLAT – the wooden platform on the outside of the engine house over the shaft pumping rods.

BORER – a steel rod with sharpened tip used for drilling shot holes in rock.

BRATTICE – timber partition work in a mine, e.g. dividing a shaft between ladderways and hoisting.

BUCKING – the breaking down of copper ore on an anvil to about 10mm in diameter by bal-maids using small hammers.

COLOUR – visible gold flakes (usually in a pan).

CORE – work shift as in 'day core' and 'night core'.

COST BOOK – the system of accounting by cost used on most Cornish mines and the books themselves in which these accounts were kept.

COSTEAN – a linear trench dug at surface to expose a vein or lode.

COUNT HOUSE – the mine office.

CROSS COURSE – a lode or vein which crosses the principle direction of mineralisation.

CROSSCUT – a tunnel or passage at right angles to the direction of a vein or lode.

DAMPER – Australian soda bread.

DIAL – a compass like surveying instrument used to map underground openings.

DRESSING – the concentration of copper or other ores contained in the rock excavated from a mine. Carried out on DRESSING FLOORS.

DRESSING FLOORS – an (often extensive) area at surface on a mine where the various processes of concentration of ore took place.

DRIVE – a tunnel excavated on the line of a LODE as the first stage of the development of a STOPE.

DRY or CHANGE HOUSE – the building within which miners changed their clothes before and after going underground. Some were heated by steam pipes connected to the engine boilers.

DUDS – waste rock.

END – a working place underground.

ENGINE HOUSE – a building designed to contain the steam engine on a mine or other works. When forming part of the framework of a beam engine, these were particularly strongly constructed.

FATHOM – six feet.

GARIBALDI – a lady's tight fitting jacket favoured by Bal Maidens on feast days.

GIBBER PLAIN – stone desert (South Australia).

GOLD CRADLE – a portable wooden box lined with carpet or sacking and set on rockers for washing gold from soil, sand and gravel. Also known as a "rocking box".

GOOK – a Bal Maiden's bonnet.

GRASS – the surface at a mine as in 'they came to grass'.

HEADFRAME – the tall construction set over a winding shaft which carried the sheave wheels over which the winding ropes ran.

HORSE WHIM – a winch with power supplied by a horse walking around a circular platform applied to an overhead winding drum.

HUMPY – a simple outback shelter commonly made of bent over branches by aborigines and other Australian bush dwellers.

KILLAS – shale.

KIBBLE – a large, strongly-constructed, egg-shaped, iron container used for ore and rock haulage.

LEVEL – a working level underground e.g. '60 fathom level' – the horizontal workings 60 fathoms from surface.

LODE – a linear area of mineralisation underground. Generally vertical or near-vertical, and often extending for considerable distances along its strike.

MALLEE – a species of eucalypt that forms scrublands in dry areas of Australia.

MULGA – a widespread hardy Australian native plant.

MUNDIC – arsenic sulphide. Also mispickel and arsenopyrite.

PARE – two to four miners working as a team.

RAISE – a shaft driven upwards between two or more underground levels.

SALTBUSH – a small, spreading grey-green, Australian shrub that withstands saline soils

SETT – the legal boundary within which a mine could extract minerals.

SETT – one of the components of timber framing of an adit where it ran through loose ground.

SHAFT – a vertical or near vertical tunnel sunk to give access to the extractive areas of a mine.

SLICKENSIDES – polished and striated rock face resulting from movement on a fault.

SOLLAR – a platform set at regular intervals between ladders in a shaft.

SPALLING – the breaking of large rocks at surface with long-handled hammers.

STAMP MILL – a machine for crushing ore.

STOPE – an excavated area produced during the extraction of ore-bearing rock. Often narrow, deep and elongated, reflecting the former position of the lode.

STURT – a rich seam of ore (Australia).

TAILINGS – the waste, sand and slime from a mine dressing floor, not containing workable quantities of mineral.

TALLOW – a candle usually made of animal fat.

TRAM – to transport underground (ususally on rails).

TRIBUTE – the system of payment whereby groups of miners (pares) bid against one another for contracts to work sections of the mine for a percentage of the value of the ore raised from that area. Hence 'tributer'.

TUTWORK – a system of payment whereby groups of miners contracted to work on a 'payment by results' system at previously-agreed rates, usually for shaft sinking or driving levels. Hence 'tutworker'.

WHEAL – a mine.

WHIM – the winding gear used for hauling from a shaft consisting of a power source and a winding drum. See HORSE-WHIM.

WINZE – an inclined shaft joining two or more underground levels.

I

FLINDERS

 'YOU KNOW THOMAS, I HAD NEVER THOUGHT TO BE so far from home.'

'Would home be Wallaroo or Penpillick, Henry?'

'Both I reckon. But Penpillick seems beyond my ken these days. Be ten years come June.'

Thomas Pascoe nods, staring south the way they have come. They followed the eastern foot of the mountain range panning the sand and gravel of every desiccated riverbed and paltry stream that crossed their path. They found colours north of Quorn and again in the riverbank at Kanyaka but neither show amounted to more than a hint of glitter in the bottom of the pan. Now they stand a thousand feet above the desert plain that stretches westward way beyond their vision. At dawn they left the horses in the camp below and climbed, following the merest trace of a trail – climbing through boulder strewn thorn-scrub and scrabbling up the rocky slopes. It has taken them two hours of hard and sweaty going. Why they have climbed Thomas Pascoe does not know. There is no gold in these hills, at least that's how it seems after all these months of prospecting. Perhaps from here he will see a future in this dry and desperate land. Should they return to the station north of Wallaroo where Maisie and the children and ten thousand head of sheep wait for his return?

They went south first off and looked for copper in the gentle hills of Adelaide, but so many had been before and they were green in those days and were at best late to every rush which mostly turned to nothing after all. And gold it seemed was all the talk in the outback bars, of more discoveries in far away Victoria, so why not here where none but the blackfellas have been before? In exchange for a mutton dinner and a glass of beer, a half-starved weather-beaten prospector showed them quartz stones tipped from a leather pouch, glassy grey and white, veined through with mica specks.

'Here, and here and here,' he said pointing with a filthy fingernail, 'Here is gold. You see it boys?'

And they stared and Thomas held the stones up to the light and yes he could see it – the faintest tracery of yellow – gold deep in the cracks and crevices.

'Where is this from?' he asked.

'Ah that would be telling, mate.'

Thomas looked at Henry across the table and said, 'I'll pay you if you show us.'

'Can't show you. Can't walk that far, got snake bit – look,' and he drew up a greasy trouser leg and showed them a suppurating sore above his ankle. 'Need a quid or two for the quack.'

'How much?'

'Ten?'

'Ten quid for the doctor?'

'Gotta live, boys. I'll draw a map for youse.'

And greenhorns that they were, they were taken in for there was no doubt that this lean leather strip of a man knew more than they. Thomas took his purse from deep within his jacket and counted out five gold sovereigns. He slapped them on the table but held his hand down. 'Make this map then,'

'Outside. I'll draw it for you.'

So they went out in blistering sunlight and with the sole of his boot the prospector smoothed a patch in the red dust of the roadway. Bending down he traced a sinuous line with his forefinger.

'This here's the hills they call the Flinders,' he said, 'and this to the west is the great salt lake. Here, close to the hills is Henry Spiers's grog shop. Take water there or grog, whatever's to yer taste and walk north for just a day. You'll find a dry creek running west out of the hills. I found gold there, mates. I did you know. That's where I found this gold.' He looked up at them holding out his hand.

'I believe you, though I don't know why I should,' Thomas said and gave the man five sovereigns.

Standing here high above that very creek, he still holds the dirt map in his mind's eye. There is the creek and stretching to the horizon, the blinding white of the great salt lake is just as it was mapped. But he knows he has been duped. He does not regret the sovereigns lost – it is the weeks, the months of weary riding and walking, the heat, the thirst and the back-breaking work of sifting sand and gravel, swirling precious water in the pan and finding nothing, nothing. There is no gold. He heaves a sigh.

Henry Hopeful Down takes his hat off and scratches his head. 'Well Thomas, what now? Which way? Should we go on?'

Thomas looks up at the big man. The pockmarked face is deeply tanned and salt rings mark the sweat-stained shirt. His beard is bleached to sandy brown.

'I think not, Henry. Fossicking like this is a mug's game and I do believe we have been mugs. It's homeward bound for us. It will take but a week or so if we ride direct.'

'I'll not be sorry to be back in Wallaroo, sheep or no sheep.'

The fact is neither man has taken to sheep farming. It started well enough. With funds from home Thomas bought a pastoral lease some miles north of Wallaroo but within easy reach of town. They cleared the mallee scrub with fire and axes and sheer hard labour and stocked twelve thousand acres with sheep, some bought from neighbours, some driven up from Adelaide. They took on a local stockman who taught them all he knew and in the third year they began to make a profit. But then came drought. The waterholes and wells dried up and they slaughtered half their flock for mutton, for which there was no market. Riding the bone-dry land, Thomas Pascoe tried and failed to banish images of lush green meadows, shadowed woods and clear-running rivers. That was home – the home to which he was forbidden to return. So he squared his shoulders, began again when the rains came back and built a homestead where Maisie bore him children – two boys and a little girl. Henry too found comfort in a wife, Jane Cottrel, the teacher Thomas hired to educate his children.

But fed up with flies and daggy ends, the two men could not stay away from mining and the miners' talk in the bars of Moonta and Wallaroo. Mining was in their Cornish blood, these Cousin Jacks and Thomas Pascoe's fame had followed him – here was the boy who beat the hangman's noose and found the richest copper lode in all of Cornwall.

So, seduced by tales of untold riches, of gold and copper in distant hills, they found a manager for the station, packed their saddlebags and roamed the desiccated back lands for half a year. But now they know it was all to no avail. And Henry worried quietly to himself about his wife; he knew she must be lonely. She'd not adapted well to station life and for reasons Henry did not understand, she bore no children.

Thomas shoulders his Martini- Henry rifle. 'Come on then.' They slip and slide down the steep and scree-strewn slopes and an hour later finds them at their camp site. But they are not alone. A band of blacks stands silent by the ashes of their fire. They hold spears and throwing sticks and are naked but for breech clouts. One taller, older than the rest, sports a great white beard that covers half his chest. He points at them and speaks. Both white men know some words of the Narungga people who come and go at Wallaroo, but this language is quite other.

Thomas shakes his head and points to the horses, mimes mounting, points south and says, "Walla Waroo. We go.'

The blacks look at each other, grin and nod and the elder speaks again and gestures to the hills and to himself.

Thomas nods. 'I think he tells us this is their land,'

'I think you're right. Best we mount up and go.'

Their horses are tethered in the meagre shade of a gnarled old gum tree, saddles, pots and pans and bedrolls piled beside them. The half-eaten remnants of a wombat Thomas shot the night before hangs fly-covered from a branch. This they leave. They load the horses, mount up and nodding to the little band, head south without a backward glance.

'They did not steal our gear,' Henry says.

'And we did not steal their land.'

II

MARY O'MALLEY

WAKENED BY THE TWITTER OF MARTINS NESTING under the eaves, Grace Clymo chases the fading memory of a dream, a vivid dream of loss, a dream of Thomas, her son so far away. Perhaps today there will be a letter. She watches the dust motes drifting downwards in a shaft of sunlight. It is summer. She woke earlier, just before sunrise, listening for a while to the dawn chorus then drifted back to sleep lulled by the endless background thump of the beam engine down at the mine. She listens now to the clatter of the cook in the kitchen below. She is raking out the coals in the range, a job Grace did herself in their miners' cottage before John Pascoe died. Her second husband lies still beside her. She raises herself on an elbow and studies the gaunt face. How he has aged. His once dark hair is grey. Deeply etched lines frame the half-opened mouth and his eyes are dark-shadowed in their sockets. She must wake him now or he will sleep on. She thinks back to those first years of their marriage when she herself was the only reason that he might stay abed of a morning and not be down his precious mine. It is not that he is old, though fifty is a good age for a Cornish miner. But Captain Mathew Clymo has neither swung a hammer nor driven steel for twenty years or more. Sure, every morning without fail he still goes down the mine and checks on machinery and men and with a practised eye judges his copper ore as rich or poor, then comes up to grass for croust. By then he is exhausted and neither he nor she know why. Doctor Couch the bal surgeon, called to stitch a miner's scalp torn open in a rock fall, listened to Mathew's back and chest, pursed his lips, shook his head and prescribed a tonic, which Mathew says does no damn good at all. His eyes move beneath the lids, his body twitches and the faintest groan escapes his lips.

She kisses his forehead. 'Wake up Mathew, wake up.'

His eyes blink open, stare at her and then he says, 'I was dreaming, dreaming.'

15

'Of what, my love?'

'Damned Scoble – the day he died. I saw the knife but Thomas had it in his hand. He held it at my throat and Scoble laughed.'

'Shush now. That's so long ago.' She strokes his forehead. 'Come, let's get up, tis past time.'

He sighs and swings his legs out of the bed and stands. His nightgown hangs loosely from his shoulders. He bends and rubs his belly then says, ' I have the damned gut pain again, Grace. Right here.'

She shakes her head. 'Oh Mathew lover, why not stay home today?'

'Grace, you know I must go down every day. It is my mine and the men expect it. If I do not, who else will make sure that they are not up to some trickery or other?'

Grace sighs and shakes her head. 'As you will, if you must. Shall I ask Mary to make you porridge then? You said it helps.'

'I don't know. Perhaps it does. It's pap enough and goes down easy.' He goes out to the bathroom.

Grace dresses quickly and hurries down the stairs and into the kitchen. 'Good morning, Mary. The master wants porridge again for breakfast.'

Mary O'Malley looks up from the range. 'Good morning to ye, ma'am. Porridge it will be. And yourself ma'am? Cheese and bread and meat or shall I cook ye an egg? And will ye eat later when Miss Emily is down or now with the Master?'

Grace smiles. 'I'll eat later, Mary and I'd like an egg.' The girl has been with them for some months now but Grace is still not accustomed to her servant's lilting speech. It makes her smile. Driven by hunger and searching for work, many Irish people have come to Cornwall's mining towns and villages and Penpillick is no exception. Mary knocked at the door on a grim winter's eve asking for work as cook.

'Have you cooked before?' Grace asked.

'Indeed I have ma'am – in the house of Mr Lethbridge in Bodmin.'

'Have you a letter?'

'No ma'am but I will get one shortly. I'm a tidy cook ma'am. You'll not regret it. I don't ask for much – sixpence a day and a roof over me head.'

Grace studied the girl. She was thin to the point of emaciation, yet she had a pretty face with straight red hair and freckles. And Grace too had worked for a pittance in her time – swinging a hammer and breaking rock when she was this girl's age and a working bal maiden. She was filled with pity. 'Wait here,' she said and went back into the parlour.

'Mathew, there's an Irish girl looking for work. Says she's a cook. I've half a mind to take her on. I've been lookin' for help ever since Jenny left.'

Her husband looked up from his fireside chair, stretched and yawned. 'You do what you think's best, lover,' he said and slumped back and closed his eyes.

'Will you cook and clean?' Grace asked returning to the front door.

The girl cocked her head. 'For how many, ma'am, might I ask?'

'There's me, my husband and my daughter Emily – so three most times. Now and then my son comes home from London town and stays a day or two.

'I'll do it, ma'am, sure I will. And I thank you.' She bobbed a slight curtsey.

'Well you come in out of the cold then, my dear. Is that all your things?'

The girl held a faded cloth bag in one hand. 'Yes ma'am, indeed it is.'

So Mary O' Malley moved into an attic room in the big house at Penpillick and became part of the Clymo household.

Mathew Clymo sprinkles sugar on his steaming porridge and covers that with cream. He looks up at Mary as she pours him a cup of tea. 'Your mother teach you to make this?' He gestures with his spoon.

'No, sir. I never knew her. It was me auntie in Omagh who brought me up.'

'And your father?'

'He died too, sir . Both of 'em in the famine, sir.'

'I'm sorry.'

'No need to be sorry, sir. Me auntie was kind enough.'

'Did she bring you to Cornwall?'

'No, sir. She died too, two years back so I came on me own. I would've starved in Omagh, sure I would.'

Mathew nods and spoons up his porridge.

'May I go now, sir?'

'Of course.'

He watches as she leaves the room. What is it about this girl that bothers him? She is a Catholic of course like all the Irish who have come seeking work in Cornwall's mines. He has many Irish miners now, and their religion bothers him not one jot. But there is something naggingly familiar about Mary O'Malley. He shakes his head. He is imagining things.

He turns his mind to the day before him. Firstly he'll visit the Pascoe lode. It's thinned downwards to the 160 fathom level and all but disappeared above the 90. But it yielded rich pickings until the copper price collapsed – damn those Americans, north and south, and bloody Australia too. What with their outlandish names – Burra Burra and Moonta and ten times as rich as Wheal Emma, or so Thomas wrote from Wallaroo. Wallaroo? Between them all they've sent the Cornish copper mines to the knackers yard. And what's worse it's Cornish miners out there digging up riches for all the foreigners. He could spit. But still his bank account and those of the adventurers grew fat on his stepson's find. He has spent thousands on improvements to his mine – a second more powerful beam engine that not only drains the mine to deeper levels but powers a stamp mill and finally a ventilation shaft and new adits just to improve the air. Yes, he has done his best. But now he is tired and his belly hurts.

Of course, the mine has only survived thanks to the sale of arsenic, much of which he doesn't even have to mine – mundic has lain there on the dump discarded all these years. It was Mr William Morris sat next to him at a counthouse dinner five years back who began it all.

'Captain Clymo,' he said, 'Some years ago I took some pretty samples home from here – mispickel it was, or mundic as I think you call it. You know it is arsenical?'

'Of course and most poisonous. They say that is why our miners'

18

hoggans have a crimpled crust – as a handle to be discarded and not eaten.

'Quite, quite. But I do not propose to eat your mundic, my dear Captain. What I want to know is how much of it is there, here at Wheal Emma?'

'Why, mountains of it, sir, positive mountains. We separate it from the copper ore and dump it, or leave it in the ground when we can. Many stopes are left lined with mundic for it is of no use to us at all.'

'Now that is where you are wrong, sir, quite wrong.' Morris forked a large slice of roast goose into his mouth followed by a gulp of claret.

'I am agog, sir. What use have you for mundic?'

'My dear Captain, I will tell you.' He wiped his beard with his napkin and belched. 'Scheele's Green, sir, Scheele's Green.'

'I am none the wiser, Mr Morris. Would that be a place in London?'

'Hah hah, Captain. Very droll. No, no indeed.' He leaned close to Mathew's ear. 'Scheele's Green, my dear Captain, is a most desirable green pigment. All my artist friends use it in their work and I wish to use it in my wallpaper manufactory. But it is most expensive being mostly imported from Germany. Now if we were to produce arsenic here at Cornish Consols we could transform it into the pigment at my works in London. It is a simple process I believe and would be highly profitable.'

'What is the price of arsenic then?'

'One hundred and fifty pounds per ton at present, so I am told. That is higher than the price of copper is it not?'

'It is, indeed it is. Well, Mr Morris, I thank you. You have given me food for thought. You may be certain that I will look into the matter and perhaps have an answer for you before our next counthouse dinner.'

Mathew heard that Geevor mine roasted tin ore mixed with mundic and thus made both tin and arsenic for sale. He took two days to ride down there and watched as women and boys raked arsenical soot from smoking flues, their heads entirely wrapped in cloths to escape the poisoned air. There must be a better way he thought. Once home he fetched an engineer from Lancashire who built a great rotating furnace and a labyrinth of tunnels where trapped gases from the roasted ore dropped white crystal arsenic like slowly falling snow on brick-lined walls and floors. Finally they built a monstrous chimney stack that none might be affected by the fumes.

He spoons up the last of his porridge, gulps down his tea and nods to himself. Yes, as always, he will spend the morning underground but this afternoon he will visit the arsenic works. He will make sure that all is as it should be, that all the workers wear the masks, the ear plugs and wrap their feet in sacks as Doctor Couch has said they must.

III

CHARITY

'"*ONCE THERE WAS A GENTLEMAN WHO MARRIED FOR a second wife the . . . the proudest and most . . . most. . .*" I'm sorry, Emily dear, what is this word here? How . . haw . . haff? I have not seen it before.' Grace stops her index finger under the offending word and slides the chapbook to her daughter who sits beside her at the parlour table.

'Let me see. Yes, "haughty". The word is "haughty", Mother.'

Grace continues, '"*most haughty woman that was ever seen. She had by a former husband two daughters of her own hu. . . humour who were exactly like her in all things.*".

Emily has been teaching her mother to read and write for almost a year now and Grace is reading the story of Cinderella from the reading primer that Emily used as a child.

Grace looks up. 'Do you think that either of my sons or even you, my dear, is exactly like me in all things?'

'Well, I believe I am not, Mother. James, perhaps a little in looks and Thomas how should I know? I was but six when he sailed away.'

Grace is silent for some minutes.

'Shall we continue reading, Mother?'

Grace shakes her head then wipes a tear from her cheek. 'I miss him so,' she says, 'Even after all this time.'

'Perhaps he will come back.'

'He has made a life out there. Ten thousand sheep he wrote, Emily. Imagine that. More sheep than in the whole of Cornwall I should think. He is a rich man. Why would he come back here? Besides he never really accepted Mathew as a father.'

'I did and so did James. Why not he?'

'You were very young and he loved his own father so.'

'I scarce remember him. I have a picture in my head of him in the bath beside the fire and you scrubbing his back.'

'I did that for him every day after he come up to grass.'

'Were we poor then, Mother?'

'No. For mining folk we were rich even then.'

'But not as rich as we are now?'

'No, my dear – much good it does us. We have no need for more money yet your father works himself to death down his precious mine. Just for the love of it, I suppose.' She shakes her head. 'Enough of this. Enough of reading too.' She goes to the window. 'Look the sun is shining. Let us walk down through the village. We will call on Jenny Tuttle.'

They put on cloaks and bonnets, take up their parasols and walk through the little garden and out of the wicket gate that separates the big house from the road between the village and the mine. They take no note of the coal smoke drifting from the engine house on the summer wind or the steady thump of the beam engine. Both are a constant in their lives. Down through Penpillick they walk, parasols held aloft, past the first row of miners' cottages and past the shuttered Bedford Arms. They nod to a group of miners' wives gossiping at the village pump who watch them pass.

'Fine lady now Grace Clymo, ain't she just?' a woman says. 'And to think ten year ago she were but a bal maiden breakin' rock.'

'She's not forgotten. You knows that.'

'What, you talkin' of her charity? We wouldn't need none o' that if our men got proper pay.'

'Ain't Grace Clymo sets the pay.'

'No it aint't but she grows rich off our men's labour down her husband's cursed mine.'

'They talk about us, mother,' Emily says.

'Yes, they do,' Grace says. 'Take no notice. It does not matter.' But it does. Grace well knows they envy her wealth and status. Mathew Clymo, Captain of Wheal Emma, is lord and master of Penpillick, his word is law and governs all their lives. Each month on setting day it is his decision how much the mine will pay for every pound of copper raised and every ton of rock dug out. And little by little, month by month the miners' pay goes down and down. Not even the riches of the Pascoe Lode have saved Wheal Emma from the falling copper price. It takes the sale of arsenic and ever lower wages to keep the mine afloat. At least that's what her husband says.

They knock at Jenny Tuttle's open cottage door.

'Hello my dears, come in, come in. A fine morning to come a visitin'. My and ain't you just the picture, Miss Emily, parasol an' all.'

Jenny is Grace's lifelong friend. As young women they worked side by side, bal maidens breaking rock. Then together served as cooks and cleaners in the counthouse until Grace up and married Mathew Clymo. That was the fist chink of the rift between them that grows ever wider, even though Jenny's daughter Maisie is wife to her Thomas in faraway Australia. Grace knows that Jenny blames her husband for Lewis Tuttle's death. He was a miner until, choking with the black lung, he could no longer climb the endless ladder ways from mine to grass. So Mathew put him to work in the arsenic flues scraping the white powder from the walls and floors and loading it in barrels. At that he lasted barely half a year before taking to his bed, a wreck of a man at forty-two. They called Dr. Couch who stood at Lewis Tuttle's bedside, measured his pulse with his elegant fingers then listened to the wheezing chest. He turned the man's calloused palm towards the light and bent to study it then turned it over and stroked the nails. With a sigh he dropped the hand.

'How long were you at the arsenic works, Lewis?' he asked.

'Six month, mebbe less,' Lewis replied, his voice little more than a feeble croak. Breath wheezing in and out, Lewis Tuttle braced himself then whispered, 'How long I got, Doctor?'

'Not long I'm afraid, not long.' The doctor continued to look down at the dying man.

'Us miners. . .us miners.' A fit of coughing racked the wasted body. 'Us miners don't live long do us, Doctor?'

The doctor shook his head, and patted the man's shoulder. 'No Lewis, no you don't.'

Downstairs he spoke to Jenny Tuttle. 'I'm afraid there is nothing I can do, Jenny. Perhaps if he hadn't been put to work on the arsenic when he stopped with mining he might have lasted yet a while.'

''Twas Mathew Clymo put him there, damn and blast him. Should've let 'un be. We could've managed.'

The doctor nodded. 'I'm sure you could. I'm sorry, Jenny, but I must be on my way. I will not charge you for this visit.'

A week later Lewis Tuttle died.

At Grace's request Mathew Clymo granted the widow a lifetime tenancy of her cottage and a tiny pension – enough to feed herself and family but no more. Grace thought this generous to a degree for it was not the norm – the poorhouse was the fate of many miners' wives and families when the breadwinner went to his early grave. For this she should be grateful, but Grace knew that she was not. Catching Jenny now and then in sideways glances at her finery, her polished button boots and her daughter's latest hat, Grace would sense the jealousy of her closest friend.

And so it is today as they sit silently in her cottage, the three of them, drinking tea as weak as waste water from the mine.

Grace puts down her cup and breaks the silence. 'No letter from Australia then?'

Jenny shakes her head. 'Not since the last, three months past when my Maisie wrote that Thomas was gone away. Gone to look for gold she said and left her and the children with just the sheep for company. But you read that one already. You've not heard neither then?'

'No. If I had you know I would have brung the letter to read to you. I do wish they'd never gone.'

'Your boy would be locked up down in Bodmin if he'd not run.'

'That's as maybe. But he could come back now. Mathew says that prosecutor's dead and gone three year ago. It's all forgot. If he were here my Mathew. . . .' Grace was about to say that her husband would not have to work and perhaps recover from whatever it is that ails him. But remembering Lewis Tuttle's death, she bites her tongue.

'If pigs could fly,' Jenny Tuttle says.

They fall into silence once again until Emily speaks up, 'Mother it is time to go. We must tell Mary what to cook for lunch.'

Grace nods getting to her feet. 'Goodbye, Jenny and thank you for the tea.'

They bob the slightest curtsies and leave the dim-lit cottage.

They walk up the hill in the summer sun, Emily's hand on her mother's arm. 'Mother, why don't we write again, tell Thomas he is needed here, that Papa is really sick and can no longer run the mine? That might bring him back.'

'Your father will not beg nor will he lie.'

'But mother, it's no lie that he is sick. Everyone knows. I heard the miners outside the Bedford Arms talking of it just last week. Thomas should come back. We must write him.'

'I don't know. Your father is too proud. He would be angry. He won't even let me call the doctor now.'

'But, mother, if he just rested perhaps he would recover. Besides we need not tell him we have written. I can write the letter for you.'

Grace sighs. 'Mebbe you're right my dear. I will think about it. Certainly if my Mathew worsens we will write to Thomas and beg him to return. But say nothing to your father. He must not know.'

IV

FATHOMS DOWN

MATHEW CLYMO STANDS ATOP THE RUBBLE PILE, HEAD back studying the rock in the roof of the tunnel. 'Hold that damn tallow closer, man,' he grumbles to the miner stood beside him.

'She'm gone Capun, clear gone. More light ain't going to bring her back,'

Mathew snorts. 'I maybe getting old, Caleb Chapman but I ain't blind nor am I stupid yet.' This is what he has dreaded. This is what keeps him awake at nights, this and his aching guts – the Pascoe Lode has disappeared; they've mined it out, up, down and along the strike. In truth, it never had much length to it but it was wide and high. From the 120 fathom level the lode soared upwards for near fifty fathom, blossoming out like a fat candle flame, then thinning until here, sixty fathoms from the surface, it has finally flickered out. Downwards too it went, a massive wen of shining copper ore until cut clean off by a great flat fault that brought it up against the killas. And there the ground was bad, soft as baby shit, all slickensided and torn about. Every foot they drove needed timber and yet more timber and water spurted from the walls, from the back and from out between the lagging boards. The men complained it was too dangerous. If they broke into water next blast or the next but one, they'd drown like rats. Knowing they were right, he abandoned working on that level, shoring up the faces and dropping down the back to block off any access. But the lode is down there somewhere, he knows it is. He's spent a fortune on surveyors making maps but they just show what he already knows – they've lost the Pascoe Lode.

'Reckon Tom Pascoe'd find her if she'm anywhere,' Caleb Chapman said.

'Not from Australia he won't.'

'Why not bring 'im back?'

Why not indeed? If he would come of course. It's not the first time the thought has crossed his mind. If Tom Pascoe when just a boy found

26

more copper than any other miner down Wheal Emma, who knows what he could he do as a full grown man? But perhaps he's lost the knack after so many years of farming sheep. Nonetheless, maybe he should write a letter. He writes to Thomas once a year with all Wheal Emma's news but that letter's not due for six months or more. He's never thought to ask for help but now perhaps he should.

'Shall us quit this face then Capun, seeing as there ain't nothin' here?' Caleb stares at him from deep-set eyes and strokes his massive beard.

'Give her one more round, Caleb, just in case. And if she don't turn kindly, then we'll quit.'

Caleb shakes his head and calls his mates back to the face and hammers ring on steel as Mathew Clymo walks slowly, head bent, back down the dark and twisting drive towards the shaft. He feels weighed down – the weight of the mine, the weight of all these men, their wives, their children, the very future of Wheal Emma and Penpillick, all rest upon his shoulders. Well, he's not done yet. They still have the old North Lode where he has an Irish gang on tutwork . They drive a tunnel at a ferocious pace to undercut the lode at 330 fathoms guided by the eye of old Jakeh James. He'll go there now and see what they have found. Though it's a long old walk and an even longer downward climb to reach them. He won't think now of the endless climb back up to grass.

Passing the adit they drove out through the hillside to bring in air and drain the upper levels, he stops and takes a deep breath in through his nose. There it is, hanging on the breeze from the tunnel's mouth – the faintest scent of woodland vegetation. How strange that is, here deep in his mine. He listens, head cocked, not moving – the plink of dripping water, his own laboured breath and from the way that he has come, a distant shout and then once more the ring of steel on steel. He turns away and trudges on. At the shaft he stops before descending, looks up at the serried ladder ways stretching into darkness, then down where he must go. For some minutes he simply stands there on the wooden sollar, watching the plunge and lift of the massive pump rods. It is a comfort to him to know that far above, the boilers are well fed with coal, his fine new engine is lovingly greased and oiled by the engineman, and that all this water showering down the shaft, soaking him even as he stands, will be sucked from the deepest depths of Wheal Emma, and driven out of the mine, out of his mine, to wend its way to the river and finally the sea. Yes, it has been worth it, all the money he has spent. But he can afford to spend no more.

He goes down, ladder after ladder after ladder. He descends without thought, settling into the familiar rhythm, the rungs beneath his calloused hands, friends to him. How many times has it been, day after day, week after week, year after year? But he loves this. It is his life; he would have no other. Finally, his searching boot lands on solid rock. He is at 330 fathoms, near two thousand feet beneath the ground, Wheal Emma's deepest level. Here in these depths is where he belongs.

It is hot and he unbuttons his flannel shirt. The air is still and stinks, not quite foul enough to douse his candle but bad enough. But he is used to it and shrugs and walks down the drive stepping on the rough laid sleepers between the rails without a thought as if it were a high road across the moor, although the back is too low for him to stand full stretch. But this too he is used to and does not care. The more rock they move that is not copper ore the less money he will make. He passes a tiny alcove in the wall used as a latrine and there he holds his breath. But he strides on now, keen to see new rock, a new face and who knows, a new discovery. Now he can hear them, shouting, calling, a man singing in a language he does not understand, the clattering of rock and beneath it all the ring of hammered steel. At first there is a glimmer far down the drive, the flickering of candles, shadows in the dark. He almost trots now still bent low and anxious to see what might be seen. Who knows, today might be the day. Then he is upon them. Here they are, Jakeh James, thin as a whippet, cheek black-scarred by an errant powder blast, levering down a slab of rock from off the back with a six foot pry bar and behind him four Irish shovelling duds into a kibble as if their lives depended on it. Two pares are drilling at the face, two more breaking great rafts of rock with hammers. And the buggers sing and shout and laugh as they work.

These Irish, driven from their homeland by famine, God, they are good workers. He has eight gangs of them all on tutwork – drilling,

28

blasting, driving drives, raising raises and sinking shafts. They are a strange addition to the hamlets around Penpillick, talking among themselves in their own language, these men from Galway, Connemara, Tipperary and County Clare, drinking their dark porter and fighting drunk on paydays. Of course his local miners grumble and complain, men who have spent their working lives down Wheal Emma, working for him man and boy for twenty years and more. "Bloody bog-trotters" they call the Irish and other epithets much worse. But their real gripe is that with Irish labour in plentiful supply and their willingness to work, Mathew has driven wages down to keep his mine in profit.

'Morning to you Jakeh. How goes it, boy?' He has to shout.

Skinny Jakeh James turns, leans on his well worn pry bar, one leg curled around it. 'Morning Capun. She ain't too bad I'm thinking – mayhap turnin' kindly. Come look at this.' He puts thumb and forefinger to his mouth and lets out a piercing whistle.

The Irish pause their labours, turn to him. Seeing Mathew Clymo, they put forefinger to the brims of mine hats and there is a chorus of 'Mornin' to yer sorr, morning' to yer.' All of them are naked to the waist, their sweat glistening in the candlelight.

He nods. 'Morning boys. So what have we, Jakeh?'

'Next round we'll cut the lode for certain, Capun. Come see.' They go to the face where the two teams of drillers stand back. Jakeh takes his hat off and holds its wavering candle close against to the rock. 'Look Capun, just here and here.'

In the face there are a wisps of quartz in the killas, and within it the yellow glint of pyrites. Mathew nods and his heart lifts. Indeed here it is. He looks closer, his nose almost touching the rock. 'Not just pyrites, Jakeh but mundic and a little copper too. You can send this up as ore. You've hit the lode, by God, you have. Lord save us.'

Jakeh grins at him and puts his hat back on. 'Reckon I'll bid this pitch come settin' day, Capun. Take these two paddies, as my pare. Work like dogs, they do. '

'You do that Jakeh. You do that. And I'll tell Kit Robin he can dial

29

this end tonight. We need to know zackly where we are.' Kit Robin is Wheal Emma's Night Captain and one of his duties is to survey new mine workings. 'I'll be down to see tomorrow. Good day to you.'

Mathew heads back off down the drive with something of a spring in his step. Perhaps their luck is turning. Now all he needs is an increase in the copper price and he'll buy two of those new-fangled Holman drill machines. He's heard they can drill a foot in two minutes – hard to credit but if it's true they'd pay their cost in manpower in no time at all. Reaching the shaft station he looks upward, takes a breath and starts to climb. On the 120 fathom sollar he stops, chest heaving hands, upon his knees. Then he vomits. 'Lord Christ,' he groans. Even in the candlelight he can see blood streaks in the curdled mess between his feet. He scrapes it off the platform with his boot, happy to see the filth blending with the falling water of the shaft – a constant rain it is, seeping out of the rocks and draining from the upper levels of the mine. Another deep breath and he starts to climb once more. At long last, he emerges into smoky sunlight, nods to the banksman and oblivious to the thump and hiss of the beam engine and the rattling whine of the winding gear, walks slowly to the counthouse. Pausing below the door he takes a breath then climbs the four steps up and pushes open the door. He loves this counthouse, his counthouse, its timber floor near white with years of holystoning, the three clerks high on their writing stools, quills in hand filling figures in the great production ledgers, the long table at which top-hatted William George sits, purser for ten years now and Mathew's confidant.

'Mornin Capun Clymo. How was it down there today?'

'Good morning Bill, and a good morning it is indeed. Jakeh James has cut the North Lode on the 330.'

'Lord be praised, Capun, Lord be praised.' William grins and claps his hands together and wrings them before his chest. 'We sorely need more copper brought to grass. Mundic's all very well but the price of arsenic is falling too.'

'I know that Bill. I know it.'

'You look exhausted, Capun.'

Mathew shrugs, unknots the red kerchief from around his neck and swabs his face. 'It's hotter than Hades down there and it's a tidy climb back up. But it's got to be done, Bill. If the miners think I'm not about, they'll be stealing us blind and that we can't afford.'

William George removes his hat and lays it on the table. He looks up at Mathew? 'And are you to the arsenic works today, Capun?'

'Indeed I am, just as soon as I have had my croust. Why do you ask?'

William glances at the clerks then mutters, 'Just thought you might need fresher air after a morning underground, Capun. Dr Couch says them fumes is mortal bad for health.'

'Couch is a maundering old woman. Mr William Morris himself says arsenic ain't that poisonous and he should know, he puts in his damn wallpaper. That's good enough for me' Mathew gestures up at the portraits on the wall where both old William Morris, the founder of his mine and his son stare down.

'I hope you're right, Capun, I just hope you're right.

V

NIGHT CAPTAIN

KIT ROBIN IS A HANDSOME MAN; HE KNOWS IT AND LIKE many handsome men is vain. Even underground he dresses carefully. Not for him the stinking clothes the miners wear – their filthy breeches stained red with mud, their verminous and sweaty shirts and boots that fill the dry with the stench of unwashed feet. No, Capun Kit wears high leather boots proofed with beeswax, dark serge trousers tucked in to avoid the mud and water, a thick cotton shirt and to top it all a fine black fustian jacket. His miners' hat is cut from the thickest ox hide and even his candle is embedded in the clay just so.

'Hold that tallow still, boy,' he yells down 320 fathom drive and kneels to bring his eye to the sighting slot in his miner's dial. God how he hates this task but bloody Clymo has made surveying the Night Captain's job and he is Night Captain – he Kit Robin once a captain at the mighty Dolcoath Mine reduced to this. He snorts. He should have left when that bugger Scoble who first appointed him was killed. But hard times hit the mines when the price of copper crashed and there was no other work. And Clymo, asserting that the mine was his took over and demoted him to this. It wasn't of course, nor is it now. William Scoble died intestate and no relatives were ever found. So his Cornish Consols stock remains enmeshed in lawyers' wrangling leaving Clymo and his cronies in control. Still, life has its compensations – Mary O' Malley for one. He first met her one night in Bodmin where she was working as a cook and suggested she should try for a place in the Clymo household, he enjoyed her company that much. Oh what a pleasure that is – bedding the Clymos' kitchen skivvy. The very thought stirs him and takes his mind off the task in hand. It's not just their coupling that excites him but her pillow talk. To all appearances she is the faithful servant but with him she admits to little love for the Clymo household. She describes her mistress as nothing but a jumped up bal maid and almost revels in Mathew Clymo's ever worsening state of health.

'Captain, shall I stay or must I move?'

'Stay, boy!' He notes down his reading of the angle, picks up the dial and one end of the fathom chain and walks to meet the boy. He levels the dial upon its tripod once again and sends the boy with candle and the chain to the tunnel's face.

'Seven fathom, four feet and three inches, Capun.' The reedy voice echoes down the tunnel.

Kit Robin sighs, wipes the sweat from his eyes and scribbles the measurement in his notebook. 'That's it, boy. That's it for tonight. Back up to grass.' He should go to check the face but simply can't be bothered. The day's advance is less than a foot and not much will change from last night. In the letter he must leave for Clymo in the morning he'll just write "*lode on 330fm level?*". Besides, he is exhausted. He has visited eight working ends on six different levels this night. Up and down ladder ways, in and out of stopes, down dark and dirty drives and in and out of crosscuts. And he has dutifully noted what he has seen and will spend an hour or so before his breakfast writing his daily letter for Captain bloody Clymo. He walks back down the drive, the boy scuttling in front of him, burdened with the tripod and the chain. God, how this level stinks – unventilated powder fumes and human shit and so infernally hot he's positively bathed in sweat. And what a bugger of a climb it is to grass. If he were captain he would put in a man engine no matter what the cost. Clymo's just too bloody mean. But he will not be captain of Wheal Emma, not now or ever, not now the boy is coming back. He had hoped that with Clymo getting sicker by the day, he'd take his place but he's learned from Mary O'Malley's pillow talk that Thomas Pascoe is returning from Australia. And that can only mean they bring him back to replace his stepfather. Not sixteen, and the boy was a legend in the mine before he fled the country, though Kit Robin barely knew him. A grown man now and as Clymo's stepson and a miner he will surely be next captain. Unless . . . unless he can persuade the next assembled gathering of adventurers that with Clymo sick, he Kit Robin, should run the mine. Yes there's a thought. He has bought a small amount of Cornish Consols stock so that he might sit with the adventurers at the quarterly counthouse meetings where such decisions are always taken. A word here and there might just do the trick. Not all the shareholders favoured Clymo's reinstatement all those years ago. Perhaps he could re-kindle that dissent. But he must move fast. The next counthouse dinner is only ten days away. He will write that London share broker Josiah Hocking. He is no friend of Mathew Clymo and has influence with the shareholders. He smiles to himself as he steps on to the first of the one thousand nine hundred and eighty rungs that he must climb to reach the surface.

'Get on boy, get up there, you lazy bugger,' he shouts at his assistant struggling a few rungs above him, hampered by the tripod slung over his shoulder.

Up and up they go, resting on a sollar now and then to catch their breath, hearing the grind and clank of the iron pump rods in the shaft beside them, not caring that they are soaked by cascading water – in fact it cools them after the humid depths of the 330 fathom level. Yes, if he is not successful at the counthouse dinner he will have to work under a man ten years his junior and that will be just too irksome. Perhaps he could get rid of Thomas Pascoe altogether, have him re-arrested for that crime in Bodmin. He was accused of the murder of some old cleric but found not guilty by some legal trickery. He'll be seeing Mary this afternoon, after his morning sleep. He'll ask her to find out more. She can't help but eavesdrop on the Clymo household and loves to gossip. She's a deep one that for all her carefree Irish manner. But she's loose and easy with her favours, likes his muscled body as he likes her lissomness and she has a pretty face beneath those freckles. They have their secret trysting place right under the Clymo family's nose – the little hayloft above their stables. She slips out of an afternoon and he slips in the back way and no one is the wiser. He grins to himself. Yes his nights down Wheal Emma may be a tiresome grind but his daytime frolics – ahh, that's another story. Up and up and ladder by ladder they climb joined at each level by men off the night core until the ladders are filled by a continuous line of exhausted miners. There's little talking just the steady thump of boots on rungs, coughing as a miner rests for a few seconds and the muttered "Mornin', Capun Kit" or the less polite "Watch it, boys. Here comes Dandy Pants." That's what they call him "Dandy Pants" – not to his face of course but well within his hearing. He does not care, in fact it feeds his vanity.

Weary to the bone he and the boy reach the final ladder. Then they are out in the fresh air. Kit Robin breathes deep then wrinkles his nose at the coal smoke blowing from the chimney stack of the engine house. He looks north and east where a splendid summer dawn is breaking and stops a moment listening for birdsong above the racket of the mine and dressing floor. He sighs as he makes his way through the throng of miners going to the dry – a long, low brick building between the counthouse and the engine house where waste heat from the engine boilers warms tubs of bathing water for the filthy men. But Kit Robin does not join them. Instead he goes in to the cold and empty counthouse, sits on a high stool at the desk that runs along the wall and opens the Wheal Emma Day & Night Book – a thick journal half filled with the hand written letters between himself and Captain Clymo. He takes a quill from the top desk ledge, dips it in the inkwell and with a sigh writes: *Night July 6th*. This he underlines with an elaborate flourish wondering if Clymo guesses how much scorn he puts into just this stroke of his quill. He then proceeds to copy out his notes detailing the progress of the various working ends that he has spent the night clambering around. This done he blots the page and shuts the journal. The day is his now – back to his cottage where his maidservant will have prepared his bath and breakfast – porridge and eggs and bacon and today being Tuesday, devilled kidneys. Yes, his night's work has left him very hungry.

VI

LETTERS FROM HOME

THEY COME DOWN OUT OF THE HILLS ONTO THE flatlands a day's ride out of Wallaroo. It is September and the winter rains have turned the land faintly green – not the intense green of the verdant valleys of their Cornish homeland but greenish nonetheless. Where the land is cleared, grass is appearing and there are new grey-green leaves on the mallee scrub On the last ridge they stand their horses and gaze west and south and Thomas imagines he can see the shimmer of the sea.

'Nearly home, Henry. We're nearly home.'

'Ah Thomas, I could do with a decent bed and my Janie's arms around me. It's been a long, long ride and not a thing to show for it.'

'I'm sorry Henry.'

'Tain't your fault Thomas. Tis just bad luck.'

'A man makes his own luck, Henry. Seems mine's run out. Lord, this country's flat. Come on.'

They ride steadily all day stopping only to water the horses at Bute and by late afternoon are on the Pascoe lands north of Wallaroo. Finally against a setting sun they see the stand of eucalypts they left to shade the farmstead, their two houses and the shearing sheds. Neither can resist the urge to gallop the last mile down the dusty track and the horses too are eager to be home. Dismounting at the gate, Thomas sees Maisie standing on the veranda in deep shadow, children round her skirts, a hand shading her eyes.

Then she runs, apron flapping, runs to him calling out, 'Thomas, Thomas my love, you are home.'

He sweeps her up in his arms and kisses her. 'How good, so very good to see you. How good to be home. Ahh you smell of children and boiled mutton.'

She laughs. 'And what else would I smell of? And you, you stink of horse and wood smoke. Just look at you – that beard. A real bushman ain't you.' She holds him away from her. 'And skinny!' She lets go of him and shakes Henry's hand. 'Henry, you've not been feeding him, nor yourself by the look.'

'Hello Maid. We run out of flour ten days past and been eating just what Tom could shoot. And I've still got no taste for kangaroo. Where's my Janie then?'

'She's down at milkin', Henry. Did you find your mine then Thomas? Tell us, is it copper or is it gold?'

Thomas shakes his head. 'Neither I'm afraid, my love, we found nothing. All that time and all those miles just wasted.' Thomas unstraps his bag and bedroll from his horse. 'Let's get these poor beasts stabled Henry. Then we'll all have supper together won't we Maisie?'

'Of course we will. Though I don't know what I'll cook if not mutton.' She runs her hand through her mop of red hair. 'And Thomas there are letters from home for you and I have had news too – my poor old father died in the summer.'

Thomas sighs. 'I'm sorry to hear that Maisie, love. He had the black lung pretty bad all those years ago. He did well to last so long.'

'Yes, but my Ma is bitter about it still. Blames Capun Clymo. I'll read her letter to you later and then you'll see.'

It is late by the time they finish eating, the children are abed and Henry and Jane are gone to their house next door. Thomas looks around the simple room he and Henry built all those years ago – blue gum planking for the walls and floor and a corrugated iron roof creaking as it cools in the evening air. Wooden table and chairs they bought in Wallaroo and two cloth covered armchairs each side of the empty fire place – no need for fires now, what goes for winter here is long gone. The oil lamp flickers on the oak dresser they brought from Adelaide three years back and another hangs from a chain above the fireplace. He takes a deep breath, smells the smells of home – the mutton and potatoes dinner, kerosene and floor polish and beneath it all the smell of sheep.

'Here, Thomas – your letters from home.' Maisie hands him two unopened envelopes and sits opposite him holding a letter of her own.

'I'll read my mother's first for you. It ain't her writing 'cos of course she can't write. I don't know who writ it for her. But listen what she says.

My Darling Daughter Maisie

On 15th day of June your poor father was taken from us. He was very poorly for many months but kept at his work in the mundic factory on Capun Clymo's orders. That work didn't do his black lung no good and he took to his bed and was dead but ten days later. We called the doctor to him but there was nothing to be done. I had words with Grace Clymo and I believe that she did tell the Capun that I blamed him for your poor father's dying as I now get his charity monthly which is enough to feed us all. I hope dear daughter that all is well with you and your family. I do miss you dear daughter.

God bless you.

Your mother.

Thomas shakes his head. 'I knew no good would come of making arsenic. That's the stuff in Coopers sheep dip that makes our stockmen sick. I am sorry for your Ma, my love, but at least she isn't in the poorhouse.' He turns his own letters in his hands. 'This one's from Capun Clymo. I wonder why he's written now. And this other I don't know. Don't recognise the writing.' He gets up, goes to the dresser and takes an ivory paper knife from a drawer. He slits open the envelope and sits down. He reads both sides of the single page then sits silent, resting his chin in his hand.

'Who is it from Thomas? Don't tease,' Maisie says.

'My mother but writ for her by Emily.'

'So what does she say? Is something wrong?'

'Yes. The Capun's sick. She wants me to go home.'

'Home? How can you? They'll arrest you. Besides our life is here now. Read it to me Tom, read it please.'

Thomas nods, stares at the letter for a few seconds then begins to read:

My Dearest Thomas,

I hope this finds you and Maisie and the children all well. I know you will be surprised to receive a letter from me as I am only now beginning to learn to read and write. Yr sister Emily teaches me every day and it is she who writes this for me. I wish I had good news for you from Penpillick but I do not. Yr dear stepfather the Capun is unwell with pains in his belly and some times a bloody flux. We do not know what it is that ails him although we have had Dr Couch to him 3 or 4 times. But the capun will not rest from working as he must every day go down into the mine. I think it is in part that he is sick with worry. He says he has lost the Pascoe lode and he must work every day to make up for the riches that are lost. Altho I was a Bal Maiden and your own father was the best miner who ever dug copper at Wheal Emma and you too understand the secrets of the earth this is all a mystery to me. I can not help my ailing husband and must watch every day as he grows thinner and weaker,

My dearest Son, If you were here I know that you would help him as he once helped you. I beg you to come home and be Capun of Wheal Emma. This would save my Mathew's life.

You need have no more fears of Bodmin jail as the prosecutor has died these six months past and the constable told the Capun all charges were dropped soon after.

I have not told the Capun I have written to you as he would be angered to know that I beg for your return to me and to the bosom of your family.

Yr Loving Mother

Thomas sighs and rubs his newly shaven chin. 'I don't know Maisie love. We must think about this. Let's see what the Capun has to say.' He opens the second letter, reads it quickly and snorts. 'Now here's a thing. Guess what – the Capun wants me to go home too. But not because he's sick. Says he needs my help to save the mine. Says it's my legacy. And just guess – he's not told my mother he has written either.'

Maisie is silent looking at her husband. She folds her arms and leans back in her chair. 'Thomas, would you want to go home?' she says quietly.

He looks across at her, thinks how beautiful she is, green eyes gazing at him, her red hair shining in the lamplight. He hears the bleating of sheep and a dog barking from the stockyard. 'You would, wouldn't you?'

She nods and almost whispers, 'Yes I would. I still miss it so. I still dream of home. And with you away these past months I've been very lonely.' She brushes away a tear.

Thomas crosses to her chair and takes her hands in his. 'Don't cry, Maisie love. We can think about it later. Come, let's go to bed now.'

She stands and puts her arms around his shoulders and kisses him. 'As long as we can be together Thomas, that's all I ask. I hated being left.'

He wakes in the night and lies still, listening to her quiet breathing and to the sighing of the wind in the gum trees. They could go home. They have the funds and with wool prices what they are they will do well at this spring's shearing. But what of the station? All the work and money they have invested here? Could he trust young Millington, the manager, if they were away for two years, or more likely three? He was happy to be away in the bush for all those months but both Maisie and Henry's Jane kept an eye out for shady dealings. What if he left Henry Hopeful Down to keep an eye Millington – his lifelong friend and the mentor of his boyhood days? But Henry cannot read or write much less understand the money matters vital to the running of the Pascoe Station. Jane his wife could help with that – she is a teacher after all. A dingo starts to howl and then the others take up the cry. It is a wild and lonely sound born of this vast and lonely land. But he has been happy here, could be still but he is restless and sheep are not for him. Now underground at Wheal Emma . . . it all comes flooding back – the smells of rust and sulphur, the sounds, the dripping water, the clang of hammer on steel. He stares into the darkness and suddenly sees again the Pascoe lode glittering in candlelight – his light, Capun Clymo's, Henry's and that of poor old Jethro Loam knifed right then and there in front of him, as if a sacrifice to the riches he had found. He slips out of bed and stands at the open window. It is a moonless night. There is the Southern Cross riding high above a horizon so flat he could be at sea, sailing the ocean in this wooden house. They say the latest clipper ships are fast, just three months from Adelaide to London. They could be back in Cornwall soon after Christmas. They could send the children to the village school which doubtless would be better than Henry's Jane whose interest in teaching leaves much to be desired. But he has grown used to life here on the station – its seasons, the easy weather, the heat, the dust and now even the flies no longer bother him. But he is not going home for weather. He is going back to bring comfort to his mother, back to Capun Clymo, the stepfather he almost hated but who saved him from the rope. His turn to do the saving now it seems. And how would it be back underground? He smiles in the darkness. Yes they will go.

'Do you know where we are, Maisie love?'

'Yes, course I do. We're on the *Rodney* in the middle of the ocean. Where we've been for the last seven weeks.' She waves her arm to encompass the deck, the vast spread of canvas above their heads and the indigo sea beyond.

'It was about here on the way out that we were married. I checked the log this morning. Three weeks and we'll be home. Maybe less, Captain Barrett says.'

'So many years ago, it's hard to believe. I never expected to go back. I thought we'd left that life forever.'

'Well, your Ma will be pleased to see you I suppose.'

'She will. But shall we stay, Thomas? Shall we stay in Penpillick for the rest of our lives?'

'I don't know Maisie. I told Henry we will come back but I do not really know. It will depend on what I find at Wheal Emma. So many Cornish mines are closing and so many miners going to Australia. Yet we are going the other way.'

They are sitting on the after deck watching the children playing quoits. It is warm – not the sweaty heat of the tropics now left behind, but warm enough for them both to be lightly dressed, Thomas in shirtsleeves and Maisie in a full but light, cotton skirt and blouse. Both wear wide hats although they are well shaded from the afternoon sun by the mizzen sail.

'Sea life suits the children now,' Maisie says. 'Just look at them – proper little sailors. They play just as if they are at home. How different from when we sailed.'

'Well they'll be getting used to a different life again once we are home in Cornwall.' Thomas takes his hat off and scratches his head wondering for the hundredth time if his decision has been right. At least he chose the right ship. The *Rodney* is a first class iron clipper, the latest of the line with the latest luxuries. He didn't stint and booked two first class cabins with hot and cold running water, something they never had at home. But he could afford it. Their wool sales were better than he had hoped and they had saved a good part of his annual share of profit from Wheal Emma. He nods to himself – yes he should be going home, if that is what it takes to save his legacy. And Henry Hopeful Down – his trust in him is total and the station will be there and waiting when they return. But he will miss him. The big man has been his constant companion since his boyhood, first underground in Cornwall then all the years in South Australia. He waved farewell from the shore when they took ship at Port Adelaide after riding down from Wallaroo. The first week all of them were badly seasick as the clipper tore its way across the Southern Ocean, breasting huge rollers in clouds of spray with seas pouring green along the decks. They stayed in their cabins sick as dogs comforting the children as best they could. But then the Pascoe family found its sea legs and made a corner of the great saloon their own where each morning they taught their children all they could of writing, reading and arithmetic. Afternoons they spent as now with games and exercise upon the deck, except on foul weather days when they and all the other passengers were confined below. They stopped a day or two at Cape Town and toured the sights and the children marvelled at the mountains having never seen the like in the flat lands of South Australia. Now they are across the equator racing northward, the ship heeling to the northeast trades. Soon they will be in the heaving grey seas of the North Atlantic and home to an English winter. How will it be he wonders and he sees again the darkness of the mine, remembers how scared he was when just a boy and how he grew to love it. He shakes his head.

'What are you thinking of my love?'

'About the mine, what else.'

'What about it then? Tell me?'

'How strange it is to be going back. I thought I had left it all forever.'

VII

ARSENIC

MATHEW COULD WATCH THE WATER WHEEL ALL DAY. It never fails to fascinate him, the great spokes almost twice his height lifting, turning and plunging, the weak winter sunlight refracted through the flying water droplets, the only sounds the rush of water and the hum of the spinning axle. They ran a brick lined leat from two miles up the river valley and even in the driest summer it carries water enough to drive the wheel. And the wheel must be driven day and night, month on month and year on year. Not only does it spin the granite millstones that grind the arsenic crystals to the fine white powder that keeps his mine afloat, but through a crafty set of gears and rods it also turns the mighty kiln that burns the mundic ore to a stinking yellow gas. To Mathew Clymo, well used to the dark and twisting tunnels beneath the hill, it is passing strange to see this once green, idyllic river valley transformed into a smoking wasteland, a labyrinth of flues and chambers where men must work masked and muffled against the poison, scraping, sweeping, shovelling and packing arsenic in barrels to be shipped to London and far away America. But just as a day cannot pass without his descent into the mine, so too he must perforce visit Wheal Emma's arsenic works, his arsenic works, to reassure himself that all is as it should be, men, women and machinery are working and production does not falter through any fault, be it mechanical or human. He leaves the waterwheel and makes his way to the change room, a brick building just beneath the great chimney stack where the workers' clothes hang on serried pegs. He dons a white, full length canvas coat from his own peg and, from the locker beneath, canvas gaiters which he ties around his legs, a cloth face mask which covers all but his eyes and finally, a felt hat with flaps that cover his ears and ties beneath his chin. Thus clad he goes back out into the open and walks along the front of the humped brick flues until he comes to one with a wooden door. This he opens. The scene inside could be from his nightmares. Lit by the flare of oil lamps, three masked men are shovelling the snow white powder into barrows while a fourth hastily knots the ties of his mask behind his neck. Their hands and ankles are wrapped in sacking and cotton wadding blocks their ears but it is the masks that make them look so eerie. He knows he must appear the same to them, perhaps more ghostly even in his clean white coat. Nonetheless he speaks boldly, just as he would if he were underground although his voice is muffled by his mask.

'Afternoon, lads. Is all well?'

They do not speak but nod in unison.

'How many barrow loads so far today?'

One ghostly figure spreads both hands five times in succession and one hand once again.

'Fifty five?' Mathew Clymo says

They nod again.

'Well done lads. Good work. Now keep those masks on all the time. They are for your own protection. Good day to you.'

They stare at him through the eye slits of their masks and do not speak. He turns away and goes out into sweet fresh air, latching the door behind him.

Taking off his mask, he gazes up at the towering chimney stack. It is near sixty feet tall and had to be so on the orders of the Duke who owns the land. Even so the fumes are killing vegetation away up the valley, or so Grace and Emily tell him from their weekend walks about the countryside. He sighs. In truth he hates this business altogether – not his mine of course, just these poisoned works. The workers too – they know just how bad it is. In the early days when neither he nor they knew what they were about, a week's work in the flues would bring their faces out in sores and after a month or so in there they'd take to their beds too sick to work. It got so bad they organised a strike and for a week he was obliged to shut the whole place down. Only when his precious miners also asked for higher pay did he relent and provided them with increased wages, the changing room, the masks and special clothes that give them some protection. But this noxious powder (they say less than a teaspoon will kill a man) has been the saving of his mine. A hundred barrow loads a day, that's near on six tons. And six times twenty eight (they work every day bar Sundays) is one seventy tons, or near enough. Half they ship to America to kill the cotton weevil and half to London for Scheele's Green. He's paid six pounds a ton which gives him the better part of a thousand pounds in just one month. Without this extra flow of cash, Wheal Emma would have to close. He hates it but he does it because he has to, or so he tells himself. He cannot bring himself to let Wheal Emma die. If only they could find another copper lode, another Pascoe lode shining in the candlelight deep down in the ground. But even then he'd carry on with this – it's easy money and that he won't forgo, nor will the adventurers and nor will Mr William Morris most of all.

Leaving his protective clothing in the change room he goes back up the valley towards Penpillick, stopping to watch the huge iron cylinder of the roasting kiln rotating slowly above its furnace. How satisfactory water power is, he thinks. Quiet almost, just the rushing sound of water and the gentle clank of meshing gears – so different from the hiss and deafening thump of the beam engines at the mine, or even worse the stamp mill he had installed three years back with its endless rhythmic hammering. But at least he need no longer have women breaking ore with hammers and the bal maidens' work is limited to sieving and sorting broken copper ore. He glances up again at the chimney stack pouring out its poisonous fumes across the landscape and wonders how Thomas Pascoe will take to making arsenic. Principled he was, even as a boy, and stubborn. It took him two years and some to accept him as a stepfather. Things were so much simpler then – just digging copper from beneath the ground and Thomas had such a nose for copper ore. Let's hope he hasn't lost that skill after eight years in Australia. Well, he'll find out soon enough. The family is arriving on the morrow, or so said the telegram the post man brought just yesterday. One day in London then the train to Plymouth and Liskeard. He'll take the Brougham to meet them. How happy Grace will be.

He walks on up the track and up through the village, past the miners' cottages anxious to be home and lying down. His guts are griping once again. He should go home and rest. Not that that makes any difference. Could it be that he too is poisoned by his pestilential product? He thinks not. He is scrupulous about his own protection, does not let the dreadful stuff ever touch his skin and stays well clear of any roaster fumes. Yes, he knows that the arsenic workers still get sick even with the protection he provides but that takes months or even years. So what can it be? Something sickly growing in his guts? Perhaps if he stayed at home and rested just as Dr Couch has said he should. With Thomas home he could. He'll tell the meeting of the adventurers that he must rest on doctor's orders and Thomas should be the Captain of Wheal Emma. They will accept it, he's sure of that though Kit Robin will doubtless be more than vexed. But what of that? The man is nothing but a dilettante.

VIII

FAREWELL

HENRY HOPEFUL DOWN WIPES A TEAR FROM HIS pockmarked cheek. Sat beside his horse on the beach at Semaphore, he watches the *Rodney* until it becomes a distant sail on the southwest horizon and wonders once again at how far he has come in so few years – he, Henry Hopeful Down, once a humble Cornish tut worker, now responsible for the Pascoe station and ten thousand head of sheep. But he cannot linger, sad though he is at the departure of Thomas and his family. 'I love that man,' he thinks, 'I've loved him since he was a boy.' And that is a strange thought to him for it is the first time in his life he has admitted it. He wishes he had gone with them. Who knows what trials and tribulations his young friend will face once back across the sea? How will he do without his protection? He shrugs and gets to his feet brushing sand from off his clothes. There is nothing he can do save what he has been asked – take care of the Pascoe lands, their sheep and their outback home, keep it safe for their return. It does not matter that he can neither read nor write or that numbers are a mystery to him. For that he can depend on Jane, his educated wife. At least it will not be for long – Thomas has promised he will return. 'One year, maybe two and we'll be back, Henry, you can be sure. We'll come back to Wallaroo.' And that is three days ride away. He mounts and with a tug on the reins, turns his horse away from the sea. 'Come on, come on there. Get up, girl.' He taps his heels on the horse's flanks and the big mare trots landward across the sandy foreshore. He will spend the night at the British Hotel in Port Adelaide and start the long ride back at daybreak.

'Would a big fella like you buy a girl a drink then?'

There is an overpowering scent of roses and a rustle of taffeta skirts as a dark haired woman sits down beside him. He looks at her – the rouged cheeks, the curls beside her ears, her slim waist and exaggerated bust. She is very pretty. He sighs. 'A drink? Yes I'll buy you a drink, lady. But nothin' else mind.'

She smiles. 'A drink will do for now, thank you kind sir.'

Henry smiles back at her. Before he married Jane Cottrell, he would have taken all this woman has to offer but not now, although her company might just assuage his loneliness. And he's drunk four beers already. 'What will it be then?'

'A gin would do nicely, thank you.'

Henry calls over to the bar, 'Barman, a gin for the lady and another beer for me.' He turns to the woman. 'You should know I have a wife at home.'

'Never knew that to make no difference. What's your name, lovey?'

'Henry. And yours?'

'Mabel, they call me. Mabel – always willing and able.' She laughs a pretty laugh and Henry cannot help but laugh as well. 'Tell me your story, Henry. Your way of talking says you're a Cousin Jack. We see more and more of your folk through this place.'

'I am. I left Cornwall eight year ago and not been back. But I ain't a miner no more and more's the pity. Now I run sheep up north of Wallaroo.'

'And where would that be, darlin'?' she slips a hand on to his knee and he doesn't push it off.

'Three days ride north and west, up on the Spencer Gulf.'

'That'd be near that Moonta mine then. We get them miners in here from time to time. Big spenders they can be.'

The barman puts their drinks upon the table. 'That'll be a shilling, Mister.'

Henry pays. He raises his beer. 'Your health Mabel.'

'And yours, Henry from Wallaroo.' She raises her glass and looks him straight in the eye as she takes the gin in a single swallow. Her eyes are very blue. He watches the movement of her throat. He should not have let her sit by him much less buy her a drink. He scratches in his beard, tries and fails to think of home and Janey, swigs his beer and bangs the glass upon the table.

'So tell me Mabel, where you from?'

'Here and there,' she says. 'Does it matter? You staying here?'

He nods.

She raises a dark painted eyebrow and smiles. Her hand is warm upon his thigh. 'Well?' she whispers.

He nods again.

Henry Hopeful Down wakes at dawn to the carolling of magpies in the street below. He is not alone as he had planned, for Mabel lies beside him still asleep. He has a fearful headache and a camel's thirst and a memory of things he's never done or even known about before. This stirs him and he turns and watches her. She is lying on her front, the sheet draped about her waist, half facing him. Her black curled hair is a tousled mess upon the pillow. Her back is bare, rising and falling as she breathes. He smells her perfume, the sharp taint of gin upon her breath and the sweaty bedding in which they've lain together. A sudden surge of tenderness makes him smile and at that same moment her eyes blink open.

'Mornin' Henry,' she says and grins at him. 'That was quite a night.'

He strokes his beard and shakes his head. 'You're some lady.'

'What could you mean? Come here.' She reaches up an arm.

He bends and kisses her then pulls away. 'I must go. It'll be a long hot ride today. And I need tea and breakfast afore I leave.' He gets out the bed, pulls on his clothes and boots. He bends over her and kisses her again, breathing in the bed smell. 'I won't see you again, but thank you, Mabel.'

'Thank you, Big Henry from Wallaro. Believe me, you'll be back.'

He smiles and shakes his head, picks up his meagre swag and goes downstairs to breakfast.

The sun rising in a cloudless sky is hot on his face as he rides the roadway across the salt flats east from the port. He tries to think only of the journey home but time and again his mind reverts to Mabel and the night just passed. He should feel guilty. He does feel guilty and his head still hurts. He thinks of Jane and shifts in the saddle and rolls his shoulders as if to rid his mind of images and words, these memories of an ecstasy he'd never known before, wishing yet not wishing to forget the night entirely. 'I could turn round, I could go back,' he mutters to himself then shakes his head, blows out his cheeks. His marriage is much less than he had hoped when Jane Cottrell, an educated woman twenty years his junior, accepted his proposal. He has always wondered why. She wanted children, or so she said, and so did he. Perhaps that made the match. But no children came. Henry thought maybe the smallpox was to blame; as a young man he'd survived it, but who knew what harm it might have done. He thought he was a simple man of simple tastes but after what passed between him and Mabel in the night just past, he's no longer quite so sure. It makes his infrequent coupling with his wife seems perfunctory at best. And he has ignored the stockmen's' sidelong looks and surreptitious grins when Bob Millington the manager is about. She's been deceiving him, he knows it, has known it all along but let it lie hidden, unacknowledged even by himself. Now his life is all awry – Thomas and his family gone, the long ride back, this guilt an extra burden that will grow in weight the closer he gets to home. And sometime soon a reckoning with the woman he must depend on to fulfil his promises to Thomas Pascoe.

Once across the salt flats, he swings north-northwest over the scrublands following the sandy track made by carts and buggies. There is no shade and already he is tempted to drink from the canvas covered water bottle dangling from his saddle. But he just wipes his gummy lips, swallows then urges the horse into a gentle trot. All day he rides, stopping only to water the horse at infrequent roadside wells. He rides dead against a hot north wind that picks up grit and dust and the mare walks head down pestered by a myriad flies. He takes off his hat and fans himself then looks skyward where a wedge-tailed eagle circles, silhouetted black against the brilliant sky. The heat is all consuming and he wishes he were going back to a damp green Cornish valley and a mist enshrouded moor along with the Pascoe family. Late in the afternoon he overtakes a bullock cart carrying three families of Cornish miners and all their baggage. Fresh off the boat they are and on their way to the Moonta Mine. He spends the night with them in the little settlement of Dublin and once again he drinks too much – this time, he tells himself, to forget the homesickness brought on by their voices so redolent of home.

Late afternoon against the setting sun he sights the smelter stacks at Wallaroo. Exhausted as he is, he could stop the night at the Globe Hotel for he doesn't like to ride in darkness. But anxious to be home, he swings north again along the familiar track to the Pascoe Station. He would gallop but his horse is all but spent and plods head down the last dark miles. Then, on the cooling wind he hears the sounds of bleating sheep and the whispered rattle of the breeze in the eucalyptus trees. The mare lifts her head and he knows that he is home. They pass the darkened Pascoe homestead and then his own where a single wavering light glows in the bedroom window. He imagines Jane abed and reading by a candle. If only he could read. He waters, feeds and stables the weary horse. A sudden image of Mabel, naked and riding him astride, rises unbidden in his mind. He shakes his head and shouldering his swag, strides towards the house. Mounting the three steps onto the veranda with a clattering of boots on wood, he goes into the house and calls out, 'Janey, Janey, I am back.'

But there silhouetted in the bedroom doorway stands a man, boots in one hand, the other pulling up his trousers.

Henry stops in mid-stride. 'What?' he roars dropping his swag and lunging forward. 'Millington, you filthy dog.' He grabs the man around his neck and lifts him clear off his feet. 'You bastard filthy dog. I'm going to kill you.' He shakes him like a rat and squeezes as hard he can.

Bob Millington, a slight and wiry figure who barely reaches Henry's shoulder, gives a strangled cry and clutches Henry's wrist with both his hands, boots and trousers dropping to the floor.

'Henry, Henry, stop, you hideous brute. Stop this now and put him down. It's not his fault.' Jane Down in flannel night gown stands screaming at him from the bedroom door.

But Henry Hopeful Down is deaf and blind to everything except his rage – rage not just at this squirming rat, nor just with Jane, he'll kill her too – but most of all with his own guilt-filled self. He roars again, 'I'll kill you, kill you both.' Millington's face is crimson, his eyes are starting from his head and his feet scrabble uselessly on the floor. But then a blinding pain sears through Henry's head, he staggers back, lets go of Millington, half crumples then falls prone.

Jane Down stands aghast, the handle of a shattered china water jug in hand, staring down at both her husband and her lover. Bob Millington squats choking on the floor and Henry lies motionless, face down, blood pouring from his scalp. 'Help me help me,' she whimpers to Middleton bending down. 'Help me turn him over. I think I've killed him.'

Bob Middleton crawls towards the prostrate man hands skidding in the blood. 'No, Jane, no he is alive. He's bleeding see.'

Together they roll him on his back and Henry takes a ragged breath and then another. A flap of skin and hair hangs over his pockmarked brow and blood is flowing from his scalp and pooling on the floorboards.

'Thank God,' she whispers. 'Get dressed and go. Come back in the morning. I'll sort this out.'

Millington pulls on his trousers and his boots and scuttles from the house. Jane Down fetches towel and water in a bowl and the candle from the bedroom. Kneeling beside her husband she wipes the blood from his face, his beard, his head and picks china splinters from his scalp. Gently she folds back the flap of skin, presses it into place then dabs away the blood still seeping from the wound.

He opens his eyes, stares at her and mutters. 'Jane, Jane.'

'Quiet. Lie still.'

He closes his eyes again while she continues dabbing blood from his scalp and hair. He sighs and tries to bring his hand up to his head but she pushes his arm away. 'You hit me,' he whispers.

'Yes, I did. You would have killed him.'

'I would.'

'Then you'd be a murderer. Hush. We'll talk in the morning.'

Henry struggles to sit up. 'I'm not sorry.'

'No. Wait, I'll get a bandage.' She comes back with bandages and tincture of iodine which she dabs on the still seeping wound. She wraps the bandage around his head and pins it. 'Can you get up?'

'I think so.'

'I'll get you to bed.'

'I won't sleep there.'

'Sleep on the couch then or where you wish. I do not care.' She takes his arm to help him up.

He shakes her off. 'I can manage.'

'Suit yourself.'

A flock of cockatoos screeching in the eucalyptus trees wake Henry Hopeful Down at dawn. He is fully dressed but for his boots which stand beside the couch. He touches his bandaged throbbing head. He would have killed a man but for his wife. Should he thank her for what she did? Perhaps, but he can no longer live with her, of that he is quite sure. He is a cuckold and all the station hands will know by now, if they have not known before of course. What should he do with Millington? Dismiss him and hire another manager? His wife walks barefoot through the room still in her blood-stained nightgown. She goes into the kitchen, not giving him a glance. He listens to the clatter as she lights the stove and puts a kettle on to boil. Is this to be a normal day then? He sits up holding his aching head in both his hands. He is completely at loss. He has promised Thomas Pascoe he will stay and run the station, manage ten thousand head of sheep, tasks he knows he cannot do alone. His wife comes in the room with bread, a pot of tea and mugs and puts them on the table.

'Breakfast,' she says.

Henry eases himself to his feet and pads across to the table and sits down. Jane comes in again this time with cheese and eggs and milk. She sits opposite him without a word. He saws himself a hunk of bread, cracks and peels an egg and eats. He is strangely hungry and pours himself a cup of milky tea. He looks at her.

'Jane,' he says.

She sips her tea and stares at him.

'Is it done then?'

She doesn't answer, but dips a crust of bread into her tea and keeps staring at him. Her face is drawn and white, her mouth turned down.

'Is our marriage done then? Do you love that man?'

She puts her tea down on the table and licks her lips. Her tongue is thin and very pink. 'Yes,' she says.

'Yes?'

'Yes to both. I do not want to live with you. We never should have married.'

'Why did you marry me?'

She sniffs. 'I've asked myself that a thousand times and still don't know the answer.'

'You and Millington must leave. I want you gone today.'

'No Henry, it is you who has to leave.'

For seconds he sits stunned. Then he says, 'No, I'll not leave. Thomas left me in charge. I say you go.'

'Well I have news for you. Your precious Mr Pascoe may have told you you're in charge but you are not. How could you be? You are illiterate.'

Henry feels his face turn hot. He has no answer.

'Besides, before he left your boss gave Bob a letter appointing him the manager. How else could we buy and sell the stock or get credit from suppliers? No, you haven't thought of that have you? I guessed as much – Henry Hopeless Down.'

With a speed that surprises even him, he leans across the table and hits her across the face with such violence that she topples from her chair and falls on to the floor. She is on her feet in seconds both hands on the table, screaming at him, her left eye and cheek already swelling from the blow. 'You swine. You great Cornish oaf. You murderer. Get out before I call the men to throw you out.'

He rocks back on his chair 'Jane, Jane, I am sorry I didn't mean to strike you. Please, please forgive me. You make me so angry. The thought of you with him. You know I would never hit a woman.'

'You just did,' she screams her lips drawn back. 'You did. And last night you would have killed Bob Millington. Out, out, get out you ugly beast. Or hit me again, if you dare. Come on, come on. Just do it.' She leans across the table.'

Henry, tears welling in his eyes, covers his face with his hands and turns away. He gets up from the table and walks into the bedroom. He does not look at the bed, just pulls a dusty leather suitcase out from beneath and opens it. The only thing inside is the miners' pick he brought from Cornwall all those years ago. He hefts it in his hand and studies it – the wooden handle still shiny from his sweat, the well-worn point that dug riches from the ground, the leather thong that looped around his wrist. He shakes his head, replaces it and covers it with spare clothing from a chest, a winter coat taken from the peg behind the door and finally scuffed and well-worn boots. From a dusty niche in the truss above his head that only he can reach, he takes a roll of notes and stuffs it in his pocket – his savings from all the years he's worked here. He quits the room and not looking round, picks up his swag from where he dropped it in his rage the night before. He walks out of the house head bent, not looking at his wife who sits bolt upright at the table, staring straight ahead.

'Come on old girl, you're rested, fed and watered. And we'll not ride far today.' The horse breaks into a gentle trot. He is anxious to be gone now, to leave the Pascoe Station and his humiliation far behind. No matter that he has let down his lifelong friend. It is far worse that he struck his wife and would be a murderer but for her. Last night, this morning, both are a fearful nightmare from which he only now awakes. He takes a dozen breaths as deeply as he can as if to purge the dreadful rage that has possessed him. Where did it come from? He's never been a violent man – intimidating perhaps, being very big and badly scarred from smallpox. But he's never hit a woman in his life before, or come near to killing. Was it jealousy, betrayal or guilt? He shakes his head and straightens in the saddle, looks around – the scrub-filled plain, flat as flat can be, the sere grass shining in the morning sun. He'll ride to the pub in Wallaroo, ease his mind with a beer or two, soothe his aching head. He presses gently on the bandage round his head and winces. 'She nearly killed me,' he mutters. 'Maybe better if she had.'

IX

HOME

 'HE LEFT A BOY. NOW YOUR BROTHER IS A MAN – JUST look at him.'

'He looks like a sailor,' Emily says.

'Perhaps. But he's a gentleman, is he not?'

'A foreign gentleman maybe.'

'A handsome foreign gentleman, I would say.' Grace cannot but agree with her daughter that her son's appearance is very different from that of his companions, the group of men who file into the drawing room. Mathew looks not just angry but more drawn and tired than usual. Wheal Emma's chairman, James Sanderson whose florid face bears witness to too much port, chats to William Morris and Thomas himself is deep in conversation with the purser, William George. Behind them all comes Kit Robin, dressed to the nines in a patterned waistcoat, flamboyant necktie and looking more than usually pleased with himself. Thomas's deeply tanned face is such a contrast to the pallor of the mining men and his slimness makes the city men look much overweight. Grace is proud and overjoyed to have her long lost son back home again – the son she thought had gone forever. She has served the finest dinner she and Mary could contrive – freshest lobsters up from Looe, poached salmon with a butter sauce and a roast saddle of mutton that was more than toothsome and made a splendid centrepiece on the dining table all lit by candlelight. Better certainly than the banquets that she used to serve at counthouse dinners when she was a bal maiden. In fact this dinner was in lieu of just that – Mathew decreed that Cornish Consols could not afford to feed the thirty odd adventurers who travelled from as far away as London to attend the reading of accounts that day. So all but this privileged group repaired to the Fountain Inn in Liskeard where no doubt they'll be carousing now. She watches William Morris gazing round her drawing room in obvious approval. He catches her eye and smiles then comes to stand beside her chair.

'Madam, I must congratulate you on your taste in wallpaper – "Indian" unless I'm much mistaken.'

'Yes indeed, sir. One of yours, of course. We do love the green – a most unusual shade.'

'Quite, quite. And this fine new house – Captain Clymo has a natural eye I'd say.'

'Thank you, you are most kind.'

'No, no Madam, it is I who must thank you for a splendid dinner and your hospitality. I have seldom eaten better even in London.'

Grace Clymo dips her head to hide her blushes. She is not really at her ease with so fine a gentleman as Mr William Morris. He met her as a bal maiden – not when she broke rock, but certainly when she cooked and served at counthouse dinners. She looks down at her hands folded in her lap – how soft they are, the calluses long gone. He treats her as a lady, which of course these days she is. She has had to learn the niceties, the manners and the social graces that befit her station as mistress of Penpillick House.

'Excuse me Madam, Miss Emily, I am most anxious to hear what that fine young man, your son, can tell me of our colonies. My goodness, what a striking fellow.'

William Morris bows to Emily and Grace and goes to the bay window where Thomas stands looking out, his hands behind his back.

'Mama, how long has Mr Morris been part of Cornish Consols?'

'Almost since the beginning, I believe. His father was a founding member and young Mr Morris took his place when he passed away. And that was but a few years after your papa began it all.'

Emily nods and looks across at her brother and William Morris. 'He is very famous now, is he not? I read about him in the Cornhill Magazine just last month. They say he is a patron of famous artists like Mr Burne-Jones and Mr. Rosetti.'

'I do not know about that, my dear but I do know that he owes his fortune to Wheal Emma.'

Thomas, deaf to the hubbub of conversation in the room, stands staring out at darkness and pondering the changes he has seen since arriving at Penpillick: this big house, the servants, his mother's role as almost lady of the manor; how Capun Clymo's aged – he barely recognised him when he and his family stepped off the train at Liskeard. And the mine itself – two new shafts, the clattering stamp mill, but most of all the changes brought about by the working of the arsenic. He knew from his stepfather's letters that arsenic had been the salvation of the mine but he never thought to see such devastation of Penpillick Valley. And he is to be Night Captain and subject to Kit Robin – well that's a joke he'd not expected when he sailed from Adelaide. At least Maisie's happy to be home. He'd tried to persuade her to attend this dinner but she preferred to spend the time with her mother and her family in the cottage. He wishes he were there.

'A penny for them, Mr Pascoe.'

He turns to face Mr William Morris whose bearded face is familiar from the portrait that still hangs in the counthouse. 'Mr Morris. My thoughts were far away in Australia, sir.'

'So tell me, how did you find it? How is life among the convicts?'

'We were to South Australia, sir. It is a free colony. There are no convicts there, nor convict labour.'

'You don't say. I was not aware of that. I must say I am pleased to hear it. Transportation was a most iniquitous business in my view. And tell me, how fares the working man in South Australia? Is he better off than here?'

'Well, somewhat I suppose. I have not given it much thought. There is great demand for labour and a shortage of supply. But that won't last long, at least in mining – not with so many miners going from here to there. But Mr Morris, if I might be so bold, there is something else I would discuss with you.'

'With me? Why of course. Fire away, dear boy.'

'Well yesterday Capun Clymo showed me the arsenic works.'

'Ahh.'

'He says it was originally your idea.'

'Hmm, yes, well I suppose that is a possibility. What of it?'

'I must say that I was somewhat shocked.'

'Why so?'

'Well first of all the valley is all a ruin. When I left it was a place of peace and quiet and greenery. Now it is a wasteland.'

'Yes, but that is the way of most industrial enterprise. You should see the Black Country. It is the penalty we pay for progress.'

'Is it? If that is so it is a great shame. But worse still, have you seen our men at work inside the arsenic flues?'

'No. I have no desire to. Nor have I ever been down the mine – not in all these years. I have never felt the need. I am content to rely on the accounts of experts such as Captain Clymo.'

'But Mr Morris, sir, we are poisoning our workers.'

'Nonsense, dear boy. Whatever gave you that idea?'

'Arsenic is a poison, is it not?'

'No, no, only in large quantities. Otherwise it is quite harmless, even beneficial, at least so I have heard.'

'It is used in sheep dip in Australia. The slightest contact makes our stock hands sick.'

'I can't imagine why. We use it in our wallpapers and my workers at Merton Abbey are never ill.'

'In the wallpaper?'

'Yes indeed. It is in the paper your mother had the good taste to put on these very walls.' Morris gestures to the room. 'It is arsenic that provides this most delightful shade of green.'

'I am dumbfounded, sir. I had no idea.'

'Yes if arsenic were so poisonous, why half the country would be sickened. If I were to be asked, I would say that the when doctors find their patients ailing and don't know what is the matter, they put it down to arsenic. In my view they ought to put it down to the water closet which I believe is the source of all illness. Now if you'll excuse me, I feel I ought to make the acquaintance of our new captain.'

'Damn Josiah Hocking. This is the second time he has blocked me on the board,' Mathew Clymo mutters to James Sanderson who sits beside him.

'Can't be helped. He carries a lot of votes and besides, he has a point.

Young Thomas has been out of the mining game for quite some years.'

'That may be so. But it doesn't make Dandy Pants over there a better Day Captain than he would be.'

'Well, with Thomas as Night Captain he can keep a close eye on things for you. And Mathew, hear me, you have to take a back seat now. I've never seen you so out of sorts. In fact you look quite ill. You should be in your bed, not clambering up and down the ladder ways. And neither of us is getting any younger.'

'It's my damn guts, not my age. I have a constant ache which nothing will assuage. And I've had a bellyful of pills and potions. None do me any good.'

'Perhaps some bed rest will. You're sure it's not from arsenic?'

'Yes. I take great care whenever I am at the works and Couch the sawbones says I do not have the symptoms. See, my hands are clear – no spots, brown or otherwise.' Mathew holds out both his hands palms upward. 'I've seen that on the workers who fail to wear their gloves.'

'It's nasty stuff, no doubt but it is the saving of Wheal Emma. '

'It is indeed. But that preening fool Kit Robin will be our downfall. He should never have been appointed. There'll be a disaster underground, you mark my words. I should never have kept the bugger on after Scoble fell down the shaft.'

'Don't be so gloomy, Mathew. In six months time we'll vote again and if by then your adopted son has justified your faith in him, we'll make him captain of Wheal Emma once and for all.'

Mathew looks across the room where William Morris chats to Kit Robin. 'You know James, in all these years this is only the fourth time I have seen Morris at Wheal Emma. You'd think that given that all his wealth comes from this mine he'd pay us more attention.'

'He's far too busy with his own enterprises, Mathew – those and his artistic circle.'

Mathew gives a derisive snort, leans back in his chair and shuts his eyes.

Kit Robin is in seventh heaven. His scheme has worked exactly as he planned. Here he is in the heart of the Clymo household, not quite as honoured guest, (that accolade belongs of course to William Morris) but certainly now as a man whose opinion is worthy of consideration. And that is what Mr Morris seeks from him.

'Captain Robin? I believe I should address you so?'

'Yes indeed, sir. How might I be of service?'

'What think you of these man engines? I have long thought that the installation of such a machine would be of considerable benefit to Wheal Emma. In fact some years ago I wrote Captain Clymo suggesting this as a solution to the exhaustion of our miners climbing hundreds of fathoms up ladder ways. But my idea has been ignored. Is it a practical solution?'

'Sir, it most certainly is. I too have suggested exactly this to Capun Clymo but he has always been against the idea. Much too costly, so he says.'

'As I understand it, now you have been appointed Captain, you could pursue this, could you not?'

'I could, sir and I will, sir, most definitely, at the earliest opportunity.'

'Excellent. And I congratulate you on your choice of necktie Captain. Quite fetching. My good friend Millais would be quite charmed. I wager he would love to paint you.'

'You are too kind Mr Morris. Ah, here comes more refreshment. You will take a coffee, sir?'

All eyes save those of Mathew Clymo, who appears to be asleep, are turned to Mary O'Malley standing in the doorway with a tray. She wears a full length black dress and white apron trimmed with lace, a white lace mob cap sits on her head. Her face is pale, her red hair is parted in the middle and drawn back into a plaited chignon. William Morris nods and Kit Robin beckons her. She stares at him then walks straight by to stand in front of Mathew Clymo. 'Your coffee, sorr,' she says, holding out a cup and saucer.

Mathew opens his eyes, sits up and takes the cup. 'Thank you Mary.'

She then serves Grace and Maisie, then Thomas Pascoe and the purser and finally Kit Robin and William Morris. 'Coffee, sorrs?'

When she has gone, they stand there coffee cups in hand. 'Irish?' William Morris asks.

'Irish,' replies Kit Robin.

X

SUSPICION

HEAD BACK AND CANDLE FLAME TRACING SOOT TRAILS across the roof, Thomas follows with one finger a white filigree of quartz that traverses the killas. Could those tiny crystals, those specks that glitter in his candlelight, be companions to the copper that he seeks? He is not sure, perhaps, perhaps, but it has been so long. He was just a boy but his eyes were sharp and the spirit of his father and his father's book guided him to the discovery that changed not just his life, but the lives of those around him. Now the Pascoe Lode, his lode, is all dug out, which is the way of all earth's natural treasures found by man, be they gold or silver, tin or copper. Now Wheal Emma's dark labyrinth extends way beyond his father's ken. It has been eight years since he has seen, touched and felt these rocks – eight years since the stink of sulphur, iron and black powder filled his nostrils. But how good it is to be back here now, back in the depths, back in the dark, alone. In the month of nights since they made him Captain he has built upon his boyhood memories and now he has a picture in his mind of all the workings of the mine, both old and new. And in that picture he can see the copper lodes, see how they lie, and where they are gone, replaced by empty caverns where water drips and slabs of rock spall off the walls and roof, unseen, unheard. He is a ferret in a rabbit warren, his quarry copper and at these depths it could be tin as well. Now if he found a tin lode – black tin they call it – as lies below the copper at Dolcoath, that would be a triumph and the saving of this mine, not the filthy mundic that poisons half Penpillick. Thomas Pascoe, chief dialler, or surveyor, as he sometimes thinks, makes maps and notes of all he sees and these he shows to Captain Clymo who is now bedridden. Which is in itself a mystery to Thomas. He remembered his stepfather as a big bold man with a scarlet neckerchief who wooed his mother and whom he could have hated just for that. Now he is half that man, bent and thin, his face so drawn and gray with constant pain. When Doctor Couch last called at the house, he spoke privately with Thomas and his mother.

'I am at a loss to know what ails the Captain,' he said. 'I thought it must be the arsenic but he assures me he was most careful to neither touch the stuff nor breath in fumes whenever he was at the works. And it is three weeks now since he was near the place, yet his symptoms still persist. I will be honest with you, I do not understand it. I will bleed him once a week and he must stay in bed the while. Perhaps time and rest will be the healer.'

But Captain Clymo has not recovered. If anything he grows worse. Thomas sighs. Although he did not replace his father in Thomas's affections as a boy, there is no question in his mind but that Mathew Clymo has become a father figure to him, a source of knowledge and authority, a figurehead and even from his sickbed, the ruler of the Clymo clan. Whatever knowledge Thomas gains from his nightly explorations underground, he shares directly with the Captain and every morning takes his breakfast in the bedroom where the Captain lies.

But look, here the colour of the killas changes from slate grey to a rusty brown and it is hardened, has a ring as he taps it with his pick. This he knows may be but a foot or two from lode rock hidden beyond the walls. But he must be sure before he discusses it with Capun Clymo then shows it to Kit Robin and they drive a cross-cut and perhaps find nothing. Earlier he dialled the end and with that finished, sent his helper, Andrew Johns a boy of twelve, back up to grass so the child might get some extra sleep. Since then he has been studying the walls, the face, the back in closest detail, noting down his observations in his little book.

'Capun, Capun Pascoe.' A call rings down the drive then comes again. Capun Pascoe, are ye there?'

'I am, Daniel.' Thomas knows the voice of Daniel Corney, a Tipperary man known to his Irish mates as Tipp. A broad shouldered fellow with black curly hair, he tributes with Jakeh James and two others on 330 fathom end, or "Jakeh's End" as they call it now. He watches the candle light come bobbing through the darkness towards him. It was strange those first nights underground to hear the Irish voices echoing in the depths of a Cornish mine but he soon became accustomed. In fact Thomas found he liked these men, their songs, their constant banter and quickly became their friend, taking when he could his night-time croust in their easy company. Perhaps it was his time on board ship and those many years in South Australia that made him more approachable than either Mathew Clymo or Dandy Pants. He smiles in the darkness at the aptness of Kit Robin's nickname.

'Capun, we cut somethin' Jakeh thinks you oughter see. Can you come down now to the three thirty?'

'I can indeed for I am finished here.' He pockets his notebook and pick in hand, follows Daniel towards the shaft. ' How are you Daniel? Did you find a proper place to live yet?'

'I did, sir, I did. Thank ye for askin'. Along with me mates we found a stable we're rentin' up by St Cleer. The farmer's a decent sort and it suits us fine.'

The resentment in the district at the coming of the Irish has lessened some but not died out. Thomas shakes his head.

'Could I tell ye something, Capun? Somethin' personal like?'

'Of course, Daniel. I'm sure you won't offend me.'

'No no, Capun, I wouldn't be doin' that. But I thought I oughter say that ye want to be watchin' that Omagh lass, Capun.'

'Omagh lass?'

'Mary O'Malley, sir. In the big house.'

They have reached the shaft and stand there on the sollar before starting the long climb down. 'Why would I want to watch Mary O'Malley, Daniel?'

'Well, sir, I don't quite know how to say this, sir. She's not quite the simple lass she makes out to be. One o' the boys met her on the ship coming across. She's an educated woman, sir. Was puttin' on airs on the ship like she was a lady. So I ask meself, if she's a lady, what she doing as a cook in the big house?'

'Well, she's more than a cook so I understand. She seems to run both house and home.'

'Indeed sir. Well placed to be makin' mischief, I'd say. And there's more that you should know, sir.' He looks at Thomas head on one side.

'Well go on Daniel.'

'Maybe it's none o' my business, but she and Dandy Pants have somethin' goin' on.'

'You mean he's courting her? That's no crime.' Thomas has started the downward climb.

'I wouldn't call it courtin', sir.'

'What would you call it, Daniel?'

'They say he's beddin' her, sir.'

'Do they now, and who might "they" be?'

'The boys, sir. He's been talkin' in the Bedford Arms and now he's the Capun sir, I thought you ought to know.'

Thomas doesn't answer and they continue climbing down in silence. He wonders what he should do with this gossip. It is true that Mary O'Malley seems to dominate the Clymo household in a quiet and unassuming way. He has noticed how his mother defers to her and his stepfather cares only for his mine and perhaps his health. But other men's affairs are not his business. After all, he knew that Henry's wife was unfaithful and kept his counsel. Should he tell his mother what he has heard? No, he'll keep it to himself for now and keep a weather eye on both Kit Robin and his paramour. It seems unlikely she could do much harm and as far as he can tell appears to be a model servant. But it brings to mind another thought that troubles him, his sister Emily. Just a child when he left for Australia, she is a young woman now and an attractive one at that. She has her mother's long brown hair and deep brown eyes and growing up in the Clymo household, she has a certain air far removed from that of a miner's daughter. Last Saturday as he walked with her down through Penpillick, they met a group of miners walking up the hill toward the mine. Thomas passed the time of day with them as he always did, but saw in passing that the eyes of an Irish lad were fixed on Emily's and hers on his. Once past he said to Emily, 'You know that boy?'

'No,' she said but blushed.

Thomas said no more and kept the incident to himself. He stops on the next sollar and waits for Daniel.

'Who was the lad with you on Saturday?' he asks.

'Which lad would that be, sir?'

'There was only one lad, Daniel. The rest of you were men.'

'Ahh, that'll be Michael, sir, Michael McCarthy. He's to start on the night core, sir with Caleb Chapman. Why do you ask, Capun?'

'I like to know our miners, Daniel, men and boys.'

Daniel Corney nods and waits as Thomas steps on to the next ladder. Then he says, 'Michael's a good lad, sir.'

Thomas answers with a grunt and forbears to say "And a Catholic too no doubt." Thomas Pascoe likes these Irish miners but brought up a Methodist he prefers not to dwell on their religion. Idolaters and Papists the preachers call them and the idea that his sister might be sweet on a Catholic pleases him not one bit. They reach the 330 fathom level and head off down the drive towards Jakeh's End. Both men must walk head bent, their eyes on the sleepers of the rail track at their feet. At this depth the simple act of walking makes them pour with sweat. Thomas unbuttons both his jacket and his shirt and Daniel takes off his shirt completely and goes bare-chested. They reach the end and clamber up a pile of rock into the timber supported stope which stretches into darkness far beyond the reach of feeble candlelight. Many tons of copper ore have been drilled and blasted down from here, hammered into pieces small enough to be shovelled into kibbles then pushed along the rail track back to the shaft. Great balks of timber support the void that's left behind and beyond these Jakeh and his gang, all stripped to the waist, are hard at, it driving steel up into the back. The place stinks of sweat, black powder and fresh sawn timber.

'Jakeh,' Thomas calls. 'Dan here says there is something here that I should see.'

The whip-thin miner leans on his hammer and turns to face him. 'There is Capun. Come see the face.' He scrabbles across the rubble pile into deeper darkness. Thomas follows, studying the rock above his head as they crawl into the gap left between the broken ore and the unsupported back. They reach the face which here is little more than two feet wide and less than five feet high, just room enough for one man to swing a hammer and another to hold a borer. Suddenly Thomas feels the unseen pressure of so much rock above him, tries to dismiss it but the image of his boyhood self trapped in just such a place as this, completely fills his mind. He hears the voice of Henry Hopeful Down, "Easy, boy, easy now." and he breathes deep and steady and the fear seeps from him. He takes a candle from the button on his shirt, lights it from the candle on his hat and holds it tight against the face. There deep within the vein of quartz that almost fills the face is a scattering of black crystals. He follows the vein towards the floor and there the crystals coalesce to form a mass that glitters in his candlelight. He sharply draws in breath. Is this just as he had dared to hope?

'Black tin, ain't she Capun. A bunch of black tin or I ain't no Cornishman.'

'I think it is, Jakeh, I think it is. And look, here is the peach that goes along with tin.' He holds the candle tight against the face where a mineral reflects pale green. But I am not certain yet. I only saw it once before and that was above the ground. Here, I'll break off a stone and take it up to daylight where we can be sure. If you've cut a tin lode Jakeh – the first at Wheal Emma, Capun Clymo's going to enjoy his breakfast in the morn.'

XI

DRUNK

'THEY SAY YOU WERE ONCE A MINER. IS THAT TRUE?'

'Could be. Who's askin'?' Henry Hopeful Down looks up at the man who has stopped in front of where he sits slouched on the veranda of the Globe Hotel. He has been drinking all afternoon and has been asking himself whether he will go back into the pub to drink himself into oblivion as he often does, or stop now while he can still walk the hundred yards to his cottage and there collapse. His decision is complicated by the stifling heat made worse by the fumes drifting over Wallaroo from the copper smelter. He squints up against the sun.

'You don't know me then?' the man says. He is almost as tall as Henry, with black hair and a great black beard that covers half his chest and even in the heat of the afternoon, wears a top hat and a long black frock coat.

Henry puts his head on one side. 'Mebbe I do.'

'You are a miner are you not?'

'I were once but now I is a drunk – for me sins.'

'You are indeed. Which brings me to my point. I am Captain Hancock.'

Henry nods. 'I knows 'zackly who you is. You is capun at the Moonta Mine – so what?'

'So what?' the big man scoffs, 'I'll tell you what, I need miners but I don't need drunk miners. You give me your word as a Cornishman and a Christian that you'll turn teetotal and come to chapel Sundays, I'll take you on tutwork or even tribute if you will – good money we're paying now. Moonta's the richest copper mine in the southern hemisphere but I'm short of men who can tell copper from cat shit in the dark.'

Henry shrugs and stares at his dusty boots. It is a month since he fled his home and his responsibilities and he has done little else but drink. He has not been short of money – in all the time he worked at the Pascoe station, Thomas paid him more than the going rate and he spent little. But he knows his savings will not last forever, even though both the grog and his one room miners' cottage are cheap enough. He has not tried to find work but sought simply to forget the failure of his marriage, his humiliation at the hands of Millington and his wife, and perhaps most of all, the knowledge that he has utterly failed his lifelong friend.

'Listen Mr Down – that is your name is it not?'

Henry nods.

'This is a small town and not much goes on in Wallaroo and certainly not in Moonta that I do not hear about. And I have heard the tale they tell about you. You're Thomas Pascoe's mate. He's gone off and left you in the lurch and your wife's run off with that scoundrel Millington.'

'She ain't run off. More like she's run me off. They're still together at the Pascoe Station and I ain't.'

'You have my sympathy, Mr Down but God works in mysterious ways. When I left the England for South Australia, the Pascoe Lode was the talk of the country from Plymouth to Penzance. I know full well that it was you and Thomas Pascoe as found it. I would have had you work for me years ago but neither of you needed me. But now I find you down on your luck just when I need you most. What do you say? Lay off the drink, and come work for me at the Moonta Mine.'

Henry levers himself off the bench and stands swaying face to face with Captain Hancock. He tugs an earlobe. 'It were Thomas Pascoe what found the Pascoe Lode, I just helped him along some. But I ain't going back to tutwork, not for you nor nobody. I'd tribute but I ain't got any mates. But tell you what, if you find me a mate or two mebbe I'll tribute for you.'

'Joe Watson's looking for a mate. You and him would make a pretty pair for he's but five feet tall.'

'You wouldn't make a joke of me would you Capun?'

'No, Mr Down. Mining ain't no joke as well you know. But what about the drink?'

Henry squints at him. 'What about it?'

'Drink and mining are a dangerous mix and I won't have it. And

70

I like my miners to come to Moonta Chapel Sundays.'

'You ask a lot of a man who's going to risk his life down your mine, Capun Hancock. But I'll be at chapel tomorrow if I must, and sober. Mebbe I'll even take the pledge.'

'Good. I have your word?'

'You do.'

'I'll see you tomorrow then, Mr Down.' He touches the brim of his top hat, turns on his heel and strides off down the hot and dusty street.

Henry Hopeful Down watches him go, sits on the bench again and considers what he has just committed to. It was six thousand miles away and eight long years ago when last he drove steel into rock, and in those long gone days he was guided in everything he did by young Thomas Pascoe. Could he, would he, remember all he learned from working side by side, day after day with Thomas? Would he still recognise good copper ore from dud rock? And how different from Wheal Emma would things be in the heat and darkness of the Moonta Mine? At least most of the miners were Cornishmen – some even came from Penpillick and St Cleer. He would find himself among friends. Or would he? Who is Joe Watson, all of five feet tall? But height is no advantage underground. Henry flexes his back in memory of those miles of walking tunnels half crouched. But Joe Watson will surely know his story and surely laugh behind his back. He will need a mate beside him before he can bid on setting day and he will need to understand the value of whatever pitch he bids. And that he has never done before. It was Thomas Pascoe did the bidding, guessing at what wealth they might gouge from this lode or that, and he was almost always right. They made money for themselves and more for the adventurers. In his mind's eye Henry can yet remember how the boy would study every detail of the rocks, trace with his fingers the veins and veinlets, the colours, textures even the very smell of minerals struck with the iron of his pick. "A rich bunch this is Henry. See here, black copper ore and no mistake" or, "Henry, look at this – it's peacock ore all blue and green." Surely he learned enough. Or was it just the drink that gave him the courage to say yes to Capun Hancock. Too late now, he cannot undo his promise. And can he stop the drink as Capun Hancock says he must? He heaves a deep sigh and gets to his feet again. 'One more I'll have, just one,' he says out loud and turns into the pub.

'Intemperance is the sin of our land and with our boundless prosperity is coming upon us like a flood, rolling through the land like a river of fire, destroying the vital air and extending around an atmosphere of death.' Captain Henry Hancock stands bareheaded at the pulpit of the Moonta Chapel, arms upraised, his great beard wagging as he speaks, voice booming over the packed congregation.

Henry Hopeful Down sits in the back row, head in his hands nursing a fearful hangover. The words mean nothing to him, save the very last – "death" . He wishes he could die, wishes he had never agreed to Captain Hancock, wishes he could take back the stupid drunken words of yesterday, wishes he was back in the pub. But here he is, sitting in Chapel just as he did on Sundays as a child with the other village children. He believes in God, the devil and damnation and has given his word that he will be a miner once again. He is not a coward nor has he ever been. It is not the fear of danger underground that grips him. It is the fear of ridicule, of failure and humiliation, and the knowledge that he must take responsibility not just for himself but unknown others whose lives and livelihoods will depend on him. This is the nightmare he will face – a nightmare of his own making that drinking will not solve, any more than it solved his abandonment of his duty to mind the Pascoe Station. If only he could read and write, he'd send a letter to Thomas Pascoe, explain what he has done and why. He hears from stockmen in the pub that Millington and Jane are full in charge and swank around the station as if it were there own, living together in the Pascoe homestead. But Henry cannot write and he is too ashamed to ask a letter writer to even send a telegram. He sighs, sits up and lifts his head to gaze across the congregation. There must be well more than a hundred people in the chapel – miners, miners' wives in their Sunday best and bonnets and people from the town. Yes, Moonta is a town now, church, chapel and The Institute all finely built in rendered brick, paved streets, far from the dusty camp that he and Thomas Pascoe found eight years back. The mine too has changed from simple holes in the ground with makeshift ladders to a proper shaft and hoisting gear and an engine house that looks as if it has come intact from Cornwall. And tomorrow he will be there as he has promised.

Joe Watson is a small man with a face like a wizened apple and two fingers missing from his right hand. He looks up at Henry and laughs. 'My, but you're a big feller, ain't yer.'

'So they say. You a miner then?'

'I am, or I was – on the gold diggings at Ballarat and Bendigo then down south at Strathalbyn on the Wheal Ellen with Captain Hancock. Gave it up for a couple of years – tried farming but it didn't take. So now I come here to tribute. I know silver and I know gold but I needs a partner who knows copper. Captain says you do. An' I see you gotta pick already.'

Henry nods and looks down at the pick laid on the bench beside him. 'Brought it with me from Cornwall eight year ago. And that's the last time I were down a mine.'

'No matter. I don't reckon a man forgets. Gold is gold and copper is copper, wherever. What do you say we go down and have a look? Captain says he wants bids for a pitch on eighty fathom.'

'I ain't never bid a pitch before.'

'Nor have I mate, but I seen it done. Gotta start sometime. Come on, let's get down there. Take a look see.'

They get up from the bench outside the counthouse at the Moonta Mine. They have been sitting there in the morning sun watching the last stragglers of the day core disappear down Taylor's Shaft. Both wear waistcoat, shirt and trousers, broad rimmed hats of hammered felt and heavy hobnailed boots.

'I got candles, two for each of us,' Joe Watson says. 'Should be enough, eh?'

'Long as we don't get lost down there.'

'Hancock says there's only the one end on the 80 fathom so that ain't likely.'

Henry heaves a sigh. 'Let's go down then Mr. Watson.'

'Call me Joe and I shall call you Hopeful Henry – bring us luck.'

'We'll need it.'

They stand for a few some minutes at the shaft head waiting for the cage. Coal smoke billows from the boiler chimney stack shadowing the morning sun. Beside them the iron pump rods rise and fall in time to the thump and hiss of the beam engine, a kibble clatters up the shaft and the banksman tips its cargo of broken rock onto a pile. He waves at the waiting pair. 'What level boys?' he shouts.

'80 fathom,' Henry shouts back.

The banksman nods and looks up at the headframe.

Henry follows his gaze and watches the greased wire rope spinning over the iron sheave wheel as the empty cage rattles up the shaft. He turns to Joe Watson. 'Last time I were down a mine we 'ad to climb down two hundred fathom o' ladders. I ain't never been in a cage.'

'Nothin' to it mate. Just step in and down we go. And tell yer what, it's a damn sight easier comin' back up. Here she is.'

With a bang and a clatter the empty cage appears at surface and an the all-clear bell rings out. They take a handful each of dampened clay from the bin beside the shaft and mould it to their hats then bed a candle in the clay.

'Ready mate?' Joe Watson says.

'Now or never.'

They step into the cage and light their candles, the banksman clangs shut the gate and rings the bell – one ring for down then four for the 80 fathom level. The cage descends slowly at first then picks up speed and seems to drop and Henry's belly drops down with it, down into his boots. He steadies both his body and his mind as the cage hurtles downward, banging and rocking in its wooden guide rails. He watches as the walls flash by too fast for him to see what rock they might be made of. At intervals they pass dark openings, hear the shouts of men echoing down the drives and crosscuts, the sound of shovelling, the ring of hammers and picks as the day core miners start their shift. Boards with painted numbers flash by at every level – 20, 30, 40 Fthm. This is another novelty to Henry for at Wheal Emma while trudging down the ladders they counted passing levels on their fingers. Finally the cage begins to slow then stops, gently bouncing on its cable.

Joe Watson unlatches the gate and they step out of the cage. 'Here we are, mate, eighty fathoms. By Christ it's hot already.' He mops his face and tugs the signal cable once and once again to tell the hoist man they've left the cage.

Henry gazes all about him. Joe is right about the heat. No longer cooled by the rush of air from their descent, he feels the sweat beading on his skin. How different this all is. No cooling water showers down this shaft. And the smells. He sniffs deep – here's eucalypt instead of pine and oak and a mustiness which could be rotting timber or perhaps the stench of bats, or age-old sweat, the sticky stench of grease on the wooden runners of the cage. But the strangest to him is the all-enclosing rock – never has he seen the like. His stomach sinks again. Thomas Pascoe taught him to recognise the Cornish killas – a grey and purple shale that yielded easily to his pick and how its colour changed where it was shot through with veins close to the lode. The granite too and elvan stones and of course the copper lodes themselves. But this rock is alien. He steps away from the cage and looks closely at the shaft walls. This is something he has never seen before, a reddish stone in candlelight with great white flakes that Thomas would call crystals. He hits it with his pick which bounces off with a ringing sound. Will copper too be a different colour here on the far side of the world? He shrugs. At least the darkness is the same and holds no fear for him. It is all enclosing, almost womb-like and Henry Hopeful Down is more at home than he has been for eight long years.

Joe Watson joins him at the rock wall. 'What you looking at, mate? No copper in the shaft, surely.'

'No. I is just looking at the rock to see if she is kindly. But I never seen the like o' this before.'

'"Kindly"?'

'That's what we say back home if a rock is like to hold some copper. This ain't.'

'Well, kindly or not, we knows that this has copper else we wouldn't be asked to bid it. Shall we go look? See if we can't find ourselves a bloody great sturt.' He points towards the opening of a tunnel, to the blackness beyond the rim of their candlelight.

Henry nods, steps out and plunges into the tunnel. It is straight, cutting through the solid rock, no breaks, no falls, no rotten ground, a crystal rock glinting in their candles, a solid roof above their heads and dry beneath their feet. But it is swelteringly hot and deathly still and the sweat streams down their bodies as they step between the rails. Henry walks head and shoulders bent, little Joe Watson strides fully upright. It takes twenty minutes of steady walking before they reach the face where Henry lights another candle. 'Lord,' he whispers

'What?' Joe Watson says.

'Richest I ever seen. Richer even than the Pascoe Lode.' The whole face shines brass yellow in the wavering candlelight.

'What should we bid then if it's so rich?'

Henry is silent, imagining Thomas Pascoe by his side. What would he say – how many shillings in the pound? The richer the lode the lower the bid. The lowest they ever bid was four shillings in the pound and on that pitch they made more money in a month than in the previous six. And this pitch looks richer still.

'How far will she go like this?' Joe Watson asks.

Henry shakes his head. 'Who knows? I don't. But Thomas always said that if she starts sudden and clean like this,' and he traces the margin of the copper lode in the wall, 'she'll carry through for many a fathom. Mebbe we should bid five shillin' in the pound.'

'So for every pound's worth of copper we send up we get five shilling, right? And this stuff's easy digging I'd say. We could do five hundredweight a day. And how much of that is copper?'

'I don't know. I ain't one for arithmatic. I just know five shillin' should see us right, if no pare makes a lower bid.'

'Captain Hancock says he ain't going to put it to an open bid. It's ours if he likes your five bob. I saved his neck in a rock fall down Wheal Ellen an' he ain't one to forget his debts.'

'Why din' you tell me this afore?'

'Listen mate, I didn't know you from Adam until today. But now I seen and heard enough to know you won't let me down, that you're an honest bloke. You been straight and honest with me. So what say you? Are we mates?' Little Joe Watson holds out his maimed right hand and Henry smothers it in his much larger paw.

'Mates,' he says and grins. 'Mates we'll be.'

'Let's go back up then. Tell Captain Hancock our good news.'

XII

BEDSIDE

CAPTAIN CLYMO HAS CALLED HIS FAMILY TO HIS bedside. It is not that he is dying, far from it. It is just that the constant griping of his guts is least painful when he's lying down and so can think. They have asked to meet him altogether. He looks from sombre face to sombre face – Grace, the worry lines draw down her mouth, Thomas, tall, still tanned, with a stubborn and determined air about him and Emily so much like her mother when he first courted her that just to look on her brings him joy.

'So Thomas, how goes my mine?'

'Not well, Capun. The copper lodes are failing on us.'

'What of the tin you found four weeks back on Jakeh's End?'

'Not more than a whisper in the dark, Capun. A hint of what might be deeper down, but no body to it. Nothing we can mine. Perhaps if we go deeper we'll find it. We could sink a winze from the 330.'

'And mundic? Surely we're not running out of that?'

Thomas doesn't answer and looks towards his mother who shakes her head,

'Come on, come on now. I'll have no conspiracies. Speak up.'

Thomas purses his lips then speaks. 'Capun, another worker died last week and five more are taken sick. We have to shut the mundic works . . .'

'God dammit, I won't have that. It's mundic that keeps the mine in profit. If we shut it down we'd have to close the mine entirely.'

'I don't think so. If we go deeper I think we'll cut the North Lode and also find the tin.'

'How can we do that when that damned fool Kit Robin spends a fortune on his harebrained scheme to build a man engine? Why did the adventurers agree to that?'

'I believe that William Morris had a hand in it. We could stop it if we buy more Cornish Consols stock. We could take back control then vote them down and I would sink a winze down from the 330.'

'Damn Morris, the interfering fool. How sure are you we'll find more copper and the tin at depth? Is there another Pascoe lode down there? Will you put your money on it?'

Thomas chews his lip. Of course he is not sure. What he thought to be the top of Wheal Emma's first tin lode was nothing more than an isolated pocket that they mined out in half a day. Since then he has spent hours and hours studying the rocks at the deepest depths of Wheal Emma, gazing at the walls, the floor, the back and every face as it's newly cut in the hope that riches lie at deeper depths. There are hints, but only that – a wisp of copper here or there, black crystal tin glinting in the candle light and the silver shine of mundic freshly broken in the rock. But none of this is certainty. What is certain is that Cornish Consols is killing men, women and their children and not by accident. In the months since his return he has made many visits to the arsenic works and been appalled at what he has found – the wooded river valley where as a child he played and later walked out with Maisie Tuttle, is a devastated wasteland; dead and dying vegetation, the earth stripped bare and noxious yellow fumes pouring from the chimney stack. He has talked with the workers, been to their homes and seen the sickness that arsenic produces – hideous warts and sores on hands and feet, hair falling out in clumps, once healthy workers taken screaming to their beds with cramps with vomiting and the bloody flux and finally, the release of death. So he has agreed with Grace his mother that although he is only Night Captain, he will challenge his step-father once again.

'I will buy Cornish Consols stock. If you do too we can stop Kit Robin's man engine and fund the deepening of the mine. But we must close the mundic works. I will not be a party to it.'

'And what do you think, Grace? Will you defy me too? Are we to risk the loss of all our hard-earned wealth just because your son has gone soft-hearted?'

'It's hard for us to hold our heads up in the village now the wages are so low. Jenny Tuttle no longer speaks to me since Lewis died and that was from the mundic.'

'Lewis was dying long before I put him on the arsenic. He always was a sickly fellow. And Emily, are you against me too?'

'No one is against you Papa. We all just want to help.'

He looks from face to face then grimaces as a spasm wracks his belly. 'And what of the workers? Shall we send them to the poorhouse?'

'If we find some good bunches of copper or a tin lode, we'll need them on the dressing floor.'

'And if we don't?'

'I'd rather see them in the poorhouse than poisoned by us for profit.'

'So be it. I will write to Sanderson instructing him to buy sufficient shares to give us back control. Have you the funds to pay for half?'

'How much do we need?'

'I do not know. Cornish Consols has been much in the doldrums of late so perhaps your scheme may not be the ruin of us all. But Sanderson will tell us.'

There is a knock at the bedroom door and Mary O'Malley comes in bearing a tray. 'Your breakfast, sir,' she says.

'Ah, Mary, what slop have you concocted for me today?'

'Tuesday's bread, sir, soaked in milk with sugar and some nutmeg.' She places the tray on the bedside table, bobs a curtsey and leaves the room.

Mathew sighs. 'Lord, how I wish I could eat proper grub. This pap is all that I can stomach.'

'Tis a pity,' Grace says, 'She's a good cook and serves up proper gentry food.'

Mathew snorts. 'Much good that does me. Emily my sweet, bring pen and paper and I'll write that letter. We'll be wagering money on your divining skills, Thomas Pascoe.' He looks up at his stepson standing beside the bed.

'Yes, Capun, we will. So I'd best get some rest or I'll be fit for nothing, least of all this night's core.' Thomas holds out his hand. 'Thank you Capun.'

Mathew nods and shakes the proffered hand.

As Thomas leaves the room he hears hurried steps on the stairs and catches a glimpse of Mary O'Malley's black dress and white mob cap in the hallway below. He pauses above the stairwell looking down.

Has she been listening at the door and if so, why? He looks back at the bedroom. He should have told them of Kit Robin's philandering but he had forgotten all about it. After that talk with Daniel Corney, the excitement of the tin discovery and his subsequent utter disappointment drove it from his mind. Maybe Kit Robin's behaviour could be used to discredit him with the adventurers and lead to his dismissal. Why had he not thought of that before? He needs more evidence. He will ask his mother what she knows about the comings and goings of her cook. But now he has more serious matters to attend to. They all depend on him now, on his ability to discover riches in the ground, an ability he himself does not really understand. It was his father who found the Pascoe Lode that saved Wheal Emma and made them rich – he just followed his father's footsteps guided by his journal. Now the future of the mine, the future of the miners and their families, of his family, his wife, his children, he will put all this at risk. The bedroom door opens and his mother and sister come out, Emily carrying the Capun's tray.

'Mother, may I talk with you a moment – in private?'

His mother looks at him in surprise. 'Of course you may, my son. Where, in the parlour?'

'In my room I think.'

Emily gives him a sideways look as she steps past him and carries on down the stairs and Thomas thinks that he should also talk to his mother about that Irish boy, Michael McCarthy, something he has intended for some time. He has not spied on his sister but merely noted her absences from home. More than once he has met the boy coming off the night core, given him a warning look and seen the boy's blush visible even under the powder grime.

He ushers Grace into the large bedroom next to the nursery where his children sleep. Maisie has gone to fetch them from dame school. He goes to the window that overlooks the front garden and gazes out over the valley towards the distant sea.

'Thank you for speaking out to the Capun about poor Lewis Tuttle.'

'No need to thank me, son. 'Twas my duty. But you didn't ask me here for that. What bothers you, Thomas?'

He scratches his chin and turns to face his mother. 'How much do you know about Mary?'

'Only that she's Irish, a fine cook and a good girl and that she worked for Mr Lethbridge the magistrate in Bodmin before she came to us.'

'So she came with a letter from him?'

'No. She came with nothing. She was half starved and it was winter so I took her in. She did say she would get a letter but never did. Why do you ask about her?'

'I believe she was listening at the door while we talked with the Capun. And there is tittle-tattle in the mine about her. But never mind. Next time I am to Bodmin I will call on the magistrate and hear what he has to say.'

'Thomas, have you not more important worries than Mary O' Malley?'

'I have, mother, of course I have. But closing the mundic works is . . . is . . . Oh never mind, Mother. Leave it all with me. No need for you to worry.'

'I am not worried about the mine. I know that like your father before you will look after us.' She puts her arms up to his shoulders and turns him to face her. 'My son, I am so happy to have you home. You will stay with us will you not? You won't take Maisie and your sweet children to faraway Australia again? I could not bear it.'

'No Mother. I know my duty lies here in Penpillick. Besides, Henry Hopeful Down looks after our interests over there. He sorely misses Cornwall and would have come with us if he could but he agreed to stay, good man that he is. I will write and tell him we might need to sell up. We'll need the money if we are to control the mine.'

'Did Henry learn to read then?'

'No, but his wife Jane reads and writes for him and helps him manage our affairs.' He turns and gazes out of the window then turns back to her. 'There's something else I think you should know. I believe Emily is walking out in secret with one of the Irish boys.'

Grace Pascoe puts her hands to her mouth and stares at her son wide-eyed. 'Are you sure?'

Thomas nods. 'Since I have been Night Captain I have time during the day to watch the comings and goings in the village. The boy works on the night core too. Have you not noticed that Emily is in the habit of walking out alone most afternoons?'

'Of course. She said to me that she just likes to be out and up on the moor, away from the dirt and noise of the mine, just as you did when you were a boy. And I do not mind for she has little enough to do here. But are you sure she is seeing this boy?'

'Yes Mother, otherwise I would not have spoken of it.'

'I suppose he is a Catholic?'

'Of course he is.'

'I will speak to her today.'

'Good. I must sleep now or I will not be fit for work tonight.'

'Sleep well, Thomas.'

XIII

SATURDAY NIGHT

THEY SIT SIDE BY SIDE AT THE BAR OF THE CORNWALL Hotel which is filled with raucous drinkers, Cornish accents and a general sense of Saturday night male revelry. Most are Moonta miners, some come straight from underground, unwashed and grimy in sweat stained shirts and greasy trousers. Amongst this rowdy mob of men there are but three women in the pub – Mabel and two others who, by their looks and dress, follow her profession. And it's clear they talk of her as they sit together at the other end of the long wooden bar, heads together and looking her way. Henry Hopeful Down takes a deep draught of his beer, sighs and wipes his mouth with the back of his hand. 'I'll tell you this much, Mabel, the heat down that mine gives a man a devil's thirst.'

'Good thing you didn't take the pledge, then.'

Henry takes another swig and gives her a slow smile. ''Tis too, though I reckon Capun Hancock would not be pleased to find me in here on a Saturday night.'

'He don't own you does he? You got your own life.'

'I have now but I got him to thank for that. I think mebbe I would've drunk myself to death otherwise. But tell us, why'd you leave Port Adelaide?'

'Just fancied a change of air and it seems like half of Cornwall was comin' here. So I thought I'd come an' see for meself.'

'When I saw you sittin' here I thought mebbe you come looking for me.'

Mabel puts a hand on her hip and leans back on her bar stool. 'Did you now? And why would that be?' She is dressed for work in a tight waisted, sky-blue dress, shorter than is considered proper in Moonta, showing as it does her small black button boots and a good part of her white-stockinged calf.

'You said I'd see you again and here you is. So I thought, well . . .

84

she musta missed me.' He takes another swig of beer.

Mabel looks up at him, her blues eyes glittering with amusement. 'Well Henry from Wallaroo, I'd not tell you even if that were the case. Fact is things have gone well for me down in Adelaide. See those two?' she looks along the bar to the two women who catch her eye and smile. 'Pretty ain't they.'

'They are too,' Henry says, 'but not as pretty as you.'

She smiles at him. 'They're my girls, Henry, if you get my drift.'

'Right. So you brung 'em up here then.'

'I did and there's two more upstairs. Truth is, seeing how you miners throw money around I thought we'd come to the source. She nods towards a group of bemused looking Cornishmen sitting at a corner table. 'We come up with them lot. They arrived off the boat two weeks back and still don't know what's hit 'em.'

'They tell you zackly where they're from?'

'They did but I forgot the place. Does it matter?'

'They might have news from home. I'd like to know how Thomas Pascoe and his family fare.'

'Why'n't you go an' ask 'em then?'

'I think I'll do that. But don't you be goin' nowhere Mabel. I'll be right back.' But as Henry eases himself off his stool and turns towards the door he stops. 'Well I'll be damned. There's that bugger Millington. What's he doing in Moonta?'

'Smart lookin' cove. Who is he?'

'Bugger stole my wife. I near killed him. Now he runs the Pascoe Station what I was s'posed to do. By Christ, I think he's comin' our way.' Henry stands to his full height and balls his fists. 'I will kill him this time.'

'Easy now big boy. You aint't killin' nobody. You're too good for the hangman's rope. Besides, I didn't come all the way up here to see you done for murder.'

Henry looks down at her then at Millington who pushes through the throng of drinkers, eyes fixed on Henry. He holds an envelope above his head. Henry subsides back on to his stool as Millington stops in front of him. 'Letter for you Henry,' he says.

'You got some cheek Millington, comin' here. I should wring your scrawny neck.'

'Just being civil, Henry. You want this letter or no?'

Henry nods and takes the letter. 'How'd you know where to find me then?'

'Oh everyone in town knows about you mate. You aren't hard to find. Henry Hopeful Down, the cuckolded Cornish giant.'

Both Henry's fists and jaw are clenched and the muscles in his arms stand out like knotted timber.

Millington leans up towards him and almost whispers 'I didn't come without protection. See there, out by the door.'

Two Pascoe station hands are lounging in the doorway and one more stands outside, a rifle in the crook of his arm.

'What did you come for you dirty dog?'

'Oh, just to let you know that all is as it should be at the Pascoe Station and to bring you that.' He points to the letter which Henry has put on the bar. 'Jane's already answered it so there's no need for you to write. Oh of course, I was forgetting – you cannot read and therefore cannot write. By the way, Jane sends her best regards.'

Even above the bar-room racket Mabel can hear Henry's heavy breathing, almost snorting like bull about to charge. She lays her hand on his thigh but he doesn't look at her. 'Your day will come Millington, you shit,' he mutters, 'Your day will come and I'll be there.'

For a moment Millington stares at Mabel then turning back to Henry he says, 'Enjoy your evening with your lovely lady-friend.' He turns away from them and worms his way back through the crowd.

'Gotta say Henry, he's a good looking fella. I can see why your missus took up with him.'

Henry snorts and picks up the letter and gives it to Mabel. 'Is this addressed to me?'

She looks up at him then down at the envelope. 'Yes, "*Mr Henry Hopeful Down*," she reads, "'*Pascoe Station, Wallaroo, South Australia*" You want me to read it to you? It's been opened already.' She lifts the flap.

'Not now, too noisy in here. Maybe later?' He looks at her.

She nods and gives the letter back to him. 'So how is it bein' a miner again. What's it like down that hole?'

'Hotter than you'd believe an' blacker than a crow's arse. But we is makin' good money my partner and me. We got two boys workin' with us and we is into some o' the best copper I ever seen. An' I seen good copper in my time back home. And the new rock drill makes a heap of difference though it fair makes yer ears ring. Christ, if we'd only had 'em back home we woulda made two fortunes. We been at it three months now an' it looks fair to carry on. An' Capun Hancock's a good 'un, fair and square though he's a chapel man and don't hold with drink. So I only drinks on Satd'y nights which is why I'se here tonight.' Henry raises his empty mug and shouts along the bar, his voice booming over the hubbub. 'Hey barman, another beer here and a gin for the lady.'

'And howse about a beer for yer mate?' Little Joe Watson taps him on the arm.

Henry turns, looks down and grins. 'Joe, you all right? You drop them borers at the smithy?'

'I did mate. They'll be sharpened ready Monday morning. Where's that beer? I'm drier than a dead dingo in the desert. Evenin' Ma'am. Ain't you goin' to introduce me, Henry?'

'This is Mabel, my friend from Adelaide. Mabel, this is Joe my partner. Here.' Henry hands Joe a pint mug of beer and the barkeep pushes a glass of gin across to Mabel.

'Your good health Mabel,' Joe says raising his mug, 'And may our good luck continue, Henry.'

Henry drinks deep, wipes his lips and says, 'Reckon it will, Joe. Ain't no reason it shouldn't. Listen, I'se goin' to talk to they Cornish boys on that table over there. They is new in town straight off the boat. Ain't they Mabel?'

She nods. 'Go on Henry, Joe'll keep me company, won't you, kind sir.'

'I will. I'll keep your seat warm, mate but don't be long or Mabel and me might just be off.'

Henry squeezes Joe Watson's shoulder with a meaty hand, slides off his stool and Joe hops on. 'You watch it, boy,' he says.

The crowd around the bar parts as Henry shoulders his way to the table in the corner. 'Evenin' boys, he says, 'Welcome to Moonta. My name's Henry Hopeful Down an' my lady friend over there,' he nods towards the bar, 'says you'm just out from Cornwall.' He holds out his hand and shakes that of each man in turn. 'Now where in Cornwall might you all be from?'

The eldest of the four, a grizzled fellow with a shaggy beard down to his chest speaks up. 'Good to meet you Mr Down. We is from Camborne and thereabouts. Worked at Wheal Tolgus till she closed down. Then there weren't no more work so we took ship an' here we is.'

Henry nods. 'Well, you'll find work here at the Moonta. Capun Hancock's needin' tutworkers and he favours Cornishmen. So show yourselves at the counthouse come Monday morn and the Capun'll take you on – you can count on it. But tell us, do you by chance have news of Cornish Consols and Wheal Emma?'

'That be they mines on Caradon Hill near to Liskeard?'

'That's right – Penpillick. I were underground there for years till I left to come over here?'

'I heard that the copper were runnin' out and they was minin' mundic. But they doin' that down Illogan way too, along with black tin.'

'You hear tell anythin' about Thomas Pascoe.'

The man shook his head. 'Not of late I didn't. You boys hear anythin'?'

Another man spoke up. 'I heard 'ee were back at Wheal Emma. Bein' famous as 'ee is, 'twere all the news up Liskeard way. Sailed the wrong direction if you aks me, Orstralia te England.'

There is a sudden ruckus from the bar and Henry swings around to see Mabel hurl her drink in a man's face. The burly miner lunges at her but little Joe Watson steps between them only to be lifted by his shirt front and slammed against the bar.

'Hang on boys, my mate's in a spot o' strife, 'Henry says. He shoves his way through the crush of drinkers, shouldering men aside, spilling their drinks and deaf to their shouts of outrage. He reaches the bar just as the miner hauls back and punches the dangling Joe full in the face. Henry roars with rage, the miner turns to face him and Henry deals him a mighty clout about the head which rocks the man on his feet but doesn't down him.

'Yer bastard,' he yells, swings back and catches Henry beneath his chin. Henry gives his head a shake and grabs the man, pinning his arms and driving him bodily backward into the crowd. Somebody pounds a fist into Henry's midriff. He doubles over clutching his gut and is hit on the head with a beer mug. He straightens up with a roar. This was the rage that possessed him that dreadful night he left his home, the rage he would have taken out once more on Millington. But now he has it entirely in his own control. He lays about him with both fists and with such fury that his opponents scatter and fall, stumbling over each other, crashing into the tables and spilling drink until the floor is awash with beer, broken crockery and glass. Then Joe Watson is at his side shouting, 'Henry, Henry, enough. That'll do, mate.'

He turns, is looking down at little Joe as if about to speak, when someone slams him twice about the head with something far harder than a fist. His vision blurs, his knees buckle and Henry Hopeful Down collapses on the bar room floor.

XIV

THREE WEEKS

HE SITS, LEGS DANGLING OVER THE BLACKNESS OF the cavernous void where once the Pascoe lode glittered yellow in the candlelight. He has set a candle now on a ledge of rock that juts beyond the lip of this pit, its feeble radiance lost in the utter darkness that lies above, beneath and before him. From far below he can hear the faint slow suck and whoosh of the pump lifting water from the depths of the mine. The air is almost fresh. It seems that somewhere down below a trick of natural ventilation draws clean air into the mine and lifts it in an updraft that whispers past his face. Some might think him foolish to sit perched so casually above a fatal fall but to Thomas Pascoe, a miner at the age of twelve, and now again accustomed to a working life beneath the ground, it holds no fears. Not even knowing, as he does, that twenty paces back along the drive behind him is the place his father died, crushed beneath a rock fall of his own contrivance. He has come here once again to peruse the rocks that enclosed such riches now mined out, to ponder on what circumstances divine or otherwise determined that here his family's fortune would be made. If only there were some peculiarity, some quirk of nature in the rocks he could discern, some colour or component that he could match deeper down in as yet unplumbed depths. But study as he might, he has found nothing here that might guide him in his nightly quest for subterranean wealth. He sighs. If this were his only problem. If only he could still his mind, could bend all the effort of his thinking to this sole purpose. But he is beset. Three weeks have passed since the family stood round the Captain's sickbed and Thomas has advanced the tasks he set himself not one jot. In fact it seems that life conspires against him and his family. To their dismay the price of Cornish Consols' share price leaped upwards just days before they planned to buy. No reason was forthcoming from their contacts in the City, just advice to hold their horses – share prices rise and fall as everybody knows. Thus control remains beyond their reach and Kit Robin stays firm in his position. This very day a letter slipped beneath his bedroom door as he lay sleeping requested his attendance at the counthouse before the night core. There he found Wheal Emma's captain, dressed in a velvet smoking jacket with frog fastenings and two-tone button boots, seated beneath the portrait of old William Morris.

'Ah Pascoe,' he said, 'we need a word. I am less than happy with the Irish on the 330 fathom level. Corney and his partners are up to some trickery, I am sure of it. Their pitch is rich as Croesus and they are bringing but poor stuff up to grass. They must be stealing.'

'I think not,' Thomas said.

'Do you suggest that I can't tell ore from attle?'

Thomas stared at him. 'No, but I think you might be mistaken.'

'That I'm not. I was down there today. There is a splendid run of copper in the face.'

'I will see to it,' he said, though he knew too well that the face the men were working was poor stuff and Kit Robin had mistaken iron pyrites for copper ore. It would not be the first time – fools gold for a fool.

'And Captain Pascoe, I am pleased to inform you that next week Wednesday we shall receive the first wagon load of parts to build the man engine as agreed. Will you please to pick five men from the night core to help with installation. I'm sure you know it is a simple system – just platforms bolted every other fathom to the pump rods – as the pump rod goes up and down and the men step on and off and so rise up.'

He nodded. He has seen a man engine working at Fowey Consols. It is indeed a simple system and in truth they should have built one long ago to save the men that long, exhausting climb. But as Captain Clymo says, he himself had always climbed the ladders and so had Thomas as a boy, so did he still. Why then should the men today not do the same and save the mine the money? He shrugged and went into the dry to change into his working clothes.

'Dandy Pants,' he mutters to himself. 'Bloody Dandy Pants. Damn and blast him.' He picks loose rock from the wall beside him, hurls it out into the darkness and listens until he hears it clatter far down below.

He's sure now that the man has a dalliance with the cook. He rose a little early one afternoon when the house was quiet and went down to the kitchen. Bread and cheese and a side of ham were laid out ready for his evening meal and a large bowl covered with muslin stood on a corner of the kitchen dresser but Mary was not there. He slipped out of the kitchen door into the yard just as the cook came in the garden gate.

'Good afternoon Mary,' he said

She was flustered and would not meet his eye, just bobbed a curtsey and hurried by. He walked out of the gate then some yards down the road from where he watched Kit Robin, swaggering down toward the mine and gazing all about him. He turned away, went back in through the front door of the house then into the kitchen. Mary was at the table tipping out risen bread dough from the bowl on to the floured surface. She looked up at him her faced still flushed and began to knead the dough, pressing with the heels of her hands, first left then right, then left again.

'Mary?' he said.

'Sir?' She did not look up nor even break the rhythm of her work.

'Mary, are you content with your position here?'

'I am sir.'

'So you would not want to lose it?'

This time she stopped her kneading and looked him squarely in the face. 'I would not, sir. Indeed I would not.'

'People talk, Mary. You should know that.'

A flush rose to her cheeks. 'Yes sir.'

'We understand each other. I think.'

She nodded. We do, sir' and bent once more to kneading.

Thomas turned as if to leave then turned back to her. 'Tell me Mary O'Malley, what was it that brought you to Cornwall?'

'Twas the famine, sir. We was starving.'

Thomas nodded and left the kitchen.

At least he's put a spoke in Kit Robin's wheel but dare he raise such tittle-tattle at the next counthouse dinner when his motive would be clear to all?

He would tell his mother but he cannot load her with another burden. She is already worried sick – not just about her husband's illness which grows worse as each week passes, but about her daughter Emily. When three weeks back he quizzed the girl about McCarthy, the Irish boy, she denied all knowledge of him – she did not even blush. He did not insist – he simply took her at her word. But after Sunday's supper just yesterday, his mother called him to the dim-lit parlour, to a scene he never will forget. A shaft of early evening sunlight illuminated just a corner of the patterned carpet beneath his sister's slippered feet. She sat bent over in the corner chair, face buried in her hands and sobbing.

'What is it Emily?' he asked.

She simply shook her head and neither spoke, nor raised her head, nor ceased her sobbing.

'Mother?' he said.

She went and stood beside her daughter, a hand on the armchair's wing. She looked up at him. Her eyes were full of tears. 'Your sister is with child,' she said in a voice not much above a whisper.

He was silent looking at them both. He listened to his breathing, watched the drift of dust motes in the sunlight, put one hand to his chin and his other arm across his chest. He turned away from them, went to the window, staring out unseeing. Of course. He turned around to face them. 'Michael McCarthy?'.

Grace Clymo gave no answer, just touched her daughter on the shoulder.

Emily raised her head and dropped her hands and folded them as if in prayer. She looked up at him. Her eyes were red with crying and the tears ran freely down her cheeks. She nodded.

'Damn,' he said and left the room.

Tonight, now, he must tackle the McCarthy boy who'll be down on the 330 with Tip Corney's team tributing on Jakeh's End. He makes as if to rise from his perch above the pitch black void, but stops and slumps back down. What shall he say? Should he just berate the boy, or knock him down or worse? As night captain he does not have the power to dismiss him from employment and he can not share this shameful knowledge with Kit Robin. No, violence is no solution – the boy must marry Emily, Catholic or not. He and his mother have agreed – there'll be no bastards in the Clymo family. They've not told the Captain – the shock would likely bring about his death. He is so weak that every day it seems his end draws nearer. His mother, though not ill herself, seems to diminish every day – her face is drawn, her shoulders hunched and the bloom has long left her cheeks. They have talked again with Dr Couch to no avail. The illness is still a mystery. He sighs again. But at least all is well with his own family. Maisie is as happy as he has ever seen her; the children have adapted easily to life in Cornwall though the weather was a shock – they had never seen such rain and they miss the sunshine and suffer with the cold. He does too if truth be told. And what a simple life he left back in South Australia. Now he does not know when he will go back, if ever. This he must admit. And what of Henry Hopeful Down – the letter from Bob Millington was such a shock. Henry a drunken down-and-out in Wallaroo? It can't be true. But at least he is assured that all goes well on the Pascoe station. He has held back from its sale as he has cash in hand to buy his share of Cornish Consols stock should the price come right. If not the station will still be waiting for him, if he returns.

'Damn it all,' he shouts out into the darkness. He takes the candle from it's niche and snuffs it out, gets to his feet and plods back towards the shaft and the long climb down.

Michael McCarthy stands head bowed before the Night Captain. One hand holds his pick, the other kneads the brim of the felt hat he clutches to his chest. Thomas called him from the face and walked him down the drive until the ring of steel on steel, of hammer on rock and the shouting of the miners was a far off clamour in the darkness. Now they stand together, isolated in the gloom relieved only by the flickering light of the candle on Thomas Pascoe's hat. Thomas, lips compressed, stands over the boy and studies him. Handsome he is, with deep blue eyes and dark curly hair and a pretty cupid's bow of a mouth. No wonder Emily fell for him. 'Well boy, you've got my sister with child. By rights

I should knock your lights out but I am not a violent man. What have you to say for yourself?'

'I'm deeply sorry, sir. I have done wrong, I know. I've done real bad.' The boy pauses studying the dirty toes protruding from his battered boots. He looks up, eyes brimming with unshed tears. 'But . . . but, sir . . . I'd gladly marry Emily if you would . . . could ever give me your permission. I do love her so.'

Thomas stares down at him unspeaking. Hands on hips he turns away, stares down the drive towards the faint light from the working face. 'I don't know, boy. You put me in a quandary. Permission is not mine to give. Besides, are you of age?'

'I am sixteen, sir but I'd need me father's blessing?'

'And is your father here in Cornwall?'

'He is sir. He stays at Camborne.'

'You will come with me to Camborne then and I and your father shall have a talk.'

'Yes sir. Of course sir. Thank you sir.' He wipes away a tear then looks once more down at his boots.'

'Back to work then, boy. Get back to work now.' Thomas Pascoe turns on his heel and strides down the drive to towards the shaft.

XV

MOONTA GAOL

'MORNIN' HENRY.'

He blinks awake, lies there gazing at the whitewashed iron roof. 'By Christ my head hurts.'

'Yeah, mate. Bloody copper eh? He caught you a couple of good ones with his billy, the bastard. Put you right out. An' you got two lumps the size of emu's eggs.'

Henry raises his hand to his head and fingers the scabbed lumps above his right ear. He groans, drags himself to sitting, swinging his naked feet to the floor and looks around – coarse brick walls, a barred door into a whitewashed brick corridor and set high in the wall opposite a tiny unglazed window. 'We in prison then,' Henry says.

Joe sits opposite on a slatted bench, his back against the wall. 'Yep. Moonta nick.'

'That's quite a shiner you got there. Where's our boots?'

'They took 'em. An' our belts.'

Henry looks down at his waist and nods. 'What next?'

'Dunno, breakfast maybe – coffee, ham an' eggs?' He whistles. 'Jeez, Henry you can fight. They was going down like ninepins. I never seen the like. Where'd you learn it?'

'I didn't. Just comes natural I suppose. I used to wrestle when I'se a boy. What made Mabel throw the drink what started it all?'

'Bloke tried to lift her dress. She didn't take to 'im I suppose.'

'What happened to her?'

'I dunno mate. Coppers dragged you an' me out. Took three of 'em to carry you. Said we started a frackarse and affray whatever that might be. We'll be up before the bloody beak tomorrow, I don't doubt. But Mabel ain't in here. You know what, I reckon she's got a thing for you.'

Henry sighs and shakes his head. 'She's too smart to fall for the likes o' me. Remember them other two girls in the pub? They was workin' for her. She brung 'em up from Adelaide, and some others, so she said.'

'Rich and beautiful eh? You got it made, mate.'

There is the clatter of keys and unlocking doors from the corridor and a policemen hatless but in uniform, shiny silver buttons down his tunic front, stands at their cell door.

'Right you two. You'll not cause trouble? Addy here has got your breakfast.'

'No, mister, we ain't no trouble, spite of all what happened in the pub And we is hungry. Leastways I am. You Henry?'

Henry nods.

A drab dressed woman bearing a tray with mugs of tea and hunks of bread shuffles up to the policeman who unlocks the door. The woman passes the tray to Joe. 'We gotta stay in here until tomorrow?' he asks.

'Fraid so. Magistrate don't work on Sundays,' the copper says and locks the cell door and leaves.

'Grub could be worse,' Joe says. 'This bread ain't more than a day old and tea's a treat. I once spent a week in Melbourne Gaol – bread was mouldy an' maggoty and there weren't nothing but water to drink.'

Henry tears off a piece of bread, chews it then takes a swig of tea. 'Why was you in Melbourne Gaol?'

'Ah, there lies a tale. Tell you what, we got all day. So I'll tell my story and you tell yours. We is mates but we know near nothin' about each other. Minin' an' conversation hardly mix specially with the racket of that new rock drill. Whatcha yer say?'

Henry nods. 'Don't know that I've that much to tell, be honest. I been minin' since I were a boy. I first went down at Wheal Trelawney at Menheniot – that were a lead mine 'tween Liskeard an' Callington. I were a big lad for me eleven years and they put me to workin' a hand pump. Standin' all day long by meself with just me candle for company, up an' down, up an' down – I worked that pump handle till me hands were one big blister an' me arms ached so hard I thought they was fallin' off. Don't mind sayin', I cried every day for a week. I done that for six month. I was took off that when they put a pump engine in – that were a sight to see I can tell you – all black smoke and hissin' steam and they great iron rods goin' up an down hundred times stronger than my achin' arms. So I got to wheelin' barrers which was a mite easier bein' as how I could rest between runs when there weren't no stuff to move. Once I were tall enough to hold a borer an' swing an 'ammer, I was at the face.'

'Was that where you met that Pascoe bloke?'

Henry shakes his head and takes another swig of tea. 'No. I got in bad with John Bryant who was mine agent at Trelawney an' a drinkin' man. Said I was an idle scoundrel. But I weren't. Just that I were bigger than him an' not yet sixteen. Told him he were a useless drunk. So I moved to Cornish Consols an' was partner to John Pascoe tributing copper down Wheal Emma. My, we made money we two. John Pascoe was the best miner I ever seen. Could find copper blindfold in the dark a hundred fathom down he could. But then I got the smallpox.' He touches his pockmarked cheek. 'Time I was better, John Pascoe was workin' secret like, on his own. Wouldn't take me back. Then he was killed by his own blast. Terrible it were. We found him near buried under broken rock. None knew what he'd done nor why. Took his son Thomas to work it out. Thomas were under my wing when he come underground. Twelve years old he were and his dad just dead. Three year later he found the Pascoe Lode – richest copper find in the whole o' Cornwall it were, lyin' hidden just beyond his father's place o' dyin'. Then we come to Australia. The law was after Thomas for a murder he didn't do. So here I is and you knows the rest. Now it's me the wrong side of the law it seems.'

'Wouldn't worry about that. I heard that Symons the beak ain't too bad – a week in here or bound over with a fine is all we'll get. I'd rather pay the bloody fine. We got the money ain't we.'

Henry nods. 'I got some saved. Now what's your story then?'

'It's a long one an' not too pretty, like so many stories in this land. But we got all day.' Joe lies back on the slatted bench, hands behind his head and eyes fixed on the roof. 'She's heatin' up out there,' he says as the iron creaks in the morning sun. 'My mum was a moll. I never knew my dad. Don't think she did either. We lived in a slab hut with a roof o' stringy bark north of Sydney Cove. Poor as bandicoots we was; too bloody poor even for an iron roof like this. Soldiers used to come and visit. I'd spend my time outdoors, playin' with the other kids. I didn't get no schoolin' leastways not then. But mum had a bit o' luck an' got took up by a rich Scotch bloke – real squattocracy he was. Had near three thousand acres pastoral up on the Hawkesbury River. Took my mum and me to live with 'im, even sent me school. Four years good livin' we had. I was doin' real good at school – proper little scholar I was, teacher's pet an' all, read an' write an' do me numbers. Then the Scotch bugger tired of mum an' kicked us out. But she went back on a dark night and stole a great wad of cash he kept hid in a ridin' boot an' we hopped it to Melbourne on the next ship. End of the gold rush it was but we didn't know that then. We went up to Ballarat an' was conned into buyin' a worked out claim an' lost all our money fossickin'. Then me mother got the yellow fever and died.' Joe sighs and shakes his head. 'Didn't have nobody in the world, just me little self. Yeah, little I was, littler than most so it was easy for me to get work burrowin' in them tunnels for gold for others. Never made much money for meself – just enough for food an' drink an' a bed in a tent. But I learned minin', that I did, though I blew me bloody fingers off.' He holds up his right hand. 'Tampin' a shot hole.'

'Seen that more than once,' Henry says.

Joe nods. 'Coulda' been worse. Anyways after three years minin' in the goldfields I'd had enough. Went down to Melbourne which was a right proper city by then – first I'd ever seen. Got a job as a clerk in a law firm but I couldn't stand sittin' on me arse all day an' the pay was bad. So I got work at a boilermakers, me bein' small enough to get inside them bloody boilers. Dirty work it was, worse than mining but I stood it for a couple of years. Used to get drunk on Saturday nights with me mates which is how I ended up in Melbourne clink – drunk and disorderly, just like now. When I got out, I shipped to Adelaide and went underground at Strathalbyn with Capun Hancock. You knows the rest.' He sits up. 'By Christ it's hot in here. I could do with a drink.' He grabs the bars of the cell door and rattles it. ' Hey, turnkey,' he yells, 'we'se bloody roastin' in here. We need a drink. Hey, hey there!'

There is no response so Joe takes up the tin mug that held his tea and bangs it on the bars.

'All right, all right. Keep it down, keep it down.' The constable appears at the cell door carrying a bucket. 'Get away for the door now. Come on, move back.'

Joe sits down on the bench and with a clank of keys, the constable unlocks their cell door and plonks the bucket of water on the floor.

'We ain't dogs you know mate,' Joe says but he squats besides the bucket and bails out a mug of water drinks deep and pours the rest over his head.

'Don't waste it now,' their gaoler says locking the cell. 'And here, this is yours I reckon.' He passes an envelope through the bars to Henry. 'We took it off you last night for safe keeping, Mr Henry Hopeful Down.' He chuckles as he turns away and marches off down the passage and shouts 'Tea at six, gents.'

Henry turns the envelope over in his hands. 'It's that letter Middleton brung. Will you read it to me?' He passes it to Joe and dips his mug into the water bucket and drinks.

Joe nods and takes out and unfolds a single sheet of paper. He studies it for a few seconds then reads:

My Dear Henry,

I write to tell you that our return to Australia is likeley to be much delayed this being due to family circumstances and the unhappy situation in which I find myself at The Wheal Emma. I will not tire you with petty detail – suffice to say that Captain Clymo has fallen very ill with some unknown sickness, Kit Robin is Captain and I am under his command as Night Captain, a duty I find most irksome particularly as the mine itself is come upon hard times.

I am applying myself with all diligence to seeking such remedies may be available to me: viz the search for new rich lodes, the removal of Kit Robin whose incompetence ill suits him for the responsibilities of his position and a cure for the Capun's malady whatever that maybe. Not knowing how long I will be occupied with these tasks I am not able to tell you when I shall return except that it is unlikely to be within the next twelvemonth.

Meanwhile I trust that all is well at the Pascoe Station.

Your friend,

Thomas Pascoe.

'Proper educated your Mr Pascoe ain't 'e?'

Henry does not answer, slumping on the bench with his head in his hands.

'C'mon, mate, it ain't that bad.' Joe taps the letter. 'He ain't comin' back for a long while an' it seems the Millington bloke is looking after the station alright. And we'll be out of here in a week or two if not before.'

'Then what?' Henry mutters not looking up. 'We won't have no job. Capun Hancock ain't goin' to take us on again, is ee. An' I let down the boy I been lookin' out for all these years.' He sits up and touches the wounds on his head. 'An my head is painin' me summat terrible.'

'That'll mend an' there's plenty more mines we can work at. There's that copper mine up at Blinman. They'll be wantin' blokes like us.' He dips his mug in the bucket and sits in silence for a while just sipping water. Then he gets up and begins to pace the cell.

'What is it Joe– you got the fidgets?'

Joe sits. 'Mate I've had this idea of going fossickin' for meself for years but I ain't never done it. Never knew no one to go with. Wot you say we go lookin' for our own selves? 'Tween us we got the knowledge. I'd like to find me own strike mate, answering to no man. Find us a copper or a gold mine. I heard there's gold north of the Flinders.'

Henry bends to the bucket, dips out another mug of water and drinks it straight down. 'I already tried that with Thomas Pascoe but we had no luck an' it's about luck, ain't it. That an' knowin' what we's lookin' for. Thomas Pascoe an' me we got took in by some old larrikin. Wasted six months or more fossickin' and half o' Thomas's dough. Took in proper we was. Didn't find nothin'. But I s'pose leastways you and me knows what we're after and mebbe we'll know it when we see it. Who knows, we might get lucky. But we'll need a grubstake. I ain't got enough money to last more'n a month or two.'

'I gotta bit saved. Reckon I can find the rest. Got a friend or two down in Adelaide. Listen, when we gets out of here we'll go to the city find us a backer, get proper gear, picks and shovels, gold pans, the works and a coupla horses and head north. Whaddya say Hopeful Henry Down? You gonna live up to your name or drown yer sorrows in drink again?'

Henry gets slowly to his feet, takes two paces across the cell and two paces back then stands towering over his friend. He nods and holds out his hand. 'You put it like that I ain't got no choice, have I.'

'It's a deal then.' Joe pumps his hand. 'But first we gotta get out o' this place.'

XVI

RIOT

'ARE YOU GOING BACK TO AUSTRALIA, PAPA?'

'No, my child, of course not. I am to Camborne only. And I shall be back tomorrow I hope. If I were going to Australia you may be sure I should take you with me, and your brother and sister and of course your dear Mama.' Thomas smiles at his wife seated beside him at the breakfast table.

'Mary has packed your bag. It is in the hallway. What time does your train leave, dearest?'

'Half past ten,' Thomas slips his watch from his waistcoat pocket and studies it for a moment, 'I shall take the gig. I have arranged to pick up the McCarthy boy at St Cleer. From there it is but three miles to the station.' He looks down the table at his mother and his sister who stares at her plate of half-eaten breakfast.

Grace Pascoe sighs and shakes her head.

'It is all right, Mother. We shall sort this out, have no fear.'

Grace merely nods. Emily looks up at him her eyes brimming with unshed tears. 'Thank you, Thomas,' she says, her voice barely above a whisper.

Thomas purses his lips, rises from his chair and walks around the table kissing the heads of his three children. 'Work hard at your schooling, now.' He kisses his mother's cheek and leaves the room. In the hallway he dons a dark tweed ulster and top hat. Taking a silver topped cane from the hallstand he catches sight of himself in the mirror – the complete English gentleman. He shakes his head thinking he'd rather be in shirtsleeves back on the Pascoe Station.

They sit facing each other on the wooden benches of a third class carriage on the Great Western Railway from Plymouth to Penzance. Thomas gazes out at the wooded valley of the River Fowey, half obscured by smoke from the engine streaming past the window. It is mid-April.

Oak and ash are hazed yellow-green with the first leaves. He looks at Michael McCarthy who sits head down and hands between his thighs. He is dressed in a brown flannel shirt, worsted jacket frayed at the cuffs and knee britches. His cap is on the bench beside him. His boots are new and polished, bought Thomas thinks with his share of Corney's team's latest tribute earnings. At least the boy doesn't drink. Or does he?

'Do you drink, Michael McCarthy?' He has to shout over the rattle of the carriage.

The boy looks up and shakes his head. 'No sir, never sir.'

Thomas looks out of the window again, then back at the youth. 'If you are to marry our Emily, how will you support her?'

'Wid me earnin's sir. I'm making good money down the mine, sir. I bought meself new boots already.' He holds up a foot for inspection.

'You'll need more than boot money to support a family.'

Michael looks at him, his eyes wide. 'I'm a good worker, sir. I'll make me way in the world, that I will.'

Thomas nods. 'Perhaps you will,' he says, thinking to himself that he'll have to take Michael McCarthy under his wing, show him the secrets of discovery, how to uncover the riches of the mine, in short how to make a life in mining, as he had done and his father before him. But Michael McCarthy is not his son. Young John Pascoe, named for his grandfather is but nine years old and if Thomas has his way, he will never be a miner. Already he reads and writes with ease, can do his numbers and should they stay in Cornwall they'll send him to the Grammar School – he'll be a gentleman. But Thomas needs to pass his knowledge on to someone; if Michael McCarthy is to be his brother-in-law at least the secrets will stay within the family. He shakes his head. He is still not used to the idea of that this Irish lad, a heathen Catholic, will be a member of his family. As a boy Thomas was a chapel-goer and many Sundays he sat and listened as the preacher railed against the Pope and pagan popery. But once in Australia his chapel going largely ceased save for christenings and the like. It seemed to him that a man's religion was his own affair. Still, an Irish Catholic brother-in-law will take some swallowing but swallow it he must if his sister's reputation is to be saved. And he has still not told the Capun that Emma is with child. He'll have to do it sometime soon, unless of course the Capun dies. Perish the very thought. How strange it is that his stepfather now takes the place of his own father, John Pascoe, whom he mourned so long while yet a boy. But it is true – he does love Mathew Clymo. Not of course as once he loved his natural father – this love is more respect and honour and gratitude. He shrugs, looks out of the window once again. High on the valley side a scarp runs rusty red with water running from fissures in the rock. A sign he knows, that within that cliff mineral riches might lie undiscovered. He's tempted to lean across, tap the boy upon the knee and say, "Look Michael McCarthy, just look at that. Iron staining that is, and here in Cornwall the red of iron may mean wealth. Though it's not gold we look for lad, but copper, tin and silver." But he says nothing. Perhaps he will go one day himself and see what there is to see.

He turns away from the window and looks across at his companion who appears to be completely absorbed in the view from the train. He studies him. Yes, he can see the attraction – the high cheekbones, the neat straight nose, full almost girlish lips and a strong jaw and that mop of black hair – the lad is beautiful.

Suddenly aware of the scrutiny, Michael stares back at him from startlingly blue eyes.

'Tell me about your family, Michael McCarthy.'

'My family, sir?'

'Yes, your family. Have you brothers and sisters? And where is your mother?'

'I've three sisters and a little brother and they all live with me mother and me daddy in Camborne.'

'And what does your father do for a living?'

'He's a timberman, sir, at the Condurrow Mine.'

'Is he now? And how did that come about?'

'Come about?'

'Well, a timberman is important job and takes years to learn. And down the mine our lives depend on the timberman's skills. I've not heard of an Irish timberman before.'

'Me father was a joiner back in Ireland, sir. 'Twas easy for him to learn timber settin' in the mine, sir.'

Thomas nods. 'So he works the day core then?'

'Aye, sir, he does.'

'So we may talk with him this evening?'

'Aye sir. I can meet him when he comes to grass. Condurrow Mine is not far from the station.'

Thomas nods and they fall silent, both gazing out at the passing countryside. The train is quite the novelty, not just for an Irish mining lad but for Thomas Pascoe too. He is more used to horseback or pony and trap and the speed of the train still amazes him. There was much talk of building railways in Australia before he left – what a boon that will be, those vast distances, those weeks of hot and dusty riding cut short by this modern miracle. They leave the wooded valleys, the train puffing north-westward up a long and gentle incline to the high bleak ground of central Cornwall. From time to time he spies the engine house of yet another mine, some with smoking chimney stacks and beam engines hard at work, others stilled, no smoke, nor any sign of men or miners. Here he knows the ore is either all mined out or too poor to merit bringing up to grass and whole villages will be starving. There is no doubt that miners and their families leave the county and the country in increasing numbers, drawn by news of family, friends and fortunes made in far-off places – the Americas and Canada, Mexico, and of course Australia. Now and then the train stops at a country station, passengers alight and climb aboard, the guard blows his whistle and off they set again. Past Chacewater they swing westward toward Redruth and Bodmin and Thomas gazes out astonished at the desolation. A pall of coal smoke lies across a wasteland of attle dumps and engine houses, sheds and dressing floors and miserable rows of blackened miners' cottages. A wasteland where not a tree nor a blade of grass is to be seen – just chimney after smoking chimney, except high on a hill just to the south where gorse and brambles sprawl about a brick-built monument, not unlike a chimney stack itself, save that the top is fashioned as a cross. 'Carn Brea – the Basset Monument,' he mutters to himself. His father spoke of this – a monument to Baron Bassett honoured for stamping out a starving miners' riot a century ago. He sighs. He is a miner through and through, a mine owner in all but name, yet is dismayed at the devastation and the misery brought on by his profession.

The train draws to a halt at Camborne Station. They step down onto the platform in a welter of steam, coal smoke, jostling passengers and their luggage. Thomas carries a small valise and Michael clutches a kerchief tied at the corners. Thomas asks a porter the way to the Condurrow Mine.

'Turn right outside the station and it's but a mile down the road,' the porter says.

Once outside Thomas turns to the youth and says, 'I will take a room in town. You go to the mine and wait for your father to come to grass. Ask him to meet me at the King's Head at seven o'clock this evening.'

'Yes sir. What should I tell him?'

'Tell him what you like. Just make sure he comes.'

Michael McCarthy doffs his cap and trots off down the road.

Thomas Pascoe sits alone at a small table set in the bay window of the King's Head. He has just finished a fine supper of venison pie and plums and custard. The sweet aftertaste of the custard is ruining his post-prandial glass of cider. Outside the grey granite of the civic buildings are cast in deep shadow as dusk falls. Inside a coal fire glows warm in the hearth and the inn is crowded with diners at the tables and noisy drinkers at the bar. The inner door of the porch is pushed open and a big man wearing a battered top hat stands there, looks around the room and then down at Michael McCarthy who has followed him in. Michael nods towards Thomas, and his father, for that's clearly who this man is, shoulders his way through the drinkers at the bar towards him. The room falls absolutely silent save for the shuffle of feet as men move away and all eyes follow the newcomers. Nobody smiles. The big man is dressed in a thick woollen shirt, tweed waistcoat, gaudy yellow neckerchief and corduroy britches. Not just big, he is broad shouldered and well muscled, biceps straining the material of his shirt. He reaches Thomas's table, takes off his hat and holds out a callused hand.

'Col McCarthy,' he says, 'Me boy says ye want to see me?'

'I do indeed. Sit down, you too, Michael. My name is Thomas Pascoe.'

'I know who ye are. There's few in the minin' business as doesn't know yer name.'

Thomas nods, 'Would you join me in a glass of cider?'

'I will.'

Father and son sit down and Thomas waves his glass towards the bar. There is no response as backs are turned and a low muttering grumbles about the room.

Col McCarthy looks at Thomas, an eyebrow raised. 'Ye might find that they don't favour our people in here.'

'Is that so? Well, we'll see about that.' Thomas gets to his feet and strides to the bar. 'Landlord,' he says, I am a guest in your inn. I require service at my table.'

The landlord stares at him. 'I can't serve the likes of them in here.'

'Why is that?'

The landlord shrugs his shoulders and glances from face to face of the dozen or so men who now stand around Thomas Pascoe.

'Because they're filthy papist bog trotters is why,' an unkempt balding fellow says. 'An' they take our jobs.'

Thomas stares at him. 'A man's religion is his own business and they get jobs because they work hard,' he says.

'What would a gent like you know about hard work?'

'More than you, I'd wager.' Thomas turns back to the landlord. 'I'll have three glasses of cider at my table, now, if you please.'

'If you must, Mr Pascoe.'

'Mr Pascoe, is it?' the unkempt fellow says. 'So you is one of us – a Cornisshman by God, consortin' with them heathens. Should be ashamed.'

Thomas grabs the man by the lapels of his dirty coat and pulls him close. 'Yes, my name is Thomas Pascoe, Captain at Wheal Emma.

Now shut your drunken mouth before I shut it for you.' He shoves the man away and pushes through the muttering crowd.

'Thomas bloody Pascoe no less. Weren't 'ee up for murder as a boy?'

'Bloody Pascoe lode – rich as can be 'ee is. Best leave 'im be.'

'Thought he was in Australia. Obviously he ain't.'

As he sits the landlord puts three glasses on the table. 'I'se sorry Mr Pascoe, but 'tis a bad business here in Camborne what with the wages goin' down an' more men than jobs.'

Thomas looks up at him but the landlord will not meet his gaze and goes back to the bar.

'Thank you,' Col McCarthy says. 'Now Michael here says that you would talk to me but he hasn't told me why.'

Thomas sips his cider and looks at Michael. 'I think you should tell your father, Michael.'

The youth looks down at the table, wipes his lips then looks away. 'I . . . I, er I have . . . .' He takes a gulp of cider, coughs and splutters.

'You have what?' his father says, 'Come on boy, spit it out now. Spit it out.'

Michael looks at his father, his blue eyes wide. 'I'm sorry father, I'm terrible sorry but I got Mr Pascoe's sister wid' a child.'

Col McCarthy bangs his glass so hard on the table half the cider spills out. 'You did what, you feckin' eejit?'

Thomas leans across the table and murmurs, 'Easy now, Mr McCarthy. I'd rather the whole country didn't know our business.'

Col McCarthy takes a deep breath and glances around the room. 'Aye you're right.' He looks at his son then says, 'So what's to be done?'

'It would seem your boy and our Emily have fallen for each other. Is that not so Michael?'

Michael nods without looking up. 'I love her,' he whispers, 'and Emily loves me.'

His father blows his cheeks out and shakes his head. 'Love!' he says.

'Yes, quite,' Thomas says. 'But listen, we'll not have a bastard in the Pascoe family so I suggest they wed.'

'By rights the boy deserves a whipping.'

'That maybe so, but it will serve nothing.'

'And shall the child be brought up a Catholic?'

'That shall be decided by the parents in due course.'

Col McCarthy drums his fingers on the table. 'And when shall this weddin' be?'

'As soon as possible I suggest.'

Col nods and lashing out across the table, fetches his son a stinging clout across the face almost knocking him off his chair. 'Eejit boy,' he hisses.

There is a muttering from the bar and from the other diners and tears start from Michael's eyes as his pretty cheek blossoms bright red. 'I'm sorry father.'

'Hah, too late for sorry, so it is. I'd not see him wed so young and certainly not to a Protestant. I wanted him to be a miner.'

'He'll be a miner. I'll see to that. And I'm not overjoyed at my sister marrying a Catholic. But needs must, Mr McCarthy. What do you say? Will you shake on it?'

Col McCarthy sits silent, looking first at his son then at Thomas. Then he sighs and holds out his hand. 'I will, if I must.'

'Good, that's settled then,' Thomas says shaking his hand. 'We will arrange for the wedding at Penpillick. Will Michael stay with you tonight?'

Col nods.

'Then I'll see him at the station on the morrow. The train for Liskeard leaves at half past ten.'

Father and son rise from the table. 'Thank you, Capun Pascoe,' Michael says.

All eyes watch them leave. The group at the bar stare at Thomas muttering as he finishes his drink and gets up to go to his room. As he passes them someone hisses 'Papist pot-lickers,' and spits on the floor.

All is quiet next morning as alone in the dining room, Thomas takes a late breakfast of fried herring, eggs and toast and tea. A cold spring rain splatters against the widow pane. He looks out at the grey stone town and sighs to himself. Well at least his sister will not give birth out of wedlock and his mother will be, if not content, at least relieved that there'll be no bastards to sully the Pascoe name. He will explain his actions to his stepfather if and when he's well enough, even though he'd rather not. His valise is packed and ready by the door. At ten he rises from the table and calls out, 'Landlord, I am away to catch the train.'

A head appears around the kitchen door and the landlord crosses the room to shake his hand. 'I'm sorry about last night Capun Pascoe but the Irish, there's so many of 'em here these days. And the townsfolk, good chapel goers that they are, they do resent 'em. Folks are threatening to burn down the Catholic Chapel, burn their houses too and chase 'em out of town.'

Thomas shakes his head. 'That's not good. We have Irish miners at Wheal Emma and good workers they are too. I don't hold with popery myself but a man's religion is his own business.'

'Indeed, sir. Let me help you with your coat.'

Thomas shrugs into his Ulster, dons his hat and picks up his valise and walking cane. 'Good-day to you and thank you for your hospitality.' He walks out into the rainy street. It takes him but five minutes to reach the station by which time the rain has stopped. The platform bustles with passengers waiting for the London train – his train too. He takes out his pocket watch – five minutes until it leaves. He scans the platform for Michael McCarthy of whom there is no sign. He goes out to the road and waits a few minutes then returns. He stops a porter wheeling a trolley full of luggage. 'Have you seen an Irish lad, by any chance, blue eyes, black hair – a striking fellow, difficult to miss?'

'No, cain't say as I 'ave but I heard there's trouble down at the Irish chapel. Maybe your man's down there. Excuse me sir, here comes the train.'

With an ear-splitting whistle and the hiss of escaping steam the train draws into the station. Thomas watches as passengers alight on the platform. 'Damn the boy,' he mutters. It can only be that something serious has delayed him. Thomas does not want to return to Penpillick without him, nor does he want to miss this train. The last passengers climb aboard, a guard waves a green flag and blows a whistle and belching black smoke, the train chugs out of the station. He stands on the platform watching the retreating carriages.

'You missed it, sir.' It is the porter standing at his side, his trolley now emptied of luggage. 'Next train's at two this afternoon.'

Thomas takes off his hat and scratches his head. 'Where's the chapel you spoke of?'

'Just down the road, sir – hundred yards or so toward Condurrow.'

'Perhaps my man is there as you suggested. Or maybe at the Condurrow Mine itself. How far is that?'

'Just a mile, sir.'

'Good, I can be there and back in time for the next train. May I leave my bag with you?'

'Indeed you can, sir.' The porter takes Thomas's valise.

As he strides away from the station, above the rattle of coach wheels on the cobbles and the clop of horses hooves, he hears a murmur that grows louder every step he takes. He stops a moment and listens. Yes, shouting, sudden cries and the sound of breaking glass and there, just on the curve ahead he sees a crowd of men and women some carrying sticks and staves and others throwing stones. He breaks into a run and reaches the mob, for that is what it is – a yelling, screaming mob of men and women blocking the road in front of a modest stone-built chapel.

'Burn it down. Burn it, burn it.'

'Out with the heathens, out, out, out.'

'Down with papists. Burn the buggers.'

Thomas clambers up on a low wall opposite and balancing precariously looks out over the heads of the mob. They are massed against the chapel steps where a dozen men or so drag pews and chairs out through the broken wooden doors. Two women emerge loaded down with silverware and a gilded crucifix, followed by the unkempt drinker from the night before who clutches a blue-painted statue of the Virgin to his chest. He hurls it from the steps and the mob surround it, beating it with sticks and stamping on the head. There is the sound of running feet and Thomas turns to see a gang of men approaching up the Condurrow Road. Some carry picks and others metal tipped staves and some are wearing miners' hats. From the mine, he thinks and there in the forefront of the gang he spies the hulking form of Col McCarthy and beside him Michael. A whistle blows and then another and another and looking the other way he sees a dozen black-clad constables, truncheons at the ready, running from the direction of the station. Trapped between opposing forces, the rioters cease their yelling, drop their sticks and stones, draw down their hats and raise coat collars to hide their guilty faces. Those at the splintered chapel doors drop their loot, slink down the steps and mingle with the dispersing crowd. Constables and miners now meet face to face. The miners stand their ground. Thomas gets down from his vantage point and sits upon the wall.

A sergeant steps forward revolver in hand. 'Arrest those men,' he shouts, pointing at McCarthy, father and son and their companions.

Two constables approach the miners.

Thomas gets off the wall, walks into the middle of the road and faces the sergeant who still holds his revolver by his side. 'Sergeant, you arrived in the nick of time. I saw it all. The mob were sacking the church. These men arrived when you did. They have done nothing.'

'And who might you be, sir? You are not a Camborne man.'

'Captain Thomas Pascoe from Wheal Emma over by Liskeard, at your service. I know these men and I can vouch for them.'

'They are Irish,'

'Indeed they are – Irish miners. But I will swear in court that other than being Irish, they had nothing to do with the riot. It's the rioters you should arrest.'

The sergeant looks around. 'What rioters? I see no rioters.' Indeed the mob has largely disappeared save for the unkempt drinker and the woman looter who loiter up the road, looking back from time to time to watch proceedings.

Thomas blinks. 'No, they've run away, cowards that they are. So you'll press no charges?'

The sergeant shrugs. 'Come men. Good day to you Captain Pascoe.' He turns on his heel and marches back towards the station followed by his men.

The gang of miners stand disconsolate gazing at their violated church and talking in low tones amongst themselves.

Col McCarthy approaches Thomas, hand held out. 'Me heartfelt thanks, Capun. But for you we'd be headed for the clink.'

'I'm glad to be of service. I was accused unjustly once and I've not forgotten how it feels.'

Michael too holds out his hand. 'Thank you Capun, thank you, sir. I'm sorry I made you miss our train. But we heard they was goin' to burn the church and Father told me I must stay to help and stop them.'

'Not to worry, Michael. There is another train at two so we'll be home tonight. What say you we go back into town and find ourselves some luncheon?'

Col McCarthy moves close and touches Thomas on the shoulder. 'Capun Pascoe, we need to talk. Ye've done us a great favour – the first an Englishman ever did me for me and one good turn deserves another. Besides we're to be related somehow are we not? That is if my son marries your sister.'

'I suppose we are. Shall we talk over luncheon?'

'I'll not be joining ye thanks all the same for I must get back to me work. But first I got a little story to tell. We need somewhere quiet and private like. The boy can hear it too. Let's go in to the church? What do ye say?'

'Hmm, I suppose so. Can't harm me can it?'

Col McCarthy gives a shout of laughter. 'Ahh you Protestants. Harm you? Might save your very soul. Come on. You'll be glad to hear my tale.'

They climb the steps where two miners clear up the broken furniture and glass and vestments torn to shreds.

'Don't let no one disturb us now, we're to have a private talk,' Col says.

They nod in unison. 'The bastards. Will ye just look at this.' The miner holds up a painting of the Virgin that is slashed across the face.

They pass through the shattered doors into the church. Both Col and Michael take off their hats, kneel in the aisle and cross themselves. Thomas too removes his hat but does not kneel or cross himself. He

114

does not know how nor what it means – it is a thing that Catholics do.

Col stands and shakes his head 'Ahh, will ye look at what they've done now. Tis all broken and smashed, the heathen gobshites. And they stole the silver crucifix and cup. Would ye believe it?'

Thomas gazes around. For the first time in his life he is in a Catholic church. He is surprised how little it differs from the chapels he attended as a boy – rows of pews with an aisle between, a pulpit, windows in the Gothic style and a high arched timbered roof. But the smell is very strange, a smell he's never come across – scented, not unpleasant but foreign and pervasive. He sniffs and sniffs again – this must be what's called incense. And even ravaged as it is, he can see that the little church was highly decorated with images of saints and gilding and there above the altar, Christ crucified stares down. He studies the dripping wounds, the crown of thorns, the protruding ribs, the pierced side. These are sights he had imagined when he read his bible as a boy but never thought to see depicted with such fidelity. Is this idolatry, works of the devil? How can that be? The finely carved confessional is reduced to matchwood, the pulpit half torn down and the organ lies in bits across the floor. A lone woman is at the altar replacing two large candlesticks. He turns to Col. 'I apologise profoundly for what my countrymen have done. This is not right.'

Col nods. 'I've seen worse, much worse. Your people have done terrible things to my people over there in Ireland. There'll be retribution one day, I don't doubt. But that's not what I want to talk to ye about. I want to tell ye a little story. Now sit ye down.'

The three sit in the back row of the pews with Col McCarthy in the middle. He starts to speak, his voice low, his Irish brogue stronger than before. 'Tis common knowledge is it not the we Irish left home and country to escape the misery of our lives – no work, no food and English landlords stealin' what little we had left.' He looks enquiringly at Thomas. 'I've known famine on and off for all me life, though in Tyrone we were luckier than most. We had food and I found work just enough to keep the family. But when I heard the rumour that good money could be earned here in yer Cornish mines, I didn't hesitate to join a group from Omagh and we come over three years ago. It's decision I don't regret in spite o' things like this.' He gestures round the church. 'Now I can see you're wonderin' Capun Pascoe, what all this has to do wid' you?'

'Indeed, I am.'

'Well, do ye remember sayin' last night that you wouldn't have a bastard in the Pascoe family.'

'I do. And that still holds.'

'Well, it does and it doesn't.'

'What do you mean?'

'You got one already, Capun Pascoe.'

'How dare you, sir,' Thomas grips the pew in front of him and turns to the Irishman. 'You'll take that back.'

Col McCarthy, grinning shakes his head. 'I'll not, for 'tis God's truth, so it is. Listen and I'll explain. Ye see Captain, I don't doubt that to you I'm just another bloody Irishman but the fact is that my family goes back to the old kings of Ireland, so it does and it behoves me to find out what I can about me son's in-laws to be. So last night I had a chat with Michael here who told me all he knows. Well, seems you were a bit of a hero yerself according to the gossip, some of which is common knowledge, is it not?'

Thomas nods still at a loss to understand where this going.

'Now in Michael's telling of your exploits, a certain name come up which took me back to the old country and sad events of long ago. You should know captain, that the owner of half the county of Tyrone which is where we're from, was the Duke of Abercorn. He wasn't the worst as English lordships go, but his agent was a bastard through and through, metaphorically speakin' as it were – a thief, a liar, and a murderer. He got a village lass with child – he raped her, so he did, the dirty swine. By the time the child was born he was long gone – stabbed a man to death over unpaid rent and scuttled back to England, back here to Cornwall. The lass died in childbirth and Mary was brought up in Omagh by the Sisters of Mercy.' He stops speaking, watching Thomas as the import of his tragic tale begins to dawn. 'I wouldn't like

116

to speak ill of the church but from what I heard, the holy sisters spend more time tryin' to beat the sin out of a child then showing mercy. Mary come outa that convent as hard as nails.'

'Are you telling me that this Mary is our Mary O'Malley?'

'Aye, that she is.'

'And the father's name?' Thomas asks although he knows the answer.

'William Scoble.'

"William Scoble, William Scoble, William Scoble." The name is drumming in his ears in time to the puffing of the train. 'William Scoble, William Scoble, William Scoble.' He shakes his head and scratches in his hair. After so long the dead man returns to haunt him. Scoble, agent to the Duke of Bedford. Scoble who stole his father's secret journal, left him for dead on Bodmin Moor. Scoble who stole Wheal Emma from Mathew Clymo. Scoble who killed poor Jethro Loam then plunged two hundred fathoms down the shaft to a grisly death. So many years have passed – he's barely thought of him save once or twice in nightmares or talking through his boyhood with Henry Hopeful Down. And now the villain's daughter is deep within Clymo-Pascoe household, working at its very heart. She may of course be innocent, may know nothing of her father's history. But Scoble died intestate while owner of Wheal Emma and none knew he had a daughter, bastard or otherwise. He must get back. He gets up from his seat, he paces to and fro, puts his head out through the window, pulls it in, and wipes smoke smuts from his eyes. He sits again takes out his pocket watch – three hours until he is home. And then what should he do?

XVII

MABEL

'FORTY SHILLINGS EACH OR ONE MONTH GAOL IF IN default.' The magistrate bangs his gavel. 'Next.'

Henry Hopeful Down and Joe Watson step down from the dock in Kadina Magistrates Court.

'Jeez, that's most of our grubstake gone ain't it?' Joe mutters. Still coulda been worse if they'd done us for more than bein' drunk.'

'You boys got the readies then?' the constable asks as he unlocks their handcuffs.

'Well, not on us. But we can get it.'

'You got twenty eight days. After that it's back inside.'

They come out of the courtroom into blazing sunshine. 'We going to walk back to Moonta then?'

Henry nods and sniffs. 'Don't see no other way. Ten mile or so'll tek us three hour if we step on it.'

'Whadd'ya say we quench our thirst afore we start?'

'I don't know Joe. 'Twas boozin' as got us in trouble in the first place.'

'Come on mate. A beer or two won't hurt. Exchange is just around the corner.

'All right, just one beer then.'

They walk down the street to the Royal Exchange Hotel. Double storied with shady deep verandas that wrap right around the corner, it is inviting. Henry cannot help but lick his lips. A group of men in working clothes lounge outside the entrance.

'Mornin' fellas,' Joe Watson says.

They nod acknowledgement eyeing the newcomers as they go in. The bar is long, extending the length of both sides of the hotel. A balustraded staircase leads to the second storey where numbered rooms open onto a balcony. Lone drinkers sit on low-backed stools and a bartender polishes glasses behind the bar. The place smells of beer, tobacco smoke and unwashed bodies.

'What'll it be gents?' the bartender asks.

'Beer for me and for me mate,' Joe Watson says.

The bartender fills two glasses from the tap. 'You'll be miners up from Moonta, eh?'

Joe nods. 'We are. But what's that to you?'

'Just that up there,' he nods towards the upstairs rooms, 'Room Twelve there's a lady who was askin' for yer.' The stress he lays on "lady" leaves little doubt as to what he means.

'That so. How d'yer know it's us she wants?'

'"Two miners – one small, one big, a cousin jack." she said. Who else would that be?'

Joe shrugs and slaps a coin on the polished counter. 'Thanks.'

They take their beers to a table by the window.

'That'll be your Mabel won't it,' Joe says looking up towards the second floor.

'My Mabel? I don't know 'bout that. She's a friend is all.'

'You gonna go up, tell her we's here then?'

Henry studies the foam on his beer. 'I dunno, Joe. She's a working girl ain't she. Might take it the wrong way.'

'Mate, she asked for us. Least we can do is tell 'er we's here. 'Sides, forgot to tell yer – fore that scrap last Saturday she was talkin' about you. What a soft old bugger y'are for such a big bloke.'

Henry shrugs and looks up towards the balcony. 'Or'll right then I'll go up.' He takes a swig of his beer and stands. As he reaches the staircase a door opens upstairs and Mabel steps out. She looks down and seeing Henry stops at the top of the staircase a hand on the newel post.

'Hello Henry. Just dandy seeing you here.'

'Barman said you be lookin' for us.'

'Did he now? Perhaps I am.' She comes slowly down the stairs, one hand on the banister the other just lifting her full black skirt which sways with each step. Reaching him she taps him on the chest. 'That was quite a fight you boys got into on my account.'

Henry rubs the side of his head and grins. 'Yes Missus, it were a fight orlright. You take a drink with me and Joe then?'

She looks across at the barman. 'They don't let women drink in here in daylight hours, Henry. This ain't Moonta on a Saturday night. But I do want to talk to you. That's why I come. There's a tea room opposite. I'll be in there.' Mabel walks out of the hotel ignoring the bartender's stare and the muttered comments from the drinkers sat in the veranda's shade.

Henry goes back to the table, sits and downs his beer. 'She wants to talk to us. Don't know what about.'

'She wants to talk to you. Sweet on you she is, like I said.'

'I dunno Joe. What say you we go and 'ave ourselves a cup o'tea then?'

'Sure, why not?'

The tearoom doorbell tinkles as one large and one small miner walk in and are gazed at in some wonder by the ladies in flowered hats sat at tables drinking tea from china cups. They watch eyes wide as the two cross the room to the corner where Mabel sits at a table with three places already laid with cake and biscuits on flowered plates. She looks up at them and laughs. 'Don't just stand there then like gobsmacked boys. Sit down and have some tea. That's a lovely shiner you got there, Joe.'

'You should see the other bloke.'

They sit. She pours them tea and cuts a cake. They each take a piece.

'You want to talk to us?' Henry says

'I do. When I heard you were going before the beak today I thought you might need some help so I came here this morning – see what I could do. You've both done time in jail on my behalf and I reckon one good turn deserves another. But I was too late for the court. I guessed that first thing you would do was get a drink so I booked in across the road.'

Both men nod and sip their tea.

'So you got a fine?'

'Beak musta been in a good mood – forty bob each.'

'I'll pay that.'

'You will?' Henry says

'Yes, least I can do.' Mabel drops her voice. 'Now listen Henry, there's another thing – that bloke Millington come in again the other night and was throwing money around like he'd won the Melbourne Cup. Went with one of the girls an' she told me next day he was boastin' that he'd sold two thousand sheep from some station up north of Wallaroo. That'd be your Mr Pascoe's station wouldn't it?'

Henry puts his teacup back on its saucer as delicately as he can manage and scratches his head. 'Could be. Must be. I'm s'posed to be lookin' after it and now I've been in prison an' if he's runnin' it down . . . aw Christ, I don't know what to do. And the dirty bugger's with my wife too.' He puts his head in his hands.

'Hold on Henry it ain't as bad as it sounds.' Mabel reaches across the table and puts a hand on Henry's arm. 'Your wife deserves all she gets and I got an idea. You and your mate Joe here, you go up there and see what's goin' on. See if the bugger has been selling stock. If he has we'll write to your Mr Pascoe tell him what's going on.'

'An' then what?' Joe says. 'What's the famous Mr Pascoe gonna do about it from fifteen thousand mile away? He writ a letter said he ain't coming back for another year. Ain't that right Henry?'

Henry nods.

'Anyway Mabel, me an' Henry, we gotta plan.' He looks around the tea room and drops his voice to a near whisper. 'We'se goin' up north find us our own mine. Had enough of bustin' our guts for Capun Hancock. 'Sides he won't take us back like as not. Henry's tops at findin' copper an I'm a minin' man through and through. Yer wouldn't fancy backin' us would yer Mabel?'

Mabel gives a little snort and smiles. 'What makes you think I have that sort of money? You been talkin' Henry or was this your idea from the start?'

Henry blushes and shakes his head. 'No, first I heard of it is now. Joe an' I just talked about goin' fossickin' while we was in the nick. Anyways, I wouldn't ask you for money Mabel.'

'Wouldn't you now? Why not? Think you might hurt my feelings?' She leans back in her chair and laughs and heads turn on nearby tables. Then she leans towards them and says in a quiet voice, 'Listen boys, I like you both. You, Henry from Wallaroo, for all your size are one of

121

the gentlest men I've ever met and in my time I've met some men. And you Joe Watson, little as you are, you stood up for me last Saturday night as if I was a lady and that I ain't, nor do I pretend to be. So tell me, what's the deal and I'll see what I can do.'

Joe swigs down the rest of his tea, plonks cup in saucer and rubs the back of his neck. 'Well, Henry's right, we ain't talked about it. The idea just come to me when you said one good turn deserves another. But I reckon we need. . . let me think . . . well, coupla a bob a day for grub. We'll need horses, picks and pans an' cookin' gear, not much else. Hundred pound should cover it.'

'Hold on Joe. How long we goin' for?'

'Six month I reckon. At least as a start. Shoulda found somethin' by then.'

'And if you do, what do I get for my hundred pounds?'

Joe looks at Henry who looks back at him a question in his eyes. 'A quarter of all we find. That's fair ain't it Henry?'

Henry shrugs as Mabel laughs again and shakes her head. 'I wasn't born yesterday? Listen boys, I've heard more miners' pillow talk than you heard stories at your mother's knee. I know the gamble I'll be taking on you two, and that's only if you'll meet my terms.' She stops and leans across the table blue eyes glinting. 'Half of what you find plus a hundredth. What d'ye say?'

The men stay silent looking first at her then at each other. Henry shrugs again.

Mabel gets to her feet. 'Perhaps you need a little conflab by yourselves. I'll be across the road. You'll find me in my room.'

They sit side by side on the veranda of the Royal Exchange Hotel chatting in low tones and sipping beer. The setting sun casts long shadows down the dusty street and the curved iron roof creaks as it cools. A scrawny dog lifts it's leg and pisses on the post in front of Henry's outstretched boot. Henry raps his heel on the wooden floor. The dog looks at him then trots away. 'Well Joe, what do we do?'

Joe Watson shakes his head. 'Jeez, Henry she's a smart lady an' no mistake. Half of everything plus a hundredth.'

'What's the hundredth for?'

'She'll be the boss – own more than us together.'

'Well that sits orlright with me though I ain't never worked for a woman before.'

'Nor 'ave I, but we'll be way outback and on our own. Women don't go minin' do they.'

'Do back home. We got bal maidens workin' at grass.'

'Yeah, well Mabel ain't no maiden is she. You wanna do what she said – go up to your old home see what that fuckin' bastard Millington is up to?'

'S'pose we should. What about her offer then. We goin' to tek it?'

' I reckon we should. What about you?'

'I do too.'

Joe looks at his companion. 'You bin with her, aint yer?'

'I have, just twice – once, in Port Adelaide an' once in Wallaroo.'

'How was it?'

Henry gives a little shake of his head and stares out into the street. 'I ain't sayin'.'

'Would you go with her again?'

'Why you askin' me 'bout this. 'Tis private ain't it.'

'Henry my friend, and you is my friend, we do this deal with her an' we is business partners, you and me an' Mabel.' He takes a drink. 'Business an' lovin' stuff don't mix. Like to come between us, an that ain't goin' to be no good if we'se out the other side of woop-woop, just you an' me an' roos and bloody dingoes not ter mention bloody flies. Know what I mean?'

Henry nods. 'Don't think she'd have me anyway.'

'She'd eat you fer bloody breakfast, mate. So let's shake on it. Do the deal with Mabel and we're fancy free. First we'll head up to your old place. Then we'll go up to Port Augusta get kitted up and head out to Blinman. No need to go to Adelaide. We got our grubstake.' He puts an arm round Henry's shoulder, holds out his hand. A long slow grin creases Henry's face as his friend's small hand is enveloped by his own.

XVIII

ARSENIC

DUSK IS FALLING AS THOMAS DRIVES THE BUGGY UP through Penpillick. He sniffs at the now familiar smell of coal smoke mingled with the sulphurous reek of the waste dumps that always hangs in the village air. Even here he can hear the steady clatter of the stamps crushing new-mined ore to fragments, ready for the women and children at the sorting tables on the morrow.

'Whoa there, whoa,' he calls out and the pony stops. He turns to Michael McCarthy sitting at his side. 'Say nothing to anybody of what your father spoke of. You understand?'

'I do sir. Yes sir.'

'I shall speak to Emily tonight, Michael, but do not come calling until the weekend.'

'No sir. Thank you sir. Might I shake your hand sir?'

Thomas nods and holds out his hand. 'Good night Michael.'

'Good night, sir.' Michael McCarthy doffs his cap as he climbs down from the buggy and disappears into the gathering gloom.

'Walk on.' The sense of urgency that has possessed him since he heard again the name of Scoble has not diminished but is tempered now by the comfort of a plan he thought out on the train. He'll say nothing to his mother, much less to Captain Clymo. He'll bide his time, watch Mary O'Malley with great care and leave Scoble's daughter as now he thinks of her, suspecting nothing. Firstly he will investigate her room. But one thing he must do with urgency – it came to him in the train. She is the cook, prepares all the family's food and feeds the Captain special dishes – gruels, porridges and pap that no other member of the family touches. Would she, could she, poison him? She has a motive and every opportunity after all. Her father William Scoble was Cornish Consols largest shareholder when he died intestate with no known relatives. The Duke of Bedford, mineral lord, appointed Captain Clymo to run the mine again and the adventurers approved. But that fell by the wayside when the Captain took to his sickbed. And now the mine is in the hands of Mary Scoble's lover – Dandy Pants, Kit Robin. And if the Captain were to die – what then? A tangled mess this is and a mess he must unravel.

The buggy's iron-clad wheels clatter across the stable yard. 'Whoa, whoa there,' he calls as the stable boy appears and takes the pony's bridle. He leaps down grabs his valise and cane. 'Thank you, boy.' He almost runs round to the front door which opens at his approach and there is his mother silhouetted against the lamplight.

'Thomas, Thomas thank the Lord that you are home. The Capun, the Capun. Oh Lord, Thomas.' She covers her face with her hands and weeps.

He drops his valise and holds her in his arms. 'Mother, what is it? He is not . . . not gone?'

'No, no but he is so sick my son, I fear now for his life.' Her body heaves with sobs as she buries her face in his coat.

Thomas hustles her inside the door and speaks in a low voice. 'Mother, listen, I believe I know what ails him. But first, where is Maisie?'

'She is upstairs with the Capun. But how could you know what ails him?'

''Tis something I heard in Camborne. Now tell me when and what did he last eat?'

She looks up at him, sniffs and wipes her eyes. 'Why, he had his usual gruel at breakfast time and said he was feeling better but in the middle of the morning I heard him cry out. I ran upstairs and found him fitting, crying out in agony then doubling up he let loose an awful bloody flux. Then he lay still, just breathing in a stupor and does so still. Maisie and I cleaned him up and have had the doctor to him but he says there is nothing to be done. Oh Thomas, what shall we do, what shall we do? I could not bear to lose another husband.'

'Call the cook to your sitting room and keep her there until I say. I believe the Capun may be poisoned. Do not ask me why. It would take too long to explain. Now, mother, please I beg you, do it now.'

She looks up at him in fear and wonder. 'Poisoned? Thomas are you sure?'

'No mother I am not sure but please do as I say.' He shrugs off his coat, drops his valise and cane. I will go upstairs and see the Capun, then I will search her room and then the kitchen. As I say, you must keep Mary O'Malley by your side until I am done. But you must pretend that nothing is amiss.'

'How can I do that? What shall I say? Oh yes, she can help me with my lace – she often does.' Grace Clymo hurries down the dim-lit hallway towards the kitchen calling as she goes, 'Mary, Mary, please come to my sitting room.'

The cook appears at the kitchen doorway dressed as usual in a black dress, apron and mob cap. 'Yes ma'am. Should I stop makin' your supper then sir?'

'Yes, Mary, I have some urgent papers to attend to. I'll come down when I am ready.'

They turn into the sitting room as Thomas takes the stairs two at a time. Standing beside his wife at the Captain's bedside he looks down upon the wasted face. Dead-white pale and drawn he is. Indeed were it not for the slow rise and fall of his chest and the faint whistle of his breath, his stepfather would be taken for a corpse. There is a stink too, not just of sickness, loosened bowels and soiled linen but something else. He bends close and sniffs the breath – onions? No, not onions, garlic, that's what is – but not quite, something else. He lays his hand upon the Captain's cold and clammy forehead and mutters.

'Is he going?' Maisie whispers.

'No my lover, not if I can help it.'

The Captain's eyes flicker open. 'Thomas,' he whispers.

'Stay with us, Capun. I'm sure I know now what's afoot.'

Mathew Clymo's eyes close again. Thomas watches him for a second or two then says, 'Stay with him Maisie till I or Mother can take your place.' He leaves the sickroom and takes the backstairs to Mary O'Malley's attic room. The door is closed but unlocked and opens into darkness. He takes the oil lamp from the landing and holds it high. A dress hangs from a curtain rail, a nightgown lies across the bed and a coat hangs on a hook behind the door. The only other furniture is an easy chair and a wooden chest beneath the tiny attic window. A wooden crucifix hangs from a nail above the bed. He puts the lamp upon the windowsill and opens up the chest. It contains a pair of button boots, an embroidered carpet bag and nothing else. There is nothing in the carpet bag. He looks around the room then kneels down beside the bed and looks beneath – there is something in the shadows. He stretches out his arm and feels the outline of a small box. He pulls it out into the light. It's locked but the key sits in the lock. He turns the key and lifts the lid. The box is empty save for a piece of yellowed paper folded and resting in the bottom. He takes it out, unfolds it and holds it to the light – a birth certificate. His eyes are drawn to the father's name, '*William Scoble*', he whispers, "*Dwelling place, Omagh, County Tyrone.*" – exactly as Col McCarthy said. He takes a deep breath, gets to his feet, folds up the birth certificate and places it in the inside pocket of his jacket. He knows who she is for certain now but what should he do? Denounce her and throw her from the house for her deception. He thinks back to the Captain's breath, his sickness, what might be the cause. If she's more than an impostor, a poisoner in fact then the poison must be in the house. He looks once more around the room. There is nothing more to see. He'll go down to the kitchen. He pushes the box back beneath the bed and leaves the room. He does not close the door and goes quietly down the back stairs, his purpose fixed. Once in the kitchen he stands arms folded and looks around. Oil lamps burn in sconces on the walls and a fire flickers in the range. A bowl of dough sits rising in a niche beside it. Utensils hang from rails above the sink and from the mantelshelf. Pots, pans, plates and dishes are lined up on the dresser. The makings of his supper – a pasty, cheese and ham and salted beef are laid out on the table. He sniffs – the smell is wholesome, yeasty. Surely this is not the workplace of a murderess. He looks again – rows of labelled tins upon a high shelf catch his eye. He studies each and reads their labels silently, lips moving, "*Sugar, flour, icing sugar, salt, ground almonds, baking powder, saltpetre, saltpeter, borax powder*". Odd, he thinks. Saltpetre's used in pickling brines but why two tins? And why the different spelling? He takes both tins down, puts them side by side upon the table and takes off the lids. Each contains a powder, pure white and crystalline – one almost full, the other three parts empty. He sniffs them both – the fuller one smells faintly acrid but not unpleasant; the other has no smell at all. He licks the tip of his little finger and dips it in the fuller tin, touches his finger to his tongue. He shudders, spits and wipes his mouth. The powder's sharply bitter. He tastes the other – no taste nor smell. Again he wipes his lips and tongue but this time goes to the sink and washes out his mouth with water. He leans back against the sink, looking at the tins upon the table and nods. Yes indeed – the bitter powder is just what it says upon the tin, saltpetre, but the other . . . the other he has seen before, but not in this kitchen nor any other. He has seen it by the shovel-full, in barrows and coating the condenser labyrinth walls at Cornish Consol's works. They ship it by the cartload to a waiting world and here it is in Captain Clymo's kitchen. He has no doubt that it is arsenic and Mary Scoble has poisoned Captain Clymo. The woman is a poisoner. What should he do – confront her now and call the constable, have her arrested for attempted murder? What of Kit Robin, now Captain at Wheal Emma? Is Dandy Pants a party to this plot? The man has access to arsenic enough to poison half the country and certainly a motive. But Thomas will bide his time, find out all he can and then decide how he must act. But first of all the Captain's life. He smiles goes back to the table, takes up the saltpetre tin closes it and puts it back upon the shelf. He takes down the tin marked icing sugar, looks inside – white powder just like arsenic. He tastes it too – yes it's sweet; the Captain will enjoy his morning gruel. The arsenic he tips down the sink, rinses the tin and dries it thoroughly with a cloth. Then he tips in half the icing sugar, closes both the tins and puts them back in their respective places on the shelf. That done he stands back a step or two and hands on hips gazes at the row of tins – all is in order. The Scoble woman will see no change. Once more he looks around the kitchen. A few white grains of powder rest on the table where he worked. He bends down and with short puffs of breath, blows them away. He stretches and heaves a satisfied sigh. Back up the back stairs now, two at a time but silently, to the attic room and the box beneath the bed to replace the woman's document and leave all as it was before. For if he's to catch her, Mary Scoble must not suspect a thing.

It is a sweet domestic scene that greets him in his mother's parlour. She sits in a cone of lamplight, lacework on a pillow on her knee while Mary Scoble sitting on a stool beside her, lifts and interweaves the wooden bobbins in a pattern too quick for him to see. They both look up to see him standing there.

'Oh Thomas,' his mother says, 'Are you all done?'

'Yes thank you. Mary, please bring my supper to the dining room as soon as it is ready.'

'Of course, sir.' She lays the bobbins on the pillow, gets to her feet and with a slight bob in his direction leaves the room.

Grace Clymo looks up at her son. 'What did you find?'

He sits down upon the stool and takes her hands in his and looking up at her speaks so quietly she must bend her head to hear. 'Mary O'Malley is William Scoble's daughter.'

She snatches her hands from his and holds them to her mouth. 'No, it cannot be.'

'It is. I was told of this in Camborne and now have verified it for myself. I found her certificate of birth in a box beneath her bed.'

'No.'

'Yes, mother and there is worse to come. I found arsenic in the kitchen. That is what ails our Captain. She is poisoning him.'

She leaps to her feet pillow, lace and bobbins scattered to the floor. 'Oh the wicked, wicked child. Thomas we must call the constable this very night.'

'Hush now Mother, hush. Listen. I am not sure she acts alone in this and she may deny all knowledge of the arsenic. Sure, she cannot deny she is an impostor but that is a petty crime at worst. No, I will find proof that she has tried to murder. But first the Capun must be cured. I've talked with Dr Couch about the arsenic in our workers. He told me that the only cure is to keep the poison from the patient. That is easily done now for the Capun. I have thrown away her stock of poison and put sugar in its place You cannot tell the difference except by taste and I doubt she has a taste for her own medicine. So from tomorrow I wager he will get better, which in itself will be at least in part a proof. Hah, she will wonder mightily at his recovery.'

'Oh my son. I am both horrified and so relieved. Let us go to him right now and tell him what you've found.'

'We will go up, Mother, but tell him nothing, not just yet. Let him rest tonight and we'll tell him all tomorrow, if he is well enough that is.' He takes his mother's arm and together they climb the stairs to the sick room where Maisie still sits at the Captain's bedside.

'He is sleeping,' she whispers.

'Come, Maisie,' Thomas whispers back, 'Mother will watch him now.' Together they leave the room and tiptoe across the landing to their bedroom.

'What is it, Thomas? You have discovered something. I know that look of yours.'

'I have indeed, my love. Sit down beside me on the bed and I will tell you everything.'

Once he is finished talking she sits in silence for a while, hands folded like a child's in prayer. Then she says 'William Scoble's daughter, here in this house, all this time. She could have poisoned all of us.'

'Indeed she could.'

'How will you catch her?'

'I am not sure yet but I will make a plan. First thing tomorrow I will send for Doctor Couch. I need very much to talk with him. Now let us go to bed.' He yawns and stretches. 'These past few days seem like a month has passed and I am very, very tired. And I must work the night core tomorrow, let's not forget.'

Thomas still dressed in a nightshirt opens his bedroom window wide and gazes out across Penpillick. The house is high enough on the hill for him to see clear across to the English Channel glinting in the morning sun. Mist hangs in the valleys below and a thrush perched in an apple tree whistles the first phrase of a song, repeats it twice then finds a new one. Thomas takes a deep breath. For once the air is fresh and clean with an easterly breeze blowing the smoke from the engine houses and the stink of the mine dumps away from the village. He turns back into the room where Maisie lies abed still sleeping, red hair splayed out across the pillow. He watches her eyes moving beneath her eyelids as she dreams. He bends to kiss her forehead. 'Wake up, Maisie love. 'Tis morning and a beautiful one at that.'

She stirs, opens her eyes, looks at him in puzzlement, smiles and reaches out to him. 'I was dreamin' my lover. Dreamin' I was.'

'Of me?'

'No. I dreamed of Wallaroo and poisoned sheep.'

Thomas shakes his head and smiles. 'I am sure that all at Wallaroo is just as it should be, Maisie love.' He hugs her to him. 'I must get dressed for I have much to do today before the night core. Not least to tell the Captain we have discovered just what ails him.'

'Of course, my lover and I too cannot lie abed. But Thomas, should we not be afeared that this dreadful woman will poison all of us? Perhaps she has more arsenic. And at this very moment she prepares the children's breakfast, and ours. How can we trust her?'

Thomas sits down on the bed. 'You are quite right, we cannot. But I need just a day or two, perhaps a week at most to catch her and her paramour.'

'Her paramour?'

'Yes. I discovered some time back that she shares her favours with Kit Robin but kept my counsel to myself till now. I suspect that it is he who supplies the arsenic and if I can catch them at it, we'll have some of the proof we need.'

Maisie nods. 'It is a risk though is it not, to let her continue in the kitchen?'

'It is but small I think. If any of us get sick at all, make no mistake, I will face her with her crime immediately.'

'I don't know Thomas. It will be hard to eat at all, let alone watch our dear children at the table.'

'It will, my lover, but just for a few days more, I promise. But listen,

I was thinking in the night. We must check every day that it is just sugar in the saltpeter tin, that she has not discovered that I changed it. I cannot do this as I must work at night and have little business in the kitchen during the day. Can you do it?'

'Of course I can and willingly. She takes a nap in her room most afternoons. I can do it then. And if she catches me, so what? I'll simply say I wish to try my hand at pickling and even ask her which tin to use.

He laughs. 'I'm sure you'll fool her. You fooled her father after all. Now do you trust our plan?'

She puts her arms around him and kisses him. 'I trust you Thomas Pascoe, I always have. Now I must get dressed and wake the children.'

'And I must tell the Capun we know what ails him and why.'

'So Doctor you have heard my tale. I am certain sure that Capun Clymo has been poisoned with arsenic. Did you not suspect that from the very start that might be the case?'

'I did, Thomas, indeed I did. I assumed he was contaminated from his visits to the works. Thus I could not understand why he did not recover when he took to his bed. It did not occur to me that he might be being poisoned in his very home. Why would it?'

'Why indeed?'

'I assumed that something else must be ailing him though for the life of me I could not discover what it was.'

'And now we know. He will get better soon will he not?'

'He will, most certainly he will. When I looked in on him this morning, I'd swear there was a blush upon his cheeks and certainly he smiled. From knowing what it was that ailed him I suspect – that and knowing too he will get better.'

The two men walk side by side along the narrow rail track from the mine that runs along the edge of Bodmin Moor, the doctor stooped with age, his white hair blowing in the breeze – Thomas tall, bareheaded too, tapping his walking cane upon the rails. 'Tis a pity you did not keep a sample of the arsenic from the kitchen. There is a test I could have done then we'd have known for certain.'

'I do not need a test. I am absolutely certain.'

'Your certainty would not hold up in court.'

'Perhaps not, but I have been thinking. How much powder do you think she uses every day?'

'A quarter teaspoon daily would be enough to cause the Captain's symptoms.'

'Hmm. I'd say I left enough sugar in the tin to last a week. After that she will be needing more. We shall watch her carefully and with luck I'll catch her in the act.'

'Thomas, you are a clever young man but you cannot do this all alone. Listen to me. Once you think she has replenished her supply you must call me day or night and together we will confront her in the kitchen. Our word, yours and mine, will stand in court, make no mistake.'

'You are right, Doctor. I shall follow your advice. I shall watch and wait and when the time is ripe, I will call upon your services. Now what say you we continue on our stroll and make the most of this splendid morning?'

Doctor Couch takes out his pocket watch. 'I have but an hour Thomas. But yes, I'll keep you company and you can tell me tales of far-off Australia.'

XIX

OF SHEEP AND GOLD

'WHAT THEY DOIN' DOWN THERE, HENRY?'

'I don't know. Wish I 'ad one o' they spyglasses. Can't see nothing for dust and sheep. Damn these blessed flies.' Henry flaps his hand in front of his face.

They lie belly down in the scrub on the only ridge that overlooks the Pascoe Station. The distant bleating of thousands of sheep is carried on the wind from the paddocks below where mounted stockmen ride amidst the milling flock, shouting and waving. 'Look, look now – a whole string of 'em is peelin' off into the paddock there. There's a bloke sittin' on the fence – looks like he's countin' 'em in. Is it Millington?'

'No it ain't. Never seen him before. Don't look like no stockman. Look, there's Millington an' my wife an somebody else with 'em.' Henry points over toward the homestead where three figures are standing at the gate. 'They're shakin' hands aint they.'

'Looks like it. They musta done a deal. Yeah, that's right. See there – they're drivin' a whole loada animals down the road. How many d'ye reckon?'

'Good two thousand, I'd say.'

'So Mabel was right. Millington is selling off your boss's stock.'

'Maybe Thomas Pascoe told him to. But if he didn't I oughter let him know. Even if he ain't my boss no more, I still owes 'im doan I.'

'Well, let's ride down to the road. Ask the buyer what's goin' on. Can't do no harm can it?'

Henry nods. 'Righto.'

They crawl backwards off the ridge and walk to their horses tethered in the shade of an ancient mallee tree. Circling first east then north they reach the road well ahead of the massive flock which pours down the roadway in a river of bleating dust. They back away from the road to let the flock pass. A black stockman reins his pony in beside them. 'G'day mate,' Joe says, 'Jeez, that's some mob o' sheep.'

The stockman takes off his hat, wipes sweat and dust from his eyes. 'Yeah,' he says and flicks a hand at the flies.

'Where ya takin' 'em then?'

The stockman blinks a long slow blink and nods towards the southeast then puts his hat on and rides on. Henry and Joe stand their horses until the flock has passed.

'Where d'ye think they're headed?' Henry asks as they trot down the track to Wallaroo.

'Who knows? Some other station I'd guess. Hold on here comes somebody who might tell us.'

A horseman pulls up beside them. 'Mornin' fellas. You out for a ride?'

'We're miners from Moonta. Just doin' a bit a fossickin' here and there'

'Any luck?'

Joe shakes his head. 'Nah, I reckon what's to be found has bin found already. What about you? That your mob o' sheep we just seen?'

''Tis now,' the man says. 'Just bought'em. Woulda bought more at that price if I could have.'

'Where you takin' 'em?'

'Adelaide sale yards. Good day to ya. Tsk tsk.' He clicks to his horse and rides off following the tracks left by his sheep.

'So now we know,' Joe says.

Henry Hopeful Down nods, says nothing and slumped in the saddle, trots slowly on.

It is late afternoon by the time they reach Moonta. They wend their way along the dusty streets between the rows of miners' cottages, past the Moonta Mines Uniting Church and the Moonta Institute until they come to their shared two room cottage rented from the mine. Inside Joe lights the oil lamp that hangs from a beam. 'Well mate,' he says, 'I reckon we needs write a letter to your Mr Pascoe.'

Henry, already sat in a wooden chair, legs splayed beside the empty hearth, nods and scratches behind his ear. 'I'll see Mabel tonight and ask her.'

'No need, Henry. I can do it for yer right away. I'se handy with a pen.'

'Okay. What shall we say?'

'Simple – tell him what we know. Millington is selling off his sheep. If he knows already he won't be worried. But if it's news to him, well, who knows what he'll do? Come back hotfoot maybe. But we gotta tell him.'

'Have to tell him why I'm not there, why I left an' all, won't I. I can't never tell him no lies.'

'Well, that's up to you. Just tell me what you wanna say. I'll write it. Think about it while I go out and get pen and paper from the store.' Joe is about to go out of the door but changes his mind and stands beside his friend and puts a hand upon his shoulder. 'No need to be so down, Henry Hopeful Down. Once the letter's writ we'll go have ourselves a drink or two and maybe talk to Mabel. We're off tomorrow or have you forgot? Up north we'll go and find ourselves that gold mine. We got the gear, the horses. All we need is grub. We'll stock up in the mornin'. Cheer up mate. It ain't the end of the world just yet.'

Henry looks at him with the beginnings of a smile. 'You're a good friend, Joe. Best I ever had bar Mr Pascoe though he were more of a son to me I s'pose. Which is why it's so hard I let him down.'

'What's done is done, mate. We got our lives to live.'

'You leave tomorrow then, Henry?'

'Yes. Yes we do.'

'When will you be coming back?'

'Six months, mebbe less if we have luck.'

'I'll be back in Adelaide by then. You'll find me at the Colonel Light Hotel. Everybody knows it.' She laughs. 'Henry, does it bother you what I do?' She runs her fingers through his hair .

'O' course not. How could it? I. . . I like to be with you. Best thing I ever known.'

'You're a lovely man Henry from Wallaroo. If I had a boy I'd want him to grow up like you.'

'I ain't got children. Wanted some with Janey but it never happened. Mebbe I'll have better luck fossickin' for gold.'

Mabel lays her head on the pillow beside his and gazing at the ceiling says, 'I wish you all the luck for I will miss you.'

Henry sits up on one elbow, head resting in his hand and looking down at her. 'You will miss me?'

She smiles, reaches up and strokes his beard then pulls his head towards her face and kisses him upon the mouth. 'I will, 'she whispers. 'Now lie back.' Henry does as he is told and Mabel sits astride him, leaning forward, the sheets falling from her shoulders, her hair cascading down around her face. She reaches down. 'Now this is something to remember me by.'

He grips her by the waist as she begins to move. Oh, Lord,' Henry groans, 'Oh Mabel.'

For three days they ride northward across the flat shrublands, the monotony broken only by the occasional sheep station with its stand of gum trees, and infrequent glimpses of the sea away to the west. They keep up a steady trot, seeking shade and rest in the early afternoons when the heat is at its most intense. On the morning of the second day they meet a small band of blacks and trade flour and hard tack for fish and swimmer crabs fresh caught from the Gulf. That evening they head down through the saltbush scrub to the shore, make camp among the dunes and saddle sore and weary, cook the fish over a blue-flamed fire of mallee root and driftwood. The crabs they boil in a billy of seawater and once cool, wrap in coarse sea grass and pack them in their saddlebags.

'Good eatin' they'll be tomorrow,' Joe Watson says.

'I ain't eaten crab since I were a boy back 'ome. They was different – bigger like without them spiky bits. I liked 'em though.'

They sit, backs rested on their saddles watching the sun sink into the sea.

'Ain't bad this is it?' Joe waves the stem of his clay pipe at the setting sun. 'I mean bein' out here and not down that fuckin' dark hole all day. Though my arse hurts somewhat. I ain't never been much of a horseman.' He takes a couple puffs on the pipe from the corner of his mouth. 'You go with Mabel the other night then?'

Henry doesn't answer, just sits staring out across the water at the sunset's afterglow.

'Did ya?'

'I did.'

'Thought we agreed you wouldn't, seein' as how we is all business partners. Talkin' of which, how much you pay her?'

'Nothin'. She wouldn't take my money.'

'Christ.'

Henry looks at his companion, the weather-beaten face, the maimed right hand, the greasy hair curling over his collar. He turns away again then says, 'I like her, Joe and she likes me.'

'Sweet Jesus, Henry, she's a bloody tart, mate.'

'I know. Don't make no difference. I ain't never met a woman like her. I don't care what she is.'

Joe Watson shakes his head and mutters almost to himself 'Got you by the cock she has.'

They sit in silence for a while then return in darkness to the embers of their cooking fire, unroll their swags and settle down to sleep.

'Good night Joe.'

'Good night Henry Hopeful Down.'

The fourth night they spend at a railway camp with hard, lean men who spend their days laying track northward to the desert and their nights hard drinking. They eat salt pork and damper baked in the ashes of the campfire. In the morning, woken by the whistle and hiss of escaping steam, they scramble from their bedrolls, frowsy from drink and stand awed as an engine up from Port Augusta hauls in rails and timber sleepers and a carriage load of top-hatted dignitaries.

'First train I ever see,' Henry says. 'She's somethin ain't she?'

'She is, mate,' a railman says. 'Some day you'll be able to ride her all the way to fuckin' Darwin.'

Joe snorts and shakes his head. 'Some day yeah, some day. I just wish it was today an' we didn't have to wear our arses out in the saddle for another three days to get to bloody Blinman. What's between here and there mate, d'ye know?'

'Not much more'n a couple o' sheep stations though I heard there's some sorta eatin' house at Wilpena. And there's another mob building a railway to the silver strike at Broken Hill but that's well east of where you're headed.'

'Thanks mate and thanks for the company and the grog last night. C'mon Henry, don't stand gawpin'. We need to be on the road afore it gets too bloody hot.'

Henry tears his eyes away from the hissing engine and they return to camp, pack up their swags and cooking gear, mount up and trot northwards towards the hills.

Late afternoon finds them riding side by side along a sandy cart track that wends its way beneath the towering scarps of the Flinders.

'Nice country ain't it,' Joe says. They are in an open woodland of spindly conifers with fire-blackened trunks.

'I ain't seen pine trees since I left home an' that were only in the vicar's garden. Strangest wood I ever saw this is. Shade makes a change though don't it.'

'Certainly does. Would you call them hills or mountains?' Joe waves an arm over to the west where a great blue-shadowed cliff looms over the bush.

'Bigger than any hill I ever see'd back 'ome. Mountains I reckon. An' it'd be a tough old climb. Was up there on t'other side with Thomas Pascoe that time we went fossickin' I told you about. Just bloody rock and thorn scrub up there, it is.'

They lapse into a silence broken only by the soft hoof beats of their horses, the creak of their saddles and the occasional flock of parrots that fly squawking through the treetops. It is dusk when rounding a bend they see a grass thatched timber shack set back from the track. 'Wilpena,' Joe says, 'just like the man said. Just hope someone's at home.'

'There's someone home alright. I smell wood smoke.'

As they approach the shack an old man with a rifle in his hands appears in the doorway. He is hatless and barefoot with a straggly white beard that covers the collar of his shirt.

'Friendly,' Joe mutters as they both rein in the horses. 'Evenin'' mister. This the Wilpena Eatin' House?'

'It is. Can't ye read?' The old man nods toward a badly painted sign nailed to a tree.

'Right. Sorry. Gettin' dark ain't it. We was hopin' to bed down here for the night. You got food?'

'We're an eatin' house, so yeah, we got food. Ain't got no beds though. You can lay yer swags over yonder.' He points with the rifle towards a grove of trees.

'Right. Any grog?'

The old man puts a dirty thumb to a nostril and blows snot out the other. 'We got grog for them as can pay for it.' Suddenly, turning towards the interior of the shack, he yells, 'Edna, two for tea.' Leaning the rifle against the door post, he sits on a stick-wood chair on the veranda. He watches as they dismount and in the gathering gloom, lead the horses towards the trees. The horses tethered and their gear unloaded, they stroll side by side to the shack.

The man looks up at them. 'Sorry about the welcome. We was robbed a while back. Two blokes on horseback just like you took near all we had. Makes a bloke careful like. Anyway, the names Mole, Tom Mole. Pleased to meet yer.' He holds out a hand.

'Joe Watson and this here is Henry Hopeful Down, a Cousin Jack all the way from Cornwall.' Joe shakes his hand.

'Fuck me. Henry Hopeful Down – that's a mouthful ain't it, even for a big bloke like you. Welcome to God's own arsehole, Henry.'

Henry bends to shake the proffered hand, nods and smiles. 'Looks alright to me. Nicest lookin' country I seen since I left Cornwall.'

'It may look nice, mate but there's nuthin' here 'cept trees and rocks and fuckin' sheep. Hot as Hades in summer and cold as a witch's tit in winter. Though I gotta say youse picked the right time o' year to visit. Come on in. Tea'll be a while yet. Edna's gone out to strangle a fuckin' roo. Nah, just jokin'. You're in luck. It's wallaby stew an dumplin's tonight.' He gets up and ushers them into the shack. Rough pine panelling divides the shack lengthways, the front room taken up with a long wood table with bush-crafted wooden benches down either side. Tom Mole takes matches from his shirt pocket and lights the oil lamp set in the middle of the table. It smokes and its orange glow sets up wavering shadows on the wooden walls. 'Sit down, sit down,' he says and goes out to the back room.

They sit across the table from each other. 'Jeez, my arse is sore,' Joe mutters looking around the room. 'I seen some outback places in my time but this dump takes the cake.'

'Hello dearies. Welcome to Edna's dinin' room.' A large black woman stands smiling in the doorway to the back room, holding a bottle in one hand and three glasses in the other. She plonks the glasses on the table. 'Grog?' She grins a wide grin, teeth shining white in the lamplight. Henry and Joe nod in unison and Edna fills each glass with oily spirit. The sharp smell of home-brewed rum mingles with kerosene fumes from the lamp.

'Here's to ya, mates.' Tom Mole comes in behind her, grabs a glass and knocks the liquor back. 'This here's Edna. She's my missus and the cook. Go on Edna, get cookin', these blokes are hungry.' He slaps her fat buttocks with a bony hand. She laughs and goes back into the kitchen.' He sits opposite them. 'She may be black but she's a fuckin' good cook is my Edna. C'mon, drink up. Good grog this is.' He pours himself another shot.

Henry and Joe knock back their drinks.

'Another? Only sixpence a shot boys.'

'Go on then.' Joe pushes his and Henry's glass across the table.

'Prospectors are ya? See ya got all the gear'

'We're miners,' Joe says. 'Up from Moonta. Goin' to Blinman, see if there's more to be found. Heard it was a shepherd found copper just stickin' out the ground. Bloke couldn't miss it even though he weren't even lookin'. Reckon there must be more.'

'Moonta miners eh? I'll be damned. I was at Moonta when she started up. Young bloke I was then full o' piss an' vinegar an' makin' good money. Rough as guts it was. I lived in a fuckin' humpy for a coupla years. But that's another story. Ain't you heard? The Blinman Mine is closed. Boys went on strike, an' shut the bugger down. Bloody ghost town it is. Buggered my business too it has. Year ago you wouldna been

141

able to move in here – teamsters, miners, fuckin' bigwig shareholders out from England on there way up or back. Now look at it – fuckin' empty ain't it.' He waves his arm to encompass the room. 'Apart from Edna, I ain't had no-one to talk to for more'n a week. Her and meself that is.'

Nobody speaks and they sit listening to the evening breeze soughing in the cypresses, the shrill of crickets and the clatter of pans from the kitchen. Joe looks at Henry then at Tom Mole then asks, 'You ever hear of anyone findin' gold up here?'

The old man wipes a dribble of snot from his nose with the back of his hand and sniffs. 'That what you're really after?'

Henry and Joe nod in unison.

'There's a strike at Teetulpa – big one so I heard. More diggers than you can shake a fuckin' stick at. That's less than a coupla days ride south an' east .'

'We heard about that. Reckon we're too late for that. What about north of Blinman?'

'If I knew anythin' an' I'm not sayin' I do, why would I tell a coupla blokes what just blew in an' I don't know from Adam?'

'Dunno mate. Why would ya?'

'Gimme a finder's fee I might.'

Henry grunts. 'My boss and me got took like that few year's back. Lost five sovereign on a dirt map o' nowhere t'other side of these mountains o' yourn. I ain't like to get took again.'

'I ain't talkin about a map. Have another shot.' He fills their glasses then shouts, 'Edna where's that fuckin' grub?'

'Comin', I'm comin.' She bustles in with a large pot in one hand and tin plates and spoons in the other. She slaps a plate and spoon in front of each of them and the pot in the middle of the table, bustles out again then returns with a charred loaf. 'Stew an' dumplins an' damper. Dig in boys. Ain't nothin' else.' She gives a great shout of laughter, pours herself a shot of rum and sits at the table.

They eat in silence until Joe, wiping his plate clean of gravy with a crusty piece of damper, leans back in his chair and says, 'Good grub that was, Edna. Thanks.'

'Told ya she could cook, didn't I. Useter be that we was known as the best eatin' house north of Augusta and south of Alice Springs. Anyway that's all over now. Washed up ain't we. You two are the first payin' customers in a week. Which is why I'm gonna do what I'm gonna do. Edna fetch the fish.'

Edna looks at Tom Mole. 'You sure?' Her deep set eyes glint in the flickering light.

'Jeez woman, fetch the bloody fish.'

She shrugs, heaves herself to her feet and goes into the kitchen.

'Fish?' Joe says. 'I ain't hungry after that stew.'

Tom Mole smiles at them, his eyes half closed. 'Just wait.' He picks up his rifle and lays it across his knees. Banging and scraping noises come from the kitchen. There is the sudden smell of soot and more banging. Then Edna returns clutching a flattish object to her chest. It is wrapped in a dirty cloth. With two hands she lays it on the table in front of her husband. He puts a hand over it and looks at Joe and Henry. 'Don't know why but I trust you blokes, but I do.'

'With what?'

'Me fish.' With a conjurer's flourish Tom Mole wips the cloth away scattering soot across the table and revealing a hand size gold nugget.

'Lord Jesus Christ,' Joe whispers. 'If that ain't the biggest nugget I ever saw. And shaped like a fish, sure enough.'

'Pure gold is that then?' Henry asks leaning across the table

'Bloody oath it is. Here, hold it if you wants.' Tom Mole picks up the nugget and passes it across the table to Henry.

'Lord,' he mutters. 'I only seen gold dust afore. And gold sovereigns o' course.' Henry turns it in the lamplight. 'This is beautiful. Feels warm don't it. And heavy. Look how she glows – shinier than copper. It's even got an eye.' He points as delicately as his large forefinger will allow to a quartz grain embedded in the gold.

Joe holds out his hand. 'Can I?' Henry places the gold on his outstretched palm. Joe moves his hand up and down in a weighing motion. 'Ten ounces or thereabouts?'

'Thereabouts.'

'What you doin' here if ya got two hundred quid in gold stashed away?' Joe asks, passing the gold back across the table.

Tom Mole wraps the nugget in the cloth and it is as if a light has gone from the room. 'Edna, fetch another bottle o' grog. I gotta a tale to tell.'

'Listen, like I already told ya, I was once a Moonta miner like you blokes – maybe that's why I trust you. Now I was a wanderin' sorta soul and after a coupla years I'd had enough o' minin' an' I come up here workin' on the Angepena station for old John Baker. Wild hill country that is, way north o' here and good for nuthin' but sheep. I was workin' with Bob Blinman the shepherd what found the mine just like you heard – a lump o' copper twenty feet wide just stickin' out the ground. He quit the station and asked me to come work on the strike seeing as how I knowed about mining. So I did an' me an' a coupla other blokes together with Bob, we put up the money to buy the lease. Eighty quid it were but more than worth it. We sold out a year later to toffs from London for twelve thousand. I was young and rich so I went down to Adelaide and for five year I just had me a good time till I woke up one morning drunk and most of me money gone. So with what I had left I come back up here and went prospectin' just like you blokes are planning. I spent a year fossickin' around Blinman but there weren't nothin left to find so I headed out east into the desert.'

He stops talking leans forward takes the smoked-grimed chimney off the lamp and picks off a charred strand of wick. He replaces the chimney and turns the lamp up. It burns cleanly now illuminating the four faces around the table.

'By meself I was and still young enough to think I knew it all. But that's hard and thirsty country out there, just scrub and sand, flies and gibber plains. I had a fine old mare and all the gear, just like you blokes. Full o' hope I was. Day after day I walked, dry pannin' in the few creeks I come across, cracking rocks with me pick, sufferin' from the sun and the bloody mirages – water I'd see, lakes and lakes of it just shimmerin' there in front o'me. Course when I come up to where it was, there weren't nuthin', just another hundred mile o' fuckin desert. Anyways I hadn't found nuthin', not a fleck o' gold did I see in that damned country. Me water was runnin' out and I ain't eaten hardly for most of a week an' I was about ready to give it up when I sees this hill picked out by the settin' sun. I thought it were just another fuckin' mirage but when I woke up next morning it were still there – one single rocky little hill in the middle of the damned desert. So I ses to meself, I'll go there and no further an' then I'll turn back. Takes me half a day to reach it and by then the sun was burnin' me an' my poor old horse up. So I crawled under a shelf of rock an' rested till near sundown. When I woke up me horse had wandered off. I followed her tracks in the sand and bugger me if she weren't down in a creek bed on t'other side of the hill drinkin from a little pool o' water. An' this time it weren't no mirage – real it was, real as us all sittin' round this table tonight. I knelt down at the water's edge and drank and drank.' He takes a swig of rum. 'So I camped there and next day started panning the banks of the creek. 'Twas still early on a morning I'll never forget long as I live, when I see the first colours glinting in me pan. Good inch an' half o' colour there were. An' I just jumped up and yelled me head off to the heavens, "I fuckin' found it, found it, I fuckin' found it" an' me voice echoed off the rocks an' I danced around like a loon. An all the time me horse just stood there lookin at me an' grazin' on the mulga scrub growin' by the creek. I stayed there three days workin' upstream followin' the colours lookin' for the mother lode. Didn't have no food but I didn't care. I had water aplenty and I was just crazed with findin' gold. By the third day I had a good six ounces o' gold dust from pannin' an' I were hackin' at the bank with me pick when I sees somethin' glintin' in the red dirt. I goes carful now, pickin' it out bit by bit until this very nugget is stickin' out the ground like it had just bin' waitin' forever to be found. I couldn't believe me eyes. I touched it. It were real. Gently gently I dug it out till I held it in me hands. I stared at it for the longest time – a golden fish shinin' in the sun.' He stops talking and uncovers the nugget. They all gaze at it and nobody speaks for a long time.

'And then?' Joe finally looks up at the old man.

'Well then I sits down by the creek, holdin' the fish in me lap, an I don't mind tellin' ya that tears were runnin' down me face. I sat there lookin' at that gold until the bloody flies were drivin' me mad. Finally I gets up an' that makes me think how damn hungry I am an' how am I goin't to get back with only a bit of dry old damper to last me a week or more. But there ain't nothin' for it but to head back an' the sooner the better. I pack up me gear, fill up all me water bottles, saddle up the old mare an' head off into the settin' sun, chewin' on me last loaf. When I'm about a mile out I stop and turn around an' stare at that rocky hill all lit up by the settin' sun – fix it in me mind like. I can see it now, long and low, a little ridge runnin' north-south with a kinda rocky knob on the north end, all alone in the middle o' nowhere, red rocks glowin' in the sunset. "Fish Hill" I says to meself an' I knew I wasn't never goin' to forget it.

I musta fallen asleep in the saddle cos' the next thing I know it's the middle of the night and the horse has stopped to graze. I looks around and there ain't no moon so I picks out the Southern Cross an' the Pointers an' carry on west towards the hills. I rode all that night an' all the next day, stoppin' only to water the horse. By then I'd eaten all me damper an' I was so bloody hungry I was chewin' on the reins, which made me thirst worse them bein' all salty with sweat. The horse is strugglin' too, jus' ploddin' along head down, pestered by the bloody flies. An' then it starts blowin' one o' them fuckin' northerlies – hot it was, like it was blowin' out of a desert furnace bringin' a red dust storm, grit in me teeth an' eyes, couldn't see nothin' not even the sun. So I gets off the horse an' tries to walk her but I lose me sense o' direction so I gets back on an' just hunker down in the saddle, wind howlin' in me ears like a banshee an' lets her wander where she will. Don't know how long it lasted. Reckon' I musta passed out. When I come to there I am in the middle of one o' them gibber plains flat as far as the eye could see, damned sun burnin' down, an all I can see is mirages, mirages, an more mirages an shimmerin' water all around and I can't even see where the sun is no more cos I daren't look at her. Poor old horse she just sits back on her haunches, an' I slide off and she lies down an' kinda whinnies her breathin' all ragged an' I know she's done. I sit for a while beside her then I gets the saddle an' me swag an all me gear off her. Then I shoot her.' He stops talking and strokes his straggly beard, rheumy eyes lost in the distance. 'Thing is I had no food, water runnin' out an' no idea where I was, nor how

146

long it would take me to walk out, or even if I could. I rigged up a bit of shade with a blanket over me shovel and tied to the horses hooves an I lay there till sundown. I had a screamin' pain in me guts, from not eatin' I s'pose, the thirst was killin me but I dursen't drink an' I just lay there by me dead horse sweatin' an' thinkin' I was a rich man but what good was that if I died out there in the desert. So I swore to God that if I got out, I wouldn't never come back gold or no gold. I'd had enough o' fuckin' desert. Then I cuts off strips of horse meat as much as I could carry along with me water, the blanket and rifle an' of course the gold. I walked all that night an' half the next day till I was tuckered out an' it was just too bloody hot. I camped again in the middle of a salt flat startin' up again at dusk. Two nights later I sees these hills like great lumps o' darkness blockin' out the starlight an' I thinks by Christ I'm gonna make it though me water was all gone. By daylight I was near dead, crawlin' on me hands an' knees an' off me head when Edna's pa found me. He was huntin' out Wirrealpa way, took me in an I stayed with their mob a while. Edna nursed me dintja Edna? Brought me back to life she did. We bin together ever since.' He looks at her and lays his withered hand on hers.

She nods. 'He was near dead all right. Skin an' bone an' near blind.'

They sit in silence, unspoken questions hanging in the air. Tom Mole pours another shot in each glass. He looks across at them unspeaking then wraps the nugget in its cloth and shoves it along the table to Edna. She picks it up and goes into the kitchen without a word. The oil lamp has burned down to a flickering rim of flame, leaving the room in deep shadow.

'You all's wonderin' why I told you my story aint'ya?'

Joe and Henry nod, look at each other and drink their drinks.

'Well, thing is I never did go back to that howlin' desert. I kept me word. I didn't want to die out there. Used the gold I'd panned to set this place up. Kept the fish so I'd always know it was real an' not like some blackfella dreamin'. But I kept it secret till now. Didn't even think about gettin' a lease – didn't want no gold rush like over east. Only people who know about it is Edna and me and our boy, David. I woulda given the nugget to him but he's more of her side than mine an just ain't interested. He's mostly with her mob if he ain't gone walkabout. But I'se gettin' old now an' it's time somebody went out to that hill again cos there ain't no doubt in my mind there's a gold mine there just waitin' to make some bloke rich.' He grins at them. 'Might as well be you two.'

'You havin' us on?'

'No mate I ain't. You give me an Edna ten percent. That'll do us nicely for the rest of our lives I reckon. That's my finder's fee. Whatdja say?'

Joe and Henry look at each other. Joe puffs his cheeks out. 'Jeez what can I say? Coupla blow-ins like us and you offer us a gold mine? I gotta say yes. Ain't that right Henry?'

'It is. And you was right to trust Joe and me, Mr Mole. We'll keep our word. But how will we find your hill out there in the desert?'

'When I was with Edna's people they asked me where I'd been. I told 'em. There ain't many hills out there an when I described it they knew straightaway. Even got a name for it which I can't call to mind right this moment. David will take you there if I ask him. We gonna shake on it?' He takes the rifle off his knees, props it against Edna's empty chair, spits in his hand and holds it out across the table.

Joe and Henry both shake his hand.

The old man smiles. 'In the morning I'll write us a letter of agreement, if that's sits right with you. I'm off to me bed now. You sleep well out there. Best get used to it if you ain't already.'

Henry Hopeful Down lies on his back eyes wide open gazing up through a gap in the pine trees at the great arch of the Milky Way. Though he has lain many nights beneath these star-dusted desert skies, he does not cease to marvel. Even on a cloudless night in Cornwall, and they were few and far between, he never saw stars like this. Myriads far beyond his counting, they make light enough to cast a shadow when there is no moon. The only southern stars he knows are those of the Cross and Pointers, a less than easy way to find your night time bearings – unlike the simple Plough and Pole Star back at home. And there in the very middle of the Milky Way is that strange dark void they call the Coalsack – a ragged pitch-black pit. He lies there watching and it is as if the earth on which he lies is moving and moving him along with it. What if they find old Tom Mole's gold mine out there in desert? He will be rich, perhaps rich enough to payback Thomas Pascoe's losses. Maybe rich enough to marry Mabel? He never knew the thing could be like it was that last time he was with her. He replays it in his mind and feels himself stir. How long till he is back with her again – months and months, maybe a year and will it be the same? She will sleep with other men, this much he knows. Perhaps she is the same with them, does with them the things she did with him. Perhaps that is the way she is, or not – he does not know. But surely those words she whispered were for him alone, that he is special to her, that she will miss him in her bed. Why else would she have trusted him and Joe with money for this doubtful scheme – for that is how he thinks of it? Less so now he must admit since his he was dazzled by gold shining in the lamplight. An owl hoots from the woodland beyond the shack – a different call to those of home, more like a night time cuckoo call. But everything is different here in this land of wonders. His mouth is dry from too much rum and he reaches for his water bottle. Joe stirs beside him. 'You awake, Joe?'

'I am.'

'You think we'll find that mine?'

'That's a prize nugget ol' Moley showed us. Got to 'ave come from somewhere.'

'You ain't afraid o' goin out there? In the proper desert I means.'

'I knows what you mean. No I ain't afraid, leastways not with a friendly blackfella as a guide. They know this land better than you an me knows the palms of our hands.'

'What about the ten percent?'

'What about it?'

'Well, I was thinking of Mabel.'

'Listen, mate, she'll still get four tenths of what we find. And four tenths of summat real is a whole load better than half o' nuthin' at all.

'Spose it is. But we never asked her, did we?'

'Jeez Henry, go to sleep.'

XX

THE MAN ENGINE

CAPTAIN THOMAS PASCOE STANDS ON THE 120 fathom sollar watching the men of the day core rising up the shaft to the steady rhythm of the twin pump rods. They beat as always up and down, up and down, their twelve foot stroke driving the pumps below sucking great draughts of water from the bottom of the mine. The men grin at him or touch their hat brims and someone calls out, 'Mornin' Capun, proper job this is,' and laughs stepping off the platform on one rod at the top of its stroke and onto the platform on the opposite rod to disappear upwards into darkness, boots last.

He has to admit to himself that the man engine is a mechanical marvel. They should have installed one years ago, even when he was a boy, for it was that far back that these machines were first mooted by old Michael Loam. They talked then of winding the men up by the bucket load but they would not have it – too dangerous by half they said. And it was true – winding ropes were known to part from time to time plunging skip and contents to the bottom of the shaft. It has been a long and tedious job, bolting the oaken platforms every twelve feet to nearly four thousand feet of elm wood pump rods. But watching the men's glee at no longer having to climb those endless ladder ways, more than makes it worth the while. Thomas is pleased too that he supervised the work, making doubly sure that all was shipshape and done Bristol fashion as they say – one snapped platform and one man falling would spell disaster. But of course Dandy Pants damn him, spoiled his pleasure, taking care that the final fixings and inauguration took place while he was off to Bodmin. And they've named it "Kit Robin's Engine" which he must admit is not unfair given it was built at his command. He sighs, waits his turn then steps on a rising platform steadying himself by the grab handle, enjoys the lift, steps off then on the other side and up he goes again. Notwithstanding the novelty, he soon settles to the rhythm of the man engine – up, step-off-step-on, up, step-off step-on. It takes near thirty minutes to raise him up to grass and that is ample time for his thoughts to wander half directed to the issues that beset his waking life. The arsenic of course – the Captain is free of it for three days now and grows better almost by the hour. The fearsome gut cramps, the vomiting, the bloody flux all are gone, though he is dreadful weak and still keeps to his bed. Which is just as well for Mary Scoble still brings his meals in the mistaken hope that he will die and she will be the mistress of Wheal Emma. Twice now he's followed Dandy Pants to the arsenic works to no avail. He stays well back and dare not follow him into the condenser tunnels where it would require the simplest sleight of hand for Kit Robin to secrete the arsenic about his person. What he hoped was that his quarry would go direct from piles of poison to the Clymo's kitchen, or even better to some secret trysting place with the Scoble woman. But no such luck – he has gone about his business in an entirely blameless, if not carefree fashion. But today must be the day that he will catch him out. In the very early hours of every morning Maisie goes into the kitchen takes down the tin, dips a finger in and touches it to her tongue – sweet to her taste again today, as was the Captain's morning porridge. But there was less than a spoonful left. She told him she could see the bottom of the tin through the powdered sugar. So today must be the day it will be replenished. He will follow Kit Robin once again. At least now he knows the man's routine – underground of a morning while Thomas sleeps, then a visit to the arsenic works after croust taken in the counthouse. So tomorrow morning surely they will catch her. He must alert the doctor, have him at the bedside when Mary Scoble delivers the Captain's breakfast gruel. She will be caught red-handed and if today he sees Kit Robin go from the arsenic works to the kitchen of Penpillick House, they'll have all the proof they need to call the constable and have both of them arrested.

He heaves a sigh – what a resolution that will be. And here he is now head rising into daylight at the collar of the shaft. He steps off the man engine onto the wooden platform, ears filled with the thump and hiss of the beam engine above his head and nostrils filled with the stink of burning coal. Yet how sweet it is to come to grass on a June morning like this, even with the clangour and stench of the mine, the crowds of workers, miners coming, miners going home, boys wheeling barrows, bal maidens and children at the sorting tables, and underfoot the red mud and slurry from the dressing floors. He strides past the clattering stamp mill to the counthouse and fairly leaps up the steps and slams open the door. 'Morning Capun Kit, morning Bill, morning Gentlemen.'

The three mine clerks and top-hatted William George the Purser turn on their high stools and chorus 'Morning Capun Pascoe.'

But Dandy Pants, sat at the white-scrubbed table, a map of the mine before him, barely looks up. He is dressed as always in a tailored jacket and dark serge trousers tucked into polished leather boots, a silk scarf at his neck – more as if he were out on a pheasant shoot with the Duke rather than ready for his daily duties as Captain of Wheal Emma.

Thomas takes off his miners' hat, unslings his satchel and hangs them on a hook behind the door. He sits on a stool back to the wall. 'Men are quite taken with the man engine,' he announces. 'So am I, come to that.'

Kit Robin looks up. 'Dare I say, "I told you so"?'

'You may dare. We should have had one long ago.'

'Quite. Were you to the 330 last night as I requested?'

'Of course. Tipp Corney and co are pleased as sixpence with their pitch. As fine a bunch of copper as I've seen for quite some time. Perhaps our luck has turned. And there's a massive lane of mundic ore in the 280 end – four tons to the fathom by my reckoning. Though it seems to me we've arsenic enough these days.'

At this Dandy Pants looks up from his map and stares at Thomas. He scratches his chin, looks down at his map again, and mutters, 'Well, write it in the Night Book then.'

Thomas turns on his stool, opens up the ledger, picks up a quill and dips it in the inkpot and begins to write, smiling to himself. Well, that was a risk but it seems the barb he could not resist has hit its mark. It takes him ten minutes to record his night time observations finishing with *"Man Engine works complete – 28 minutes travel 330fm up to grass."* and signs his entry with a flourish. 'Right Gents, I'm off to the dry and thence to breakfast. A good day to you.' He leaves the counthouse through the back door which leads directly into the adjacent dry where rows of miners sit amidst the steam of drying clothes, their feet in tubs of hot water chatting between themselves. A bal maiden tidies discarded, dirty mining clothes the men have simply dropped upon the floor. Thomas changes quickly into his day clothes and leaves his night shift wear upon the peg. The bal maiden will have it washed and dried for him by tonight. He does not bathe in the dry for unlike the miners, he has a hot bath at home. 'A good night's work,' he says to himself as he walks up through the village in the sunshine.

But his mood is sobered by a letter come that very morning post marked "*Moonta, South Australia*". It sits unopened by his breakfast plate of eggs, hot scones with cream and butter. He pours himself a cup of tea and eats. Finally replete, he opens it and starts to read just as Maisie comes into the dining room pink and flustered from her walk to take the children to the dame school. 'Good morning, my lover', she says and bends to kiss him on the cheek, 'News from Wallaroo?'

He nods. 'From Henry. Somebody has written it for him. Sit and I will read it to you.'

She sits down at the table and pours herself a cup of tea as he begins to read.

Dear Capun Pascoe

I am deeply sorry to tell you that I left my post at the Pascoe Station. My wife Jane was carrying on with Bob Millington. This I could not abide and besides she bade me leave as I do not have my letters so could not carry out my duties witout her help. I was unwell for some time but then found work at the Moonta Mine and it is my mining partner Mr Joe Watson Esq who writes this letter on my behalf. Yesterday Mr Watson and myself we did visit the station to see that all was as it should be. We discovered that Millington and Jane have sold a large number (5000 or thereabouts)of your sheep at a very low price. If this is at your instruction then all is well but if not I think it be my duty to tell you this. I hope that you and Mrs Pascoe and your dear children are all well.

Your humble servant
Henry Hopeful Down.

'Damn. And I was thinking how well this day had started.' Thomas folds the letter replaces it its envelope and looks at his wife. 'What are we to do Maisie?'

'You believe it's true, then?'

'I am not sure. I find it hard to believe that Henry would lie to me. And I recall Millington making sheep's eyes at Jane Cottrell on more than one occasion.'

Maisie nods. 'I heard the telegraph to Australia is now complete. We could send a telegram – ask Mr Millington why he sells our stock?'

'I'll go to Liskeard tomorrow. First I must sleep. This afternoon I will follow Dandy Pants again. Is the sugar in the tin all gone.'

'It is. It seems we are beset by evil people, husband.'

'It does, Maisie, indeed it does.'

Kit Robin and William George stand on the bob plat gazing out over the dressing floor and the shafts of the mine. 'You heard him Bill, "We should have had one long ago." Even bloody Pascoe is for it now it's working.'

The purser takes off his hat and scratches his head. 'Yes, Captain Kit, I heard him well enough. But his opinion does not fill the mighty hole it's made in Treasury. We'll not be paying dividends this month nor the next. Our adventurers will not be happy come the counthouse dinner, I can tell you. We may even have to ask for funds.'

'Not while I am Captain. What if we sell more arsenic? Would that help?'

'It might. At least the price is not in the dumps like copper. Can we mine more?'

'Perhaps, if what Pascoe says they've found on the 280 is correct. I can start a night core at the condensing works – that's not a problem. The buggers work there in near darkness anyway.'

'So be it. Now I must get back to those lazy clerks – make sure their accounting is correct.' He puts his top hat on and goes back inside the engine house, climbs down the ladder and thence into the counthouse.

Kit Robin stays there watching the great iron bob lifting up and down. Arsenic – he shudders at the very word. How has it come to this? How did she draw him in? He nods, of course he knows full well how – those love-soaked afternoons in the Clymo stable loft, that lilting accent, the laughing admiration of his prowess and her willingness. God, if only she were with him now. He breathes deep to calm himself, tries to ignore the tightening in his britches. He is possessed with lust, or is it love? That time she said, 'If I do that for you, what will you do for me?'

And he said, 'I'd do anything for you Mary O'Malley.'

'Would you now?'

'I would,' he said, 'I would.'

And later she said 'Would you get me some o' that arsenic?'

'What for?' he asked.

'Rats. But don't say nuttin'. I wouldn't be wanting the Lady Clymo to think I'd let rats in her precious kitchen.'

So he took a tin mug down to the works – simple it was to dip it in an open barrow load while no-one watched. He took care to wear old leather gloves so he'd not touch the stuff himself. But twice she'd asked for more until suspicious he asked her outright. 'Is there a plague of rats in Penpillick House then Molly?'

'Not a plague, Kit, me love. Just one rat in particular I'm tryin' to kill. But he's a tough old bugger, sure he is.'

And he thought, two and two make four. Mathew Clymo lies dying and none knew why and the cook is using arsenic in the kitchen supplied by him. But why, why would she?

He shakes his head. Today will be the last time, the very last. He swears it to himself out loud 'God damn, this will be the last time,' even though he loves her. And Pascoe – does he suspect? What did he say? "We have enough arsenic these days." The thought of discovery makes his bowels churn. And he's had a sense of being followed these last few days – that unseen eyes were watching him. But when he's turned he's seen no-one. He shrugs – it must be his imagination.

He spends the morning underground, visiting the working places, inspecting timbering and making sure that all is safe, although his attention today is cursory. He goes to the drive on the 280 and indeed the southern wall is solid mundic glittering steely grey in his candlelight. Odd, he thinks to find such poison buried in the ground but they will mine it to line the adventurers' pockets with yet more money.

Finally he returns to grass on Kit Robin's Engine and his sense of pride puts paid to his earlier despondency. I am a splendid chap he thinks and eats croust with a pint of cider in the counthouse with more than usual relish. Then its off to the blasted landscape of the arsenic works. His does not like to enter the condenser's brick-lined tunnels – all that poison on the walls and on the floors and the workers bundled up in their protective rags, all lit by candlelight – it haunts his dreams. But he does as he must and on his way out slyly dips the mug into an open barrel and holds it beneath his coat. Once outside and out of sight, he stuffs crumpled paper in the mug and puts it in his pocket. He stops, looks around at the massive spinning water wheel that turns the roasting kiln shimmering with heat, at the closed doors leading to the tunnels and the stunted trees up on the ridge. Was that a movement there? No, surely not – he must be seeing things. He walks back towards the mine and looking once more behind him, turns off on the path that leads to Penpillick House. As he approaches through the stable yard he starts to whistle a tune he knows she likes. There she is, Mary O' Malley, his love, his lover, standing prim in the kitchen doorway in her black housekeeper's dress, white lace apron and white mob cap. She comes quickly to the garden gate and he slips her the mug and turns away muttering, 'The last time, Mary, the very last time.'

'To be sure,' she whispers, 'to be sure, sweet boy.'

He goes quickly now but just as he turns on to the road leading down to the mine, he looks back to see Thomas Pascoe standing at the corner of the stable yard watching him. How long has he been there? Did he see him at the gate with Mary? How did he come there? Not from the house for he would have seen him cross the garden. He must have followed him, in which case he must know. He stares at him then turns away and walks off down the road, guts churning and his scrotum tightening with fear. He knows – the bugger knows. He must warn Mary. But how? He daren't go back to Penpillick House tonight. Tomorrow then when Pascoe sleeps. Together they could flee but where? Away from Cornwall, to Ireland perhaps – no the place still starves. Australia then – Plymouth is but three hours ride away and there take ship. But Pascoe could pursue him there. And he would lose this role he loves so much – Captain Kit Robin, captain of Wheal Emma. He does have money enough at least to last a while. No, it is unthinkable. He will stay. They do not know – it is all in his imagination. But fetching poison for his lover – no, that was the last.

They sit there in the evening light around his bedside – Grace and Thomas and red-haired Maisie, and Emily. He sits propped up on pillows still grey and gaunt but with a smile upon his face. 'Thomas Pascoe, clever as a fox you are and no mistake.'

'Not so clever Capun. Once I knew she's Scoble's daughter it didn't take too much to work out she means you harm. But let's not count our chickens till tomorrow morning. Now I must leave you for the night core. You'll like the man engine Capun. At least some good's come out of Dandy Pants as Captain of Wheal Emma.'

'Well, he'll not hold that post much longer will he? He'll be hangin' from a post more like if I have my way.'

'Hush, now Mathew. You're still not well enough to get excited. Oh, but it's good to see you as yourself, my lover.' She takes his hand in hers and kisses it.

'I'll not be myself till I'm back underground, down that bloody mine of mine.'

XXI

FISH HILL

THEY WATCH IN SILENCE AS THE SLIM FIGURE TROTS away westward to the flat horizon where the sun sets in a blaze of desert glory. He carries a spear longer than he is tall and two gourds strung on bark strip around his waist. He is barefoot and wears just a pair of tattered trousers cut off at the knees. He turned down their offer of food but filled the gourds with water from the creek.

'What will he eat?' Henry asks.

'Berries, grubs and roots and you've seen how handy he is with that bloody spear.'

Henry nods. Three days earlier he watched astonished as David held up a hand to halt their little cavalcade, stood unmoving as a statue then hurled the weapon a good forty yards at something neither white man could even see. He ran forward then and with a whoop held up the spear, a large goanna dangling from the tip. They ate it that night and the next day and its roasted flesh tasted much like chicken. But he has left them now and Henry feels a sudden surge of loneliness – this land, this desert land just goes on forever. Far to the west, the way they've come, more than a hundred miles he reckons, lies Wilpena and the Flinders Ranges which, from this solitary hill, seem civilised. Another week beyond are Wallaroo and Moonta which he now calls home, more so when he thinks of Mabel. And then beyond again, oceans and a world away his real home – damp green England and beloved Cornwall. But what lies north of here or to the east and even southward he does not know, save that somewhere is another ocean. He is a bug crawling on this sere desert tableland, his vision entirely limited by flat horizons. And the daytime heat is beyond imagining. David kept them moving even through the hottest part of every day when he and Joe slumped on their horses, broad-brimmed hats drawn low, the only flesh exposed their sunburned, blistered hands. He seemed immune the boy, his near naked body protected only by a film of desert dust, trotting out in front of them, unerring in his course. He'd stop once every hour or so, look back and wait for them, help water both the horses and the mules that carried all their food and mining gear. It seemed miraculous how he found the water holes marked at best by a slightly denser patch of scrub or perhaps a gentle hollow in the land, near invisible to Henry. Now he has gone and Henry Hopeful Down and Joe Watson must make do entirely on their own. He listens to the desert wind hissing in the scrub. A solitary crow calls far in the distance and something rustles in the boulders at his back – a small animal perhaps. He shakes his head in silent wonder and watches the setting sun.

'Come on Henry. Lets build camp before it gets too dark.'

They scramble down the rocky eastern slope of Fish Hill which stands perhaps three hundred feet above the desert plain. Horses and mules are tethered to an ancient gum tree that grows beside the creek. They unload their gear – two good rifles, their swags, a tent they bought in Blinman not so much for sleeping but more for rest and shade in the blistering midday heat. Pots and pans and shovels, broad gold pans one each and what they hope will be their money maker – a wooden cradle to sieve pure gold from sand and soil and gravel. And of course their picks and shovels, the tools that are part of their lives, and a wooden keg of black powder, miners that they are. They have flour enough to last a month – salted mutton, and strips of dried kangaroo, two bottles of Edna Mole's grog in case of celebration, two pounds of sugar and a bag of potatoes. They pitch their camp in the shade of the biggest gum tree and Joe Watson builds a small camp fire and boils water in a billy can for tea.

They sit there on the bank, boots off and feet cooling in the water, sipping tea hot enough to sting their sun-cracked lips.

'Bloody paradise this is mate,' Joe Watson says waving his mug at the wide green pool, the rocky foot of Fish Hill and the red-lit clouds above. 'And the fuckin' flies have gone to bed thank Christ.'

'Tis too,' Henry says. 'Bit like a dream after crossin' all that desert. You'd never a thought it'd be here, water an' all.'

'From what I saw from up the top there ain't nuthin' but sand

and scrub out eastward too. Ridge an' this creek run north and south jus' like ol Moley said. Tomorrer we'll start to work both upstream and down. What d'ye say?'

'You be the prospectin' man Joe Watson. I did try it before as you know but never saw a lick of gold. So you tells me what to do and I will do just as you say.'

'Well, the chances of finding another nugget like Moley's fish you can forget. They come once in a hundred years. We'll find small nuggets and gold dust in this here sand and in the gravel in the creek – that'll make us money specially with that there rockin' box. But what we're really after mate, is the mother-fuckin' lode, excuse my French.'

'An' how do we find that?'

'Work the up the creek till the colours run out then climb the bloody hill. Somewhere up there,' he waves his mug uphill and to the north, there'll be the bloody quartz reef what's shedding gold into the creek. We gotta a month or so to find her.' He takes his pipe from a trouser pocket, stuffs it with tobacco from a pouch, lights up and smokes in silence.

Henry Hopeful Down digs a shovel full of deep red soil and sand from the bank and dumps it in the pan. He takes this to the creek, squats down and sinks the pan until it fills with water and stirs it with his hand. He sets a swirling motion going, tipping the pan just slightly, just enough for liquid mud to slop over the outer edge, taking with it slurried soil and floating mineral flakes. Rocking slightly on his heels, pan held in both his hands, round and round he moves it, releasing suspended sediment until only heavier minerals, gravel and rocky fragments remain. Yesterday he spent with Joe, watching, trying his hand, failing, trying again and yet again until towards the end of the day Joe, squatting beside him said, 'Yes, yes mate, you've got it. Look there, and there.' And sure enough three, tiny gold nuggets the size of wheat grains, half obscured by black lees of iron, rolled in the bottom of the pan. He cried out in joy and that elation fed his dreams and has stayed with him overnight. A magpie warbles bell-like in the early morning air. This is the time he loves the best, the cool of the desert night still over the land, the smell of the gum trees along the creek, his back, his thighs, his calves not aching yet, as they surely will before this day is out.

He watches the last layer of mineral dross slide across the bottom of the pan, picks out the pebbles, gravel stones, tilts the pan again, knocks the edge with the heel of his hand and sends a slosh of ripples through the slurry and tips again. Yes, here is gold. This time a larger nugget, the size of his little fingernail and an inch long streak of gold dust. He picks out the nugget, holds it between thumb and forefinger, turns to see it glow in the light of the rising sun. Is this rich? Is he close to the mother lode? He has no idea. He loosens the drawstring of the leather pouch suspended from his belt and drops the nugget in. The gold dust he washes into a screw-topped jar and holds that too up to the sun, swirls it and watches, laughing at the glinting flakes of gold. He calls out, 'Joe, Joe Watson, get over here,' puts two fingers to his mouth and lets out a piercing whistle. 'Joe, Joe,' he shouts again. Taking up the shovel and the pan, he goes to the bank and digs exactly where he dug before. He fills the pan and squats in the creek again, flinching as the water fills his boots.

'Found something already have you, Henry?' Joe is at his shoulder.

Henry nods without looking up, 'I have but let's see what's in this here lot.' He works the pan while Joe squats silent at his side. Ten minutes it takes him until gold shows once more but this time a string of pea-sized nuggets and a two inch tail of gold dust.

'Jesus, Henry, you've got beginner's luck, no question.'

Henry grins up at his companion. 'So this is rich then?'

'Too right mate. There's two ounces in that pan. Near ten quids worth. I aint seen that since Ballarat. Not bad for a mornin's work. Tell yer what – we'll work this bank with the cradle for a coupla days, see how we go. Make enough money to make this whole trip worth our while. Then we'll go lookin' for the reef. I didn't find no colours upstream so I reckon the mother lode ain't too far away.

The cradle is a four foot wooden box, part open at the bottom and sat on rockers on a sloping frame. A metal sieve is slotted in a hopper at the upper end and below it a sloping wooden bed. They brought it out dismantled, wrapped in sacking and strapped on to a mule. It takes them less than fifteen minutes to set it up beside the creek at Henry's find.

'This here goes on here,' Joe Watson says and bolts a wooden lever to one side of the box. 'And now Henry old friend, we'se set an' ready.'

'So how's she work zackly?'

'Simple as can be. We puts a shovel full o'dirt in the hopper, you rock the handle to and fro as I pour water in, not too fast and not too slow but steady like. All right?'

Henry nods goes to the bank digs in deep, returns and drops his shovel load into the hopper. Joe stands beside the cradle and tips in water from a bucket. 'Start her rockin', easy now, easy.'

Henry grabs the handle, works it crossways to and fro and watches as gravel, sand and silt disappear through the sieve to the sloping bed below, leaving stones and rubble on the top. It takes several minutes of steady rocking, Joe slopping water in from time to time before the hopper's empty save for stony debris rattling on the surface of the sieve.

'That's it. Hold it now, mate. Stop rockin'. We needs to clean the crap out of here.' Joe lifts out the hopper peers in and runs his fingers through the detritus on the sieve. 'Just checkin' for fish-sized nuggets. Ain't none.' He empties the hopper in the creek and washes it. 'Now let's see how we done.' They squat down on either side, looking in the cradle. The sloping floor is crossed by wooden riffles and lined with strips of carpet where black silt, reddish sand and heavy gravel fragments lie drifted.

'Don't see no gold,' Henry says.

'You ain't lookin'. There and there.' He points with his single forefinger, rolls a pea-sized nugget then another half obscured by silt. He picks them out, drops them in his shirt pocket. 'We'll pan all this and then you'll see.' He lifts the cradle, and slops sediment first into his pan then into Henry's. 'Right, let's go.'

They both squat in the shallows of the creek, panning in silence. By now the sun, risen clear of the sheltering eucalypts, beats down upon their bended backs and sweat seeps through their shirts. Flies crawl on their faces and buzz about their ears and eyes but their attention stays fixed on the swirling liquid in the pans. From time one or the other grunts, or stretches or tilts his pan's lip in the water or flaps away a more persistent fly. Finally Joe rocks back on his heels. 'At least an ounce o' dust I reckon. How's yours?'

'Ounces I don't know. But four nuggets maybe more – look here.' He holds out his pan, gold glinting clear in the bottom.'

'Lord lifting Christ, Henry. I can't hardly believe it. We'se gonna be rich, boy. And we ain't hardly started.'

Henry grins. 'Good old Mr Mole. He done us a right good turn, did'n he?'

'You ain't wrong there, boy. Now let's get back to it.'

By midday they've filled and cleared the cradle half a dozen times and are both elated and exhausted. It seems to Henry that gold is pouring from the ground. His excavation in the bank is now a red dirt cave, a treasure trove that never in his sweetest dreams has he imagined. Although working in this dizzying heat takes dogged fortitude and grit, it is nothing compared to driving steel in the stygian depths of the Moonta Mine or of Wheal Emma. The leather pouch suspended from his belt is heavy now – he weighs it in his hand. It is his, all his this gold, and not like copper or tin tributed for mere shillings in the pound to make the rich still richer. He could dance. He strides across to where Joe Watson stands staring up the hill and puffing on his pipe. 'Joe my friend,' he bellows, 'we is rich, boy. Aint't we so rich.' He picks the little man up by the waist and holds him high.

'We are and we'se gonna be richer still. There's a mother lode up there that'll be Ballarat and Bendigo in one.' He points wildly up the hill. 'Now put me down yer lummox. I need some grub.'

They quit and seek the shade of their encampment, stretching out their aching bodies and drying out their shrivelled calloused feet. They eat damper baked the night before in the ashes of their fire and strips of salted mutton washed down with tea boiled in a billy can.

Joe lies back in the tent, his rolled up swag his pillow. 'Wake me when the sun is down behind the hill and then we'll start again.'

Henry too lies down but does not sleep. The future fills his mind. How will he spend his riches? Perhaps he could buy the Pascoe station, get rid of Middleton and his faithless wife, have it ready for Thomas's return. He shakes his head – he does not really know how rich he is, how rich he will be nor what that means. And of course the gold is not all his, nor even his and Joe's, who lies snoring by his side. In his joy he has forgotten. "Half of what you find plus one hundredth," that's what Mabel said and they all agreed. But if Mabel were his wife her half would be his too? 'I am a fool,' he mutters to himself. Why would she want him anyway? Besides Jane Cottrell is his wife, for better or for worse. He lies eyes open staring up at pinpricks of sunlight shining through the canvas. Then too there is the journey home. Joe seems sure of the way back but all that Henry knows is that it's four or five days travel westward. Without a guide how will they find the waterholes and how avoid the blinding salt flats? He sighs, closes his eyes and drifts off to sleep.

'What does a mother lode look like Joe?'

'Mate, they all look different but we'll know it when we find it, believe you me.'

They have stopped half way up the hill both to catch their breath and fossick around with their picks in the shaly rubble at their feet. Below them lies the creek, its still waters glinting in the sun, its tree lined banks the only greenery as far as they can see. A red stained hollow on a bend marks the diggings where they worked until last evening when finally their pans yielded nothing more than iron-sand and silt. They've left their leather pouches filled with nuggets and six jars of gold dust hidden deep in a cleft in the boulders above their camp. 'Can't be too careful,' Joe said. ''Pears there ain't nobody around but who knows out here?'

Henry studies the ground beneath his boots and picks up a fist-sized grey-white stone and hands it to his mate. 'What about this here?'

'Yeah, quartz alright,' Joe says, tapping it with his pick. 'But nuthin' in it – dry as bloody desert dust. You wanna look for stuff like this but with a bit of iron in it – fools gold, mispickel and maybe copper too. Leastways that's how it was on the diggings back east.' He hurls the rock away and they stand and watch it clatter down the slope, kicking up little rills of shale and gravel.

They carry on climbing, stopping now and then to pick up a rock, study it briefly and then discard it. As they climb their random paths diverge, Henry's to the south and Joe Watson's to the north until once up on the ridge, they are more than two hundred yards apart. Henry squats looking at the naked rock beneath his boots – hard, black and faintly banded. He hits it with his pick and listens to its ring. He shakes his head and doubts that even Thomas Pascoe would know what he was looking at and whether it held gold or not. He stands and stares away to the west – nothing, not a soul and the only sound the faint hiss of the wind in the scrub below. The sky is a vast blue bowl and there, there just at the limits of his vision something else – another living being, a black speck circling and circling, drifting nearer, tilting, circling ever nearer until he makes out the fingered feathers tipping the great black wings and the wedge-shaped tail. The eagle calls and calls again and swings over his head and follows the line of the ridge southward. He watches it until once again it is nothing more than a black dot moving across an empty sky.

'Henry. Henry Hopeful Down. Henreeee.'

He turns at the shout to see Joe Watson waving his arms in the air and beckoning to him. He scrambles along the ridge his head filled with images of golden veins, of him and Joe swinging their picks digging pure gold out of the ground. But when he reaches the spot where Joe now kneels amidst fragments of broken rubble, he can see nothing more than a rusty mass of rock laced with stringers and blebs of quartz.

'This could be it, mate. It's a good six foot wide and runs right across the hill.'

Henry follows his partner's pointing finger towards a red-stained bluff that juts out on the western flank of the hill.

'An I think there's another lode up there, see?' This time he points northwards where the ridge dips then climbs again to a peak.

Henry shakes his head. 'Is this a lode? I don't see no gold.'

'Just like before, you ain't lookin. Here. Hold it in the sun. Look close. Get yer eye in.' He passes up a piece of rocky ironstone he's cracked wide open.

Henry turns it in his hand, peers at it, catches sunlight glinting off crystal faces, traces round a quartz fragment with his little finger then he sees it – filaments of gold yes, and tiny nuggets buried in rusty vesicles and there a golden filigree, fine as cotton thread half-buried in rusty flint. He holds the sample out, looks at it again and measures with his eye the breadth and length of the rock mass on which they stand. He nods.

'See it?' Joe asks.

'I do. How rich?'

'Dunno – rich but we'll bag up a load an', crush it, an run it through the cradle. Then we'll know. An' if that runs too,' he points towards the rusty peak, 'we got ourselves an even bigger mine, no question.'

'Good thing we brought powder and steel. This stuff's as hard as a whore's heart but she's got gold all right.' Joe whangs the rock face with his pick. 'We'll have to drill and blast her tomorrow.'

'How d'ye know?'

'Cos I know whores.'

Henry snorts. 'I'll throw ee down the bloody hill yer little bugger. I mean how d'ye know there's gold here?'

'I knows what yer mean. Same rock as down there. Just harder.'

They are standing on the peak of Fish Hill after a morning spent panning samples from their discovery of the day before. Henry stretches, groans and wipes away the sweat trickling down his face. 'Lord, I ain't never been so hot.' He takes a swig from his water bottle and passes it to Joe. 'Aint no breeze neither, not like yesterday – 'twas almost cool up here.'

Joe Watson sniffs the air. 'Reckon there's rain about.' He drinks, turns and shades his eyes against the sun. 'Yeah look, way out there.'

He points to sun-lit thunder heads towering far off on the southwest horizon. 'Storm coming I reckon.'

They sit in silence staring out across the endless flatlands watching as dust devils whirl their way across the scrub. The thought of being out there day after sweltering day makes Henry's mouth feel drier than it already is. He drinks again and cannot help himself from thinking of Tom Mole delirious with thirst, half dead, lost and alone. Well, he will not be alone. They have their horses and the mules and more than food enough and water. He need not worry, they will get home. Lightning flickers far away and now he too can smell the rain. He smiles – months it's been since he felt raindrops on his face.

'Best get down to camp, Henry.'

He nods, gets wearily to his feet and follows after Joe who scuttles down the scree slope like some kind of biped goat.

Sat before the campfire that night they broach the home-brewed rum they brought to celebrate. Wind rustles in the eucalyptus trees and to the north the thunder booms and lightning skitters across the sky.

'What you going to do with your share Joe?'

'Dunno mate. Have to think about it. But first we'll have to get a mineral lease. Do that in Adelaide. I'll ride down there soon as we get back. Won't be no problem – I know the Lands Office clerk from when I was at Strathalbyn – bloke by the name of Scrivener.'

'So we goin' to mine this ourselves – be mine owners, wear them top hats like Capun Hancock?'

'Capun Henry 'an Capun Joe. How about that. Here, have a drink – good stuff old Moley's missus makes.'

Henry upends the bottle, pours the oily spirit down his throat, swallows and wipes his mouth. He lets out a breath. 'Bloody light that stuff, boy.' He passes the bottle back. 'We've had some luck ain't we Joe, you an' I? First Mabel with her money, then Mr Mole, now this. I can't hardly believe it.'

'Deserve it don't we. Minin' down that fuckin' dark hole then trekkin' halfway across Australia an' livin' like blackfellas. Not to mention that week in gaol where we dreamed this up. Here's to us matey.'

Henry is silent for a while, staring into the fire, watching the flames sawing in the wind and sparks whirling upwards into the dark. It is not home but he is comforted – the vastness of this land reduced to a fire-lit circle, his friend beside him, the inward glow of rum. The Pascoe family once the very centre of his life are long gone, now just a distant memory of someone he used to be. And his life will change again. If only he and Jane had children perhaps things would not have gone so wrong. But then he'd not be here, he'd not be rich. He's never dreamed of riches but here he is, a wealthy man.

'You ever wanted children, Joe?'

Joe takes a swig from the bottle. 'I left a boy back in Melbourne. I was hooked up with this workin' girl for a year or two. But she ran off with another bloke when I was in the clink. Took the boy with her. Lovely kid he was. We called 'im Joseph. I looked for them but they was gone. Near broke my bloody heart it did. That's why I come out to South Australia.'

'That why you think Mabel ain't for me?'

'You'se a lovely bloke Henry. Sorta bloke that women take advantage of just like that bloody wife o' yours. Blokes like us we're mates. Won't let each other down. Mabel? Christ knows. Here, finish it.' He passes him the bottle.

Henry drinks and lays the empty bottle down, lies back on the sand and shuts his eyes watching the swirling after images of flames. Good to be drunk again he thinks – rich, no worries, just the long trip back . . . then Mabel. He grins to himself.

'Best sleep in the tent tonight, mate. It may not be raining now but it surely will before this night's out.'

He rolls over, staggers to his feet and collapses in the tent beside his friend.

Neither the near continuous rolls of thunder nor the constant lightning flashes wake them from their drunken sleep. They do not hear the braying of the mules, the terrified whinnying of tethered horses or the rush and tumble of water rising in the creek. Not until the spreading flood sends wet fingers seeping beneath his swag does Henry Hopeful Down jerk awake. For a second he lies there wondering where he is and what is happening. He sits up and in a single lightning flash sees dark water swirling past the opening of their tent.

'Joe, Joe wake up wake up,' he shouts shaking the body of his friend. 'The creek's in flood. Wake up.' He bellows now, 'Joe, Joe, wake up boy,' and grabs his boots already filled with water and jammed against the inside of the tent by the muddy rising flood. He hauls them on, tumbles out of the tent into a rainstorm the like of which he's never seen. He stands up and in another lightning flash sees their quiet little creek a roaring foam-flecked torrent. The wind is roaring in the trees, the boom of thunder continuous and lightning zips and rips and crackles across the sky. Joe crawls out behind him barefoot, stands up and yells above the storm, 'Jesus Christ, me fuckin' boots there gone, there gone. Quick we gotta get out of here before we drown. Up the fuckin, hill.'

But they are too late. The flood is now knee deep, tugging at their legs as they slip and skid up the crumbling bank, blinded by alternating utter darkness and dazzling lightning. Henry throws his body against the current, feels rocks and boulders sliding beneath his feet, takes one great stride and he is out, clutching at roots and skinny branches to haul himself, gasping above the flood.

'Henry, Henry, Henry,'.

He turns at the last despairing wail and in a lightning flash sees Joe Watson, head just above the water, spinning, one arm waving. Then he is gone.

XXII

PORRIDGE

DOCTOR COUCH SLIPS HIS WATCH FROM HIS waistcoat pocket, flips open the cover, studies it then looks at him sat up in bed. 'Eight prompt, you said. That gives us ten minutes to decide how we shall confront her.'

'You sit just where you are beside the door. The hussy will not see you. Thomas will stay beside the bed which she'll not find untoward. Once she's given me the gruel, Thomas will take good hold of her and the two of you will march her down to the cellar and lock her in. Thomas will then send hotfoot for the constable. We'll have the poisoned gruel, the arsenic from the kitchen and you will have observed her in the act. Not so Thomas?'

'Indeed Capun. She'll be caught red-handed.'

'What about her accomplice? Dandy Pants you called him?' The doctor chuckles. 'How came he by that name?'

'The miners gave it him. Apt is it not – he dresses like a fop. We'll deal with him later.'

Mathew Clymo leans back on his pillows, sighs and smiles. How good it is to be once more in command. And good too to have his stepson at his side, this clever upright man, this peerless miner. He grasps the forearm resting on the bed. And best of all that dreadful griping in his guts is gone. For the first time in months and months he's free of pain, thinks no more of dying. He could wring the Irish bitch's neck, she's put him through such agony – wring her neck with these, his own two hands. He holds them up – liver spotted, withered before their time, the veins stand out like twisted tunnels burrowing beneath the skin. Arsenic flowing in his veins – no more.

'Capun she's here,' Thomas whispers just as a knock comes at the door.

Mathew nods and closes his eyes.

'Come in Mary,' Thomas calls.

The door opens and Mary Scoble enters, holding high a tray which bears a glass of water, a slice of bread and butter and a bowl of gruel still steaming. 'Morning Captain, sir. Morning Captain Pascoe.' She places the tray on the bedside table. 'Will you be having your porridge first as usual Captain?'

Mathew opens his eyes, holds out both hands and nods. As she passes him the bowl he smiles and whispers 'Good morning Mary Scoble.'

She jerks back. Thomas seizes her arm. She spins around just as the white haired doctor leaps to his feet takes two paces and grabs her other arm. 'The porridge is poisoned is it not, woman?'

'Ah ye bastards, bastards. Let me go. Let me go.' Her voice rises to a scream. 'Let me go ye bastards.' She tugs and turns but they lift her from her feet and drag her backwards through the open door.

He puts the bowl of poisoned porridge on his bedside table and swings his legs out of the bed. Feet on the floor and using the bed head for support he hauls himself to standing. His head swims as he totters towards the door and clutches at the jamb. He stands there in his crumpled bed-smelling nightgown watching as the doctor and his stepson half carry, half push the screeching maid down the stairs. She twists violently, bends her head and bites the doctor's hand. He cries out and lets go of her as she wrenches herself from Thomas's grasp, kicking his shins with all her strength. He stumbles and she leaps down the remaining stairs two at a time, races along the hallway to the front door, black skirts flying.

'After her,' Mathew shouts, 'don't let her get away, the murderous bitch. Thomas, get after her.'

But Thomas clings to the banister rubbing his leg before hobbling down to the hallway, by which time Mary Scoble is out of the door, slamming it behind her.

Mathew sighs and exhausted turns back to his bed. He sits, staring at the open door and shakes his head. She's got away. Scoble's daughter has got away – Scoble's daughter who for all these weeks has fed him arsenic. He remembers swimming up from some dreadful dream some morning past, opening his eyes and seeing Thomas at his bedside. His mouth was dry and filthy tasting, yet suddenly he knew the endless griping in his guts was stopped. It was then that Thomas told him Mary O'Malley was William Scoble's daughter and he thought he must be dreaming still. 'Impossible,' he whispered.

'No Capun, it's true and I have proof. She's been poisoning you with arsenic from the mine.'

He closed his eyes, thought back to when he last felt well. O'Malley was not with them then. It could be true. He rubbed his belly, pressed his hand against his guts – yes, the pain was almost gone, a memory now of what it was. He breathed the deepest breath, felt the air lifting up his chest and knew that he would live. And now, sitting on the bed, he looks down at his bony shanks outlined by the thin stuff of his nightgown, wondering if they'll carry him down, and more importantly up, three hundred fathom of ladders. I must get down there, he thinks, see what that bloody Dandy Pants has been up to.

'Mathew, Mathew, what you doin' out of bed my lover.' Grace bustles in with a plate of porridge in her hand. 'Get back to bed. Here I've brought your proper breakfast.'

'Bugger that, Grace Clymo. I've spent more than enough time abed. Bring me some clothes now and I'll take my breakfast in the dining room like a proper human being.'

She puts the porridge on the table and hugs him to her breast. 'Oh Mathew, Mathew, it's so good to have you back. I thought . . . I thought . . . .'

'I thought so too but never mind. It didn't happen thanks to that boy of yours. It's all over now and I'm still living. Did the woman get away?'

'I don't know. Thomas took after her on horseback.'

He nods. 'And the doctor?'

'He's in the parlour dressin' his wound. She give him a dreadful bite. Don't they say a human's is worse than a dog's?'

'They do, they do. But come Grace, help me dress and I'll go down. I must talk to him. Will you bring the poisoned porridge.'

'Of course. But first, let's get you dressed.'

Captain Kit Robin sitting alone in the count house, leans back in his chair and puts his hands behind his head. The purser and his clerks are out on the dressing floor sampling parcels of sorted copper ore ready for the smelters' agents due on Monday. He has decided that he will not go underground today but will spend the morning studying the accounts to determine how much more arsenic needs to be produced to put the mine in profit. The account ledgers lie open on the desk in front of him but try as he will, he cannot concentrate. He slept little last night, waking time after time, unable to rid his mind of the image of Thomas Pascoe watching him from the stable yard. He sees him now, standing tall and motionless, staring at him his height exaggerated by his hat. He looks at his own hat, a high crowned bowler hanging on the peg behind the door and thinks perhaps he too should adopt the top hat favoured by Cornish mine captains. But somehow a bowler goes much better with the silk-embroidered waistcoats he so loves. He tugs at the tips of the one he's wearing and admires the snug fit around his waist. Climbing all those ladders all these years has kept him trim – he'll have to take care now, eat less heartily perhaps. He bends to study the ledger once more, turns a page and sighs – the last sale of arsenic was at one hundred and twenty pounds per ton. He looks up as the counthouse door bangs open. Mary O'Malley stands in the doorway, panting, red in the face, her mob cap askew.

'Kit me darlin', I needs yer help. I needs to hide. They're after me.'

He jumps to his feet. 'Who's after you?'

'Damn Pascoe and the bloody doctor, ' she pants.

He feels a sickening lurch in his guts. He need not ask her why for he already knows the answer but he asks her just the same. 'Why?'

'They say I tried to poison old Clymo. Quick now. Where can I hide?'

He looks at her, his mind a whirl. Then he has it. 'Come in, quick. Shut the door.'

She looks around. 'In here?'

'No.' He unlocks a drawer in his desk and takes out a single large key. 'Come.' He takes her by the hand, leads her out the back door of the counthouse, through the empty dry and out into the open behind the engine house. Skirting the vast rubble pile of the attle dump they come to a low stone building with a single sturdy padlocked door.

'What's this?' she asks.

'Magazine,' he says undoing the padlock. 'You'll be safe here until tonight. I have the only key.' He opens the door. 'Go in. Sit on the floor. Are you afraid of the dark?'

'No, Kit me darlin', I'm not.'

'That's good. If you strike a light you'll blow yourself to kingdom come. The barrels are full of black powder.'

She goes in, sits astride a barrel and grins at him. 'Go off like a rocket would I?'

He shakes his head. 'I'll bring you food and water when I can.'

'Will yer leave with me tonight?'

He doesn't answer leaning his weight on the open door looking at her.

'Give us a kiss then.'

He leans in and kisses the upturned mouth.

She puts her hand between his legs and fondles him. 'Don't leave me in the dark too long. I'll get lonesome, darlin'.'

He closes and locks the door, stands and looks around. No one has seen them. He walks back to the counthouse deep in thought.

Thomas shades his eyes against the sun and scans the moor. If she has come this way he should see her, unless she has seen him first. Perhaps she lies hidden behind some tussock or in a peaty gully. She cannot have gone far, outdistanced him by much for he was but minutes behind her when he galloped from the stables sure she was headed for the moor. His horse stands quivering, breath quieting after the gallop up the hill. Where would she go from here – north across the moor to Bolventor or west along its southern margin? Neither, he realises. She's not on the moor. He sees her kicking him on the stairs – shiny pointed boots, hardly footwear for trekking through the bogs of Bodmin Moor. More likely she went down through the village and the lane to Liskeard. He twists in the saddle and looks back the way he came – there is no sign of her. He turns the horse and trots back down the hill. Someone will have been seen her running through the village; all he needs to do is ask.

Half a dozen miners' wives stand chatting at the village pump, amongst them Jenny Tuttle. He stops his horse and doffs his hat. 'Good morning, ladies.'

They look up at him. 'Mornin' Capun Pascoe.'

'Heard Capun Clymo's on the mend,' Jenny Tuttle says.

'He is, thank the Lord.'

'It's all right for some.'

'Quite.' He coughs, hesitates then says, 'Did any of you see Mary O' Malley pass this way perchance?'

They look at each other. Jenny Tuttle grins. 'Lost your housekeeper have you Capun?'

'Mm, yes, you might say that.'

'Well she ain't been by here, not this mornin'. Ain't that right, maids?'

The women nod and one says, 'No, no Capun, we ain't seen her an' I been here since sun-up doin' me washin'.'

'Thank you ladies. Good morning to you.' He doffs his hat again, turns his horse and rides slowly back up through the village. The only other places she could be are somewhere on the mine or down at the arsenic works. He stops outside Penpillick House uncertain whether to stable the horse or ride on. But the clatter of the stamps, the smoke and bustle of the dressing floor all upset the beast so he dismounts, walks the horse to the stable yard and hands him to the stable boy. 'Brush him down and feed him oats,' he says, 'then tell the missus I'm gone to the mine.' He strides down the cindered track, stops at the engine house and puts his head through the open door. For a moment he watches the ponderous rise and fall of the massive iron beam driven by the pistons sliding almost silently in their polished cylinders. He shouts out above the hiss of steam, 'Anybody here?'

The engineer, oiling can in hand and a dirty kerchief around his head, leans over the gantry above him. 'Mornin' Capun Pascoe. Is aught amiss?'

'Anybody been in here this morning?'

'No Capun, only me.'

Thomas nods and waves, leaves the engine house and is walking towards the dressing floor when above the clatter of the stamps he hears a shout.

'Captain Pascoe, Captain Pascoe.'

He turns to see Kit Robin standing on the counthouse steps, beckoning to him. He walks across. 'Captain Kit?'

'Captain Pascoe, I need to talk to you – in private if I may.'

'I am sorry Captain, but I am in somewhat of a hurry. Could we not talk later?'

'It's about . . .,' He hesitates.

'About?'

'Mary O'Malley.'

'You have seen her?'

'I have.'

'Where?'

'She came here half an hour ago.'

'Where did she go?'

'I locked her in the magazine.'

Thomas blinks. 'Did you now?'

'I did. Will you come in?'

Thomas nods and follows Kit Robin up the steps and into the empty counthouse. 'Well Captain?' Thomas says once he is seated across the desk.

Kit Robin swallows. His Adam's apple bobs above the silk cravat. 'She rushed in here looking for a place to hide. Said you and Doctor Couch were after her for poisoning Captain Clymo. Needless to say, I was astonished.'

Thomas puts a hand to his mouth, strokes his chin and regards the man across the desk. 'Astonished.'

'Indeed I was. I thought I should detain her so I locked her up . . .

as I said in the magazine. I was just coming to call you.'

'Were you Captain?'

'Yes, yes I was.'

'You know that yesterday I followed you to and from the arsenic works.'

Kit Robin nods. 'Yes, I thought you had.'

'You brought arsenic from the works to the house just yesterday, did you not?'

He nods again.

'And gave it to Mary.'

'I did. I thought it was just for rats. She told me Mrs Clymo would dismiss her if she discovered rats in the kitchen. I believed her. I swear it.'

Thomas shakes his head. 'She is your lover, is she not?'

Kit Robin nods once more, head bent, eyes fixed on the opened ledgers on the table.

'You are complicit in attempted murder, Captain Kit.'

'I knew nothing of it, I swear. Why would I lock her up if I was her accomplice?' He takes the key to the magazine from his waistcoat pocket and holds it out to him. 'Let us call for the constable and have the woman arrested now.'

Thomas takes the key but shakes his head. 'I will call for the constable in due course. When he arrives, Doctor Couch and I will accompany him to the magazine and arrest the woman. But I will have to tell the constable that I followed you and saw you take arsenic from the works, bring it to the house and give it to Mary Scoble.'

'Mary Scoble!'

'Yes, Mary Scoble, William Scoble's daughter.'

Kit Robin collapses in his chair, his mouth drops open and he puts his hands to his head. 'It cannot be – all this time . . . I thought she . . ..' He sits silent, head bowed.

'You thought what?'

'I will not say.'

'Come, Captain Kit, if you are not open with me how can I believe that you did not know the woman's purpose?'

The man looks up at him, his mouth set in a grim line. Finally he speaks. 'I loved her. I planned to marry her. Yet all along she was deceiving me.'

Thomas purses his lips and nods. 'Yes, she deceived us all but now she is unmasked and will answer to the law. You will be needed as a witness and I suggest you do not leave Penpillick.'

'Am I to remain as Captain of Wheal Emma?'

'That is for Captain Clymo and the adventurers to decide. Mercifully the Captain is on the mend and anxious to resume his duties.' Thomas gets to his feet. 'I will inform you when the constable arrives. Meanwhile I will keep the key.' He holds it up then slips it in his jacket pocket.'

'You do not trust me, Captain.'

'No, I do not.' Thomas turns on his heel and leaves the counthouse.

It is midday when the constable arrives at Penpillick House. Thomas Pascoe, Mathew Clymo and Doctor Couch sit with him in the parlour and tell their tale.

He shakes his head. 'Such villainy I can scarce believe. And you say she is violent?'

'She bit the doctor and kicked me. That is how she escaped.' Thomas pulls up his trouser leg to show the bruises on his shin.

'Then I may need your help to apprehend her.'

'Of course. The doctor and I will accompany you. Kit Robin too.'

'You think him innocent?'

'I do not know. If we take him with us and confront her perhaps we shall find out.'

'A good idea. I shall observe him closely. Well gentleman, let us get to work.'

'I shall not go with you, Constable,' Mathew Clymo says. 'I am far from myself as yet and not too steady on my legs. But I will surely be well enough to see her accused in court. What think you Doctor?'

'Captain Clymo, by all rights you should be in your grave. To be frank I do not understand why you are still alive. She served you arsenic enough to kill an ox.'

'Ah, we Cornish captains are made of strong stuff. A little mundic never killed a miner.'

The four men stand silent in front of the oaken door. The constable puts a finger to his lips. Thomas holds up the key and the constable points to the doctor, stands on one side of the door and motions Thomas to stand on the other. Thomas passes the key to the doctor and stands where he is bid. The constable gestures to Kit Robin to position himself in front of the door and nods to the doctor. As he inserts the key in the lock a quiet voice comes from within, 'Is that you, Kit me darlin'?'

'It is,' Kit Robin says.

The doctor unlocks the padlock, unloops it from its hasp and swings the door wide open. Mary Scoble steps out blinking in the sunlight. 'Ah Kit, 'twas awful dark in there,' she says just as Thomas comes from behind, grabs one arm while the constable seizes her by the other. She shrieks and struggles, twists and turns, losing her white mob cap. But this time their grip is firm and the constable clamps on handcuffs.

She squirms in their grip. 'Ye bastards. Ye bastards. Let me go, let me go. I done nuttin' at all.'

'Mary Scoble, you are charged with the heavy crime of attempted murder. I shall take you before the magistrate at Bodmin. Will you come peacefully?'

'I will not. 'Twas him the lyin' cheatin' English bastard. 'Twas all his idea.' She spits in Kit Robin's face. 'Ah yer traitorous English pig. I hates yer, by Christ I do.'

Kit Robin wipes saliva from his face. 'You said it was for the rats, Mary.'

'Don't yer "Mary" me yer bloody swine. Ye planned it all. Ye want to be owner o' this damned mine. Well yer never will be now. Besides by rights 'tis mine.' She stamps. 'Dis mine is mine for it was me da's – yes William Scoble was me father and he was kilt by dat swine Clymo. Ah by God I'd liked to see him. . . .' she twists and struggles in their grip.

Thomas looks across at the constable. 'See him what, Mary?' Thomas asks.

'Ahh,' she says shaking her head. 'Ye don't know do yer. You bloody English you starved us and you don't even know. Starved us for generations. Stole our land and I come here to take back what is rightly mine and now look at me.' She shakes her head again and begins to weep.

'Come Mary Scoble,' the constable says.

She nods and walks weeping, head bowed beside the constable, down the track toward the engine house, her red hair glossy in the sunlight. Couch the doctor, Thomas Pascoe and Kit Robin follow in single file. When they reach the policeman's pony trap hitched outside the counthouse, he hands her up and climbs in to sit beside her. 'You'll come quietly now?' he says. 'I do not have to tie you?'

'No. Where would I, a woman, go with these?'She holds up her handcuffed hands and wipes away her tears. 'But what about him? He put me up to it, I swear.'

The constable looks to Thomas and the doctor. Both shake their heads.

'Captain Robin, do not leave the county. You will be called as witness at the trial. Walk on,' he says taking up the reins. They watch as pony, trap and policeman and his prisoner disappear around the bend toward Penpillick.

'Well Thomas, that is a job well done.'

'Indeed, doctor. I thank you for all your help. And thank you Captain Kit. I fancy that without your assistance our task would have been more onerous.'

Kit Robin gives a slight bow. 'The least I could do Captain. I much regret my foolish part in this affair.' He stops and looks around and coughs into his hand. 'Er Captain, am I to continue with my normal duties?'

'For the time being. At least until Captain Clymo is fit to resume his post. This evening I will take the night core as per usual.'

'Thank you Captain. Good afternoon. Good afternoon, Doctor.' He takes the three steps up to the counthouse goes in and shuts the door.

'You believe him then?' Couch asks as they walk up towards the house.

'My mind is not made up. He may be a villain or just a fool. What think you?'

The doctor takes off his hat and runs a hand through his mop of white hair. 'If he's a villain he's no fool. If he did conspire to murder your stepfather it was a master stroke to lock the woman up once the plot came out. But the woman's trial will tell. You do not suppose he'll run away?'

'To do so would be to admit his guilt. There'd be a hue and cry. And Kit Robin's known from coast to coast, fop and philanderer that he is. He'd not get far.' They reach the house. 'Doctor, I must to Liskeard and send a telegram to Australia where my affairs need my attention. This business has quite taken my mind off all else and tomorrow is Sunday. But will you go in and pass our news to Captain Clymo, my mother and the family?'

'I will. I do not doubt that Captain Clymo will be much bucked up at our success.'

'He will indeed, Doctor, he will indeed.'

Kit Robin sits once more alone at his desk in the counthouse. He sighs. He was right in what he did – giving up the woman. She deceived him, made him look a fool although in his heart of hearts he knew – had known all along. But that is a thing that he must hide, deep down in the darkest recesses of his mind, as deep as the deepest levels of the deepest mine where few miners dare to go. Yes he will hide it even from himself and it shall not come out – not ever. He sighs again a weary sigh. He is tired, exhausted, as if he has been on the rack. He loved her and she is gone. He could weep but does not. Turns instead to the ledgers, takes up a quill dips it in the ink and returns finally to calculating how much mundic will turn the mine to profit.

XXIII

SALTBUSH, MALLEE AND MULGA

HENRY HOPEFUL DOWN HAS NOT SLEPT. RESTED perhaps, curled up in the hard and meagre shelter of a granite boulder at the foot of Fish Hill. He is wet to the skin, his body wracked with shivers. From time to time a sob rises in his throat and the tears flood his eyes as he sees again Joe Watson spinning in the current and in that flash of lightning, the final despairing wave. Towards dawn the rain stops, the storm rumbles off towards the north and lightning no longer flashes in the coffin of his shelter. He dozes for a while, more to forget his sickening loss than anything else until the carolling of the magpies in the trees across the creek wakes him. Crawling from beneath his boulder like some sodden desert beast, he stands joints creaking, facing the rising sun. He breathes deep and long, rubs his face and head and runs his fingers through his beard. He looks around. All is gone – their camp, their pots and pans, their picks and shovels, the rocking box – nothing is left, not even the remnants of their campfire. And in their place a pall of mud and gravel, sand and silt, the banks torn out, the gum tree roots exposed. Yet the creek itself flows quietly now, if on a somewhat different course. A massive tree trunk lies athwart the stream lodged between the rocks. It was never there before – it must have come from way upstream. So downstream perhaps he will find the wreckage of his life, some items he can use, perhaps the body of his friend, perhaps the bodies of the horses and the mules. The gold they hid well deep in a crevice high above the creek. Surely it will not have washed away but what use is that to him? He shakes his head as the tears well once again. First of all, he will search downstream until he finds Joe Watson's body. He sets off working his way along the hillside somewhat above the creek to get a better view of both the banks. Stopping every now and then, he shades his eyes against the sun and studies the scene below. He finds nothing until the first the first meander where a sack of flour has fetched up against a gravel shoal.

182

He scrambles down and paddles through the water to drag the sodden sack up onto the sand. At least he will not starve – the flour will dry out in the sun and he'll make damper. He shuts away the thought of how he is to get back home, alone, across the wasteland, without beasts to carry food and water for surely they will have drowned. The flour now safe upon the sand, he crosses to the eastern bank and roots amongst the sodden logs and vegetation. He turns over a splintered plank and with a cry holds up a rifle, his own, battered but still serviceable, if only he can find some ammunition. Leaving the rifle propped against a tree, he walks a short way to the next turn in the creek, crosses over once again and decides to climb the hill to gain a better view for he has never been this far downstream. A short way up he sits down on a boulder, his clothing steaming in the warming sun. He gazes now toward the east, eyes half closed against the glare – a vast flat plain, no movement, no bird nor beast and certainly no humanity. A darker patch in the middle distance might be scrub and could that be another hill on the far horizon? His guts constrict as he is beset by utter loneliness and fear. He has no knowledge of what lies out there. Joe Watson spoke of Melbourne, Sydney, Bendigo and Ballarat but to Henry Hopeful Down they might be a million miles away. Sighing and getting to his feet he looks once more towards the south and down at the creek. He starts – is that movement? Yes, there it is again, a hundred yards downstream or more. He cannot make it out, but something surely moves. There is no wind; the air is still, already heating up. It must be something living and then so faint he fears he is mistaken, there comes a cry, 'Henreee, Henree.' And now he runs downhill, skidding on the scree, on to the creek bank, runs, jumping over driftwood logs and leaping across the gullies to finally wade across the creek, panting, laughing to where Joe Watson lies half reclined, his back against a solitary ghost gum.

'Joe, oh Joe, I thought you was a goner. I thought you was gone for good.' He stifles a sob, kneels down and holds his partner in his arms.

'I thought you was too mate. Easy now, I think me fuckin' leg is broke.' He points to his outstretched leg. 'I tried to stand an' just fell over. Guess I did it tumblin' down that bloody flood 'fore I washed up here.'

Henry sits back. 'Lord Jesus it's good to see you boy. But what we goin' to do? You can't walk an' all our gear is gone.'

'I dunno, but first things first. I need to drink an' then we need some proper shade or we'll be bloody roastin' come midday.'

Henry goes to the creek, cups water in his hands and brings it back to Joe who laps it up as if he were a dog. 'More,' he sighs and Henry repeats the process several times until Joe nods and leans back against the tree. 'Thanks mate,' he says.

Henry squats beside him. 'I was lookin' for our stuff when I heard you call. I found a rifle an' a sack o' flour already. There must be more.'

'There will be. This creek'll die out in salt pan somewhere south o' here so everything'll be dumped before it gets there. But Henry, mate, we need to make a humpy. I got me knife. Can you climb the tree? If you can break off branches and chuck 'em down, I'll sharpen 'em an' we can stick 'em in the sand and bend 'em over against the trunk. Make room enough for two.'

It takes them most of that morning to make the shelter, Henry shinning up the bleached white trunk and breaking down the skinnier branches. Once in its shade they rest a while, exhausted. 'Have a gander at that leg, will ya Henry. I ain't dared to look – just know it hurts like buggery.'

Henry rolls up his trouser leg. 'The skin ain't broken but there's a mighty lump an' it's all bruised and swelled just here below yer knee.'

'Ahh, Jesus that hurts. Christ, let's see if I can stand. Here, help me up.'

Henry lifts him up. Joe stands tottering on one leg, puts the other down, then with a shriek collapses on the ground. 'It's no use,' he gasps. 'Maybe if we can splint it.' He sits up and backs himself into the humpy. 'But listen, first you go off down the creek, see what more you can find. I'll drag meself about here, get a bit o' firewood for tonight. We can see to me leg later.'

Henry Hopeful Down spends the whole of a sweltering afternoon working up and down the creek and bringing anything useful he can find back to their new camp. As the sun disappears behind the hill he sits with Joe in front of the humpy sorting the results of his labours which includes the shattered remnants of the gold cradle and haunches hacked from one of the two drowned horses.

'Looks good,' Joe says surveying Henry's finds.

'I don't know. How long you reckon we can survive on this lot? More important, how we goin to get back if you can't walk? An' what about yer boots?'

'One thing at a time, mate. When I come to this mornin', found meself washed up here all alone, I thought I was done for. Now look – we're both alive, we got a working rifle, a box of ammo, a keg of powder, sack o' flour, a bucket, most of our tent so we can fix up the humpy better, no shortage of lumber, saddles and harnesses, an axe, a pick an' a shovel, even a bloody pot to cook in and meat to put in it. And mate, don't forget, the bloody gold. We'se still rich. C'mon, lets get a fire goin', I could eat a fuckin horse.' He laughs and claps his mate upon the shoulder.

Henry nods and smiles. It's true, they could be much worse off. And he thinks back to that moment of sheer elation when he put his arm deep into the crevice in the rocks above the old camp and pulled out gold nuggets in two leather bags and the jars of gold dust. But he looks across at Joe's outstretched leg and his heart sinks again at the impossibility of their walking out. Even so he says, 'Shall we try and fix your leg afore the light is gone?'

'Okay. You know what to do?'

'I seen it done more than once. Here roll up yer trouser. Lets have another look. Like I said, the skin ain't broke and your leg ain't swelled no more than it was. But she ain't straight. Reckon I should try an' straighten her?'

Joe nods. 'Yeah, do it.' He grits his teeth and looks away as Henry takes hold of his leg at the ankle and the knee and gives a steady pull. Joe lets out a hiss of pain and says, 'Fuckit,' through his teeth.

'Looks about right. Lie back now' Henry selects a plank from what had once been the base of the gold cradle, sizes it up against Joe's leg, splits it in two with the axe and chops both halves to length. With strips of canvas and rope cut from the tent, he pads and binds the planks, one each side of the leg. 'That too tight?' he asks.

Joe shakes his head. 'Nah, it's okay. But Jeez it hurts. Wish we still had some o' that rum.'

'You rest there a bit. I'll get a fire goin' an' we can cook some 'o that there horse.'

They sit before the fire grilling strips of horsemeat on sharpened sticks.

'Christ, I'm hungry,' Joe says.

'Me too. Smells good don't it.'

'Reckon this bit's done.' Joe pulls his stick from the fire, blows on the meat and pulls it off with his teeth. He puts another strip of meat on the stick and holds it to the flames. 'Listen Henry,' he says between chews, 'I been thinkin'.'

Henry looks at him watching the blood trickling into his beard.

'If tomorrer you cut off all the meat you can from the carcasses, we can dry it in the sun. I reckon we can last a week or two on damper an' horsemeat. Ain't much but it'll keep us alive an' we ain't short of water. I'll make meself a crutch an' at least I'll be able get around a bit. Coupla weeks, maybe sooner, I'll be able to walk proper.'

'All day? And only if I find yer boots?' Henry says, chewing on his own piece of horse.

'Mebbe, mebbe not. But I got another idea. While me leg is mendin' you could make a fire, you know a smudge – like, on top o' the hill. If anyone's out there there'll be bound to see it. Come over here, help us get out.'

'Ain't very likely though, is it. We never saw a livin' soul on the way here.'

'True enough. But, mate, we gotta try.'

Early next morning Henry spends an hour or two chopping branches off the eucalypts along the bank and lugging them to the foot of the hill. He binds them in bundles with strips of bark, puts a one on each shoulder and clambers up the hill. It's hard and sweaty work and he pants in the morning heat. At least he has a sort of hat he's made from eucalyptus leaves threaded on a piece of wire. At the top of the hill he dumps his load and gazes westward. 'What?' he mutters to himself. He shades his eyes. Yes, there is no doubt – there in the middle distance what was once was an arid plain is a vast lake shimmering in the morning sun. This was the way they came so many weeks ago with David as their guide. He remembers the last afternoon when, crossing a low-lying area, they skirted blinding white salt pans holding central pools of pinkish water. And now, as if their troubles were not enough, the way back to Wilpena and their passage home, is barred by yet another obstacle. He sits down on a rock his shoulders slumped. It is impossible. He counts the problems on his fingers: one – he has to find Joe's boots; two – he doubts Joe will be able to walk more than a mile or two each day and it is at least a hundred miles back to the Flinders; three – with no pack animals they cannot carry enough food and water and four – neither he nor Joe are certain of the way across, nor capable of finding the water holes that David located with such ease. All he knows is that home lies westward and now that way is blocked. He sits chin in his hands watching a mottled brownish lizard on a nearby rock that watches him with its black and beady eye. Fat tailed and ten inches long it is. Henry remembers the chicken taste of the goanna David speared. He picks up a stone but quick as a flash the lizard rises on its legs and scuttles under a boulder. With a sigh he gets to his to his feet and builds the fire, dry sticks first in a pyramid then green branches from the gum trees and finally the leafy branches. Not that he really believes there is a single soul out there in that forbidding landscape to see the smoke that billows up in a satisfying cloud of white. He watches it rising high, charred flecks and sparks racing skyward when, with a woosh and crackle, the leaves ignite, blaze up, the smoke swirls brown and black then disappears completely in shimmering heat. He backs away and shakes his head, sits down once again and waits until the fire dies down and all the fuel he so laboriously gathered and carried to this lookout, is finally consumed. He breathes in the now familiar minty smell of eucalyptus, recalls how strange it was to him in those long gone days when he first set foot on Australian soil.

Back at the camp he finds his partner already hobbling about using a crutch made from a forked gum tree branch and padded saddle leather.

'How'd it go,' Joe asks. 'I couldn't see much smoke.'

'No. We shoulda known – these gum tree leaves go up like tinder. Smoke lasted not more'n a minute or two. Waste o' time it were. Ain't nobody out there neither. An' there's worse news.'

'Sit down, mate. Drink some water. You look hot. An' look what I found.' He gestures with his crutch to three potatoes in the pot beside the humpy. 'Found 'em floating in the creek. Meat an' potato stew tonight. An' I made some damper.' Two blackened loaves sit in the ashes of their fire. 'So what's your bad news?'

Henry sheds his hat of leaves, sits in the shaded doorway of the humpy and drinks from the bucket of water just inside. He looks up at Joe. 'There be a bloody great lake where we come across. Don't see how we'll cross it.'

Joe lowers himself down to sit beside him. 'Wouldn't worry about that, mate. Water'll disappear in a few days.' He chews his lip. 'Unless there's more rain o'course. Then it'd be a problem that's for sure. But I been thinkin'. You remember that night at the railway camp?'

'I does.'

'Remember they were talkin' about some mob building a railway eastward to the silver strike at Broken Hill.'

Henry nods although he has no idea where the silver strike might be.

'Well, mate, I reckon that railway can't be more than forty mile south o' here. Look.' He smoothes a patch in the sand between them and with two fingers marks a line. 'This here's the Flinders. We is here, a hundred miles or so due east.' He marks the place with a pebble. 'Now that silver strike is way northeast o' the railway camp, maybe two hundred mile. I heard some bloke talkin' about it in the pub that night in Moonta. That puts it here across the border into New South Wales.' He places another pebble close to Henry's thigh. 'If yer draws a line from the railway camp to Broken Hill it passes not far south of us. Like I say, not more than forty mile.'

'We don't know the railway's built. What if she ain't?'

'Bloke said she was bein' built an' that were two month ago.'

'But what if she ain't?'

'Jesus Henry, you're a fuckin' Jonah aint yer. Here, have some damper.' Joe bends to the remnants of the fire, picks out one of the loaves, breaks it and gives half to Henry.

He tears into it with his teeth and between chews says, 'I'll go downstream and cut more meat an' see what else I can find. Gotta find yer boots anyway or we ain't goin' nowhere.' After another swig from the bucket, Henry puts his hat back on, picks up the rifle which leans against the tree and walks off downstream still munching on the bread. Although he finds nothing new, the search for useful flotsam in and around the creek takes his mind off their plight until he finds some more potatoes floating in a pool. He puts them in his pockets, sits down, takes off his boots and rests his feet in the water. Maybe Joe is right. Perhaps the railway is only a few days walk away but if it's not they'll be walking into the unknown. This is not his country. If only he had stayed at home, had never left; if only he were back now in his miners' cottage in Penpillick. If only. He shakes his head, sighs and puts his boots back on. He must deal with where he is and what he must do with what he has. He had best go and cut more dead horse before the ravens, crows and magpies scoff the lot.

Some distance down beyond the camp he rounds a bend and to his surprise, fifty yards away, he spots a large grey kangaroo bent down drinking at the water's edge. He doesn't hesitate to kneel right where he is and bring the rifle to his shoulder. He is no marksman, never having hunted, but knows just enough to sight the foresight bead into the back sight notch and line them up with the poor beast's head. He squeezes the trigger. The recoil punches into his shoulder, the sound of the shot echoes and re-echoes off the rocky hill and to his complete astonishment the kangaroo drops to the ground. He runs to it, squats beside it and watches as the eyes glaze over and the animal's back legs give a final kick. Taking out his knife he slits the beast wide open, pulls out the steaming guts and flushes out the body cavity with water from the creek. He hoists the animal across his shoulders and using the rifle for support, grunts as he heaves himself to standing. One arm over the kangaroo, his rifle in the other hand, he staggers back up the creek with sweat pouring down his face. Before he reaches camp he sees barefoot Joe Watson hobbling as fast as he can towards him swinging the makeshift crutch as if he were born with it.

'What yer got Henry?' he shouts. 'What yer got? A fuckin' kangaroo, no less. I heard the shot. God's truth, Henry, you're a bloody hero. Here let me carry the rifle. Oh my, we're gonna eat well now an' no mistake.'

Henry grins. 'Maybe our luck has changed. I ain't a gamblin' man, Joe Watson, but mebbe you are right. Our best bet's to go south an' find that railway.'

'Too right it is. But listen, I been thinkin'. When we gets out – an' we will get out, make no mistake, we don't say nothin' about what we found here. Not until we got the mineral lease all signed up an' in our names. Then the rush'll start – this here,' he waves an arm encompassing both up and down the creek and the hill beyond, 'will be crawlin' with miners, prospectors, no-hopers, not to mention Cousin Jacks, mark my words. But we'll have it tied up. It'll be ours.'

'And Mabel's.'

'An' Mabel's, yeah. But don't forget – no talkin' once we're out.'

Eight days later they set off at dusk. They both feel chipper, full of hope, well fed, well watered but both are burdened down with water, food and gold. Joe carries a makeshift back-pack fashioned from rope and canvas, the final ragged remnants of their tent. It contains the food – sun-dried kangaroo and horsemeat, six loaves of damper a single tin mug and the jars of gold dust. Slung from both their waists are their canvas-covered water bottles. Knowing that carrying enough water to last them perhaps a week would be their greatest challenge, Henry spent day after day scouring the creek for their belongings. He found Joe's boots half buried in a mud bank. One water bottle he found wedged beneath a tree root which encouraged him to continue searching until he found a second more than a mile downstream. But just one bottle each was nowhere near enough so they emptied out the powder keg and left it two days in the creek to rid it of the taste of nitre. Now Henry has it hoisted on his shoulder, two thirds filled with water, which is as heavy as he can bear. And his trouser pockets sag with the leather pouches filled with nuggets and a dozen rounds of ammunition.

They stand for some minutes gazing across the creek and watching the sun sink behind the hill in a blaze of red and orange.

'We make it out, that hills's gonna make us richer than you ever dreamed.'

'If we make it out I'll be happy with what I got. You lead on Joe Watson. I'll follow you.'

Joe turns south, shifts his pack on his shoulders, leans into his crutch and begins to walk. Henry some steps behind watches him, wondering how long his friend and partner, his mate as he has come to call him, can really last. At least now he can bear his right foot on the ground but still most of his weight is carried by the crutch. He ponders too how far he himself will manage with the barrel on his shoulder. He's made a pad of sacking filled with grass but his shoulder already aches and he must walk with his neck bent all awry. At least the weight will lessen day by day. In his right hand he carries the rifle.

Night falls fast and soon the sky is lit with stars. Still, even after so many many nights out in the bush, Henry does not cease to marvel at the sight – stars beyond counting strewn like glittering dust across the heavens and the great arch of the Milky Way near overhead, its light so bright it even casts the faintest shadow. He has no trouble now in picking out the Pointers and the Southern Cross, nor in drawing the imagined lines across the starscape to find that point on the horizon which is south and where lies their destination. He is comforted when Joe Watson picks out the very path and the direction that he would choose were he the leader. But even with Joe near crippled, Henry trusts him more than he would trust himself to succeed in what he thinks is near impossible – to reach the railway and human habitation that may or may not exist. Shutting thoughts like these entirely from his mind, he bends to his task and plods on through the night behind the limping figure.

They've stopped for rest a dozen times and still the night drags on. Both are weary to the bone but before the dawn they must find refuge from the sun and heat to come. The barrel is a monumental burden and both Henry's shoulders are blistered raw but he dare not lighten it by emptying out the smallest dash of water. Poor Joe Watson stumbles on, bearing down more heavily upon his crutch, the tip of which all too often sinks into the sand. From time to time a night bird calls and once they heard the scuttle of some small beast about its nocturnal business. Finally just as dawn begins to tint the eastern sky, they slip and stagger across a gully towards a patch of scrub.

'It ain't much but it'll do,' Joe gasps. 'I'm fuckin' whacked an' me water bottle's empty. We'll stop here for the day.'

With a massive sigh, Henry eases the barrel from his shoulder and lays it on its side beneath the spread of a scrubby mulga tree. There is just room enough beneath the tree for both of them to sit, their backs against the trunk, the lowest branches almost touching Henry's head. From his makeshift pack Joe takes out strips of meat, a loaf and the single mug they rescued from the creek. He holds it to the barrel and Henry eases out the wooden bung. They both lick their lips as water gurgles in the mug.

'You first, mate. You carried it.'

Henry would down the water in a single swig but he lets it swirl inside his mouth then swallows, sips again and then again. He sighs and says, 'That's the best water I ever tasted, Joe. Here.' He refills the mug and hands it over.

Joe wipes his lips. 'You ain't wrong. Don't even taste o' powder.' They eat meat and damper and drink another mug of water each then stretch out on the sandy soil. Henry digs a hollow for his hip, lies on his side, head cradled on his arm. The last thing he sees before exhaustion overcomes him is a fly crawling round Joe Watson's open mouth. Their sleep is fitful, each wakes from time to time disturbed by heat and flies and a thirst which neither will assuage alone. By late morning they are both awake, Henry lying on his back, eyes open watching the way the sunlight filters through the grey-green mulga leaves and Joe sitting up, legs outstretched and back against the trunk.

'I gotta mortal fuckin' thirst, Henry. You wanna drink?'

Henry sits up, stretches and rubs his blistered shoulders. 'Yes. I ain't never been so thirsty. But we needs be sparing. One mug each would make three today already.'

'Yeah, I know but there ain't no point in dyin' of thirst out here. Reckon we done twelve mile last night so if I'm right we got three more nights to go. Here.' He holds out the mug.

Henry nods and they broach the water keg again and drink.

'Christ, don't move mate,' Joe whispers. 'Fuckin' snake. Just there, behind you.'

Henry freezes. Joe takes the rifle from its place beside the tree, and in one smooth movement, works the bolt, aims and fires. 'Gotcha,' he says and Henry, ears ringing from the shot, turns to see eight feet of snake laid out behind him.

'King Brown. If he'd a bit yer would've been bloody curtains for us both I reckon.' Joe says. 'I'd never walk and carry water.'

Henry shakes his head, marvelling at the length of it, its glistening copper scales and paler belly.

The second night is harder than the first, Joe stopping with increasing frequency and falling more than once. Two hours they take to cross perhaps two miles of ancient dunes part stabilised with scrubby growth but near impossible for Joe to walk on with his crutch. Once they are back on stony desert ground, he stops, sits down and looks up at his companion. 'Sorry mate, can't do no more,' he gasps, 'I'm whacked. Reckon we done ten mile though.'

'Wait here, I'll look for shade,' Henry says lowering down the water barrel. He walks on and in a hundred yards or so spies the silhouette of trees against the starlit western skyline. He goes back for Joe. 'Not far, mate. Leave your pack. I'll come back for it.'

Joe pulls himself to standing with his crutch but cannot bear to rest his weight upon it. He holds up his arm and even in the darkness Henry can see his shirt is blood-soaked from his armpit to his elbow.

'Here, rest your weight on me.' Henry puts his arm around his friend and together they stagger three-legged to the trees which line a dried up river bed. 'Lie, here. I'll go get the water and your pack.'

Joe, prone upon the ground and almost weeping, looks up. 'Thanks,' he says, lies back and shuts his eyes.

They wake at dawn and once they have drunk and eaten, Henry looks at his companion's leg.

'How is it?'

'All swolled. Don't look good at all. Wait, let me take the splint off and get a proper look.' He unties the strips of canvas and pulls away the splints.

Joe sighs. 'Ah, that feels easier.'

Henry shakes his head. He is amazed his friend can walk at all. The skin beneath his knee is purple and stretched to near bursting. 'We'll leave the splint off until tonight. But what about yer armpit. Take off yer shirt.'

Joe does as he is bid and holds up his arm to reveal a horrid mess of blood, hair and blistered flesh.

'Lord, Joe that must hurt some.' He sniffs. 'Don't smell too good neither. I'll bathe it then you'd better put yer shirt back on – keep they bloody flies off.' He takes a mug of water from the barrel and lets it trickle over Joe Watson's armpit.

'Thanks Henry. Who'd a thought a big bloke like you would make a nurse?'

'I ain't never seen a nurse. Nearest I ever got was Crouch the bal surgeon back in Penpillick. Watched him patch up many a miner – broken legs an' arms. Once saw him sew up a man's guts stove open by flyin' rock. Silly bugger 'ad stood around to watch a blast.' He sighs. 'Best try and sleep now Joe. If you is right we got near twenty mile to go.'

In the middle of the third night when their way south is blocked by a dark shadowed hill, Joe Watson stumbles, falls on his face and finally admits defeat. 'Fuckin' crutch,' he cries, flinging it away. 'Fuckin leg.

Henry mate, I can't do no more. I've had it. Find me some shade and leave me.'

Henry lays down the barrel which is a lighter burden now and sits beside his friend. He pours him a mug of water. 'Drink boy, and we'll rest awhile.'

Joe gulps down the water. 'I'm sorry mate. You'll have to go on without me. Reckon it's only fifteen mile now. On yer own you'd get there sometime tomorrer night.'

Henry pours himself some water, drinks and sits silent. If the railway is really there then Joe is right, he could walk it easily in twelve hours, four more tonight, rest up as usual, then the final stretch tomorrow evening. He could leave the barrel and take both water bottles which should be just enough to see him through. But he hears again old Tom Mole's voice, his tale of being lost, deranged and without water and knows he cannot face the outback all alone; it is Joe Watson's self-belief that has kept him going all along. Besides, if he left him now, here, how would he find him again? All he knows is south by the stars and south again. Landmarks are few and far between and one rocky hill looks much like another. 'I won't leave you, Joe.'

'You gotta. I can't go on. I told yer.'

'I'll carry you.'

'You can't.'

'O' course I can. You're a little feller. Ain't much heavier than that barrel I been carryin' and you'll be sight easier on my shoulders.'

'What'll we do for water?'

'We drink all we can afore we set off and hope a bottle each'll see us there. An' maybe we'll find a water hole.'

'That ain't likely.'

'Just as likely as I makin' it on me own an' comin back to find yer.'

'You sure?'

'I'm sure. We'll leave the rifle. Just you, me, the water and the gold.'

They sit for a while drinking mug after mug of water until both feel bloated. They fill both water bottles to overflowing and finally Henry gets to his feet. 'Come on, up ye get.' He holds out a hand. Joe puts the

195

pack on and pulls himself to standing, wobbling on his good leg. Henry bends to let him scramble up onto his back and puts his arms under Joe's thighs. Leaning forward, he sets off up the hill. 'Light as a feather,' he grunts. Once over the hill he walks steadily until an hour after dawn when they rest up again in the shade another patch of mallee scrub.

Late that afternoon Henry leaves the shade and stares toward the south. Flat it is, flat as flat can be – a vast plain of red sandy soil and knee-high, grey-green saltbush. Easy walking, he thinks. Nothing breaks the skyline, nothing at all. But out there somewhere is a railway – in that he must believe. He wakes his friend, they both sip from their bottles and once again Joe climbs upon his back. He walks now, his stride an easy rhythm, the weight familiar, almost comfortable, his shirt already soaked with sweat. He looks away toward the west where sparse clouds are lit with blazing pinks and reds and the saltbush is tinged with a reddish glow. There is the faintest breeze whispering across the darkening landscape, the only other sounds the soft crunch of his boot steps and the scrape of brush against his trousers. Settling to the task ahead, he shifts the burden on his back – twelve hours walking, maybe less, one last long night.

Four hours and he is thirsty, thirsty as he has never been before. His mouth is dry, his lips gummed and split, his tongue swollen and he has only half a bottle of water. He swallows, dismisses drinking from his mind and walks on towards the unmarked point on the horizon that he knows is south.

'All right, mate?' The voice comes softly in his ear.

'I'll stop. I have to rest.' He feels Joe shift, he breaks his stride and stops, kneeling down until the weight is lifted. 'Ah.' Lying back he stares straight up at the cloudless, starlit dome, his sense of wonder still there despite his desperate thirst. Sitting up he uncorks the bottle, trickles water on his desiccated tongue and wets his lips. Lord, he will drink it all, right now but no, he cannot. He must go on but knows he's almost spent. His thighs and calves are burning. Another mile, another five? He does not know and why would there be water at the railway track – a thought he has not dared to face but now fills his mind with horror.

'Have mine. You need it.'

He turns to the little man beside him, takes the offered water, drinks one deep draught and hands it back.

'I'll keep it for you. I won't drink. Not long now Henry Hopeful Down, not long.'

He tries to smile but the movement pains his lips. Tears well behind his eyelids and he whispers, 'I'm almost done, Joe. Not sure I can go on.'

Joe stares out into the darkness. 'We got more to live for you an' me than we ever had before. Let's give it one more go. I'll hop if you can't carry me.'

'No you won't. Get on.'

Head bent, mouth open, gasping, one foot before the other and all the water gone, he's walked and walked and still no sign of dawn. From time to time he staggers and almost drops the burden clinging to his back. His way is no longer straight but with subtle movements of his hands Joe Watson guides him ever southward muttering quiet encouragement in his ear. Utterly exhausted, racked with desperate thirst, he thinks he hears the sound of running water, sees before him a crystal stream and hears the voice of Thomas Pascoe calling, echoing down the passages of some dark mine. 'Stop, Henry stop. Look.'

He stops and shakes his head. The visions disappear and it is Joe Watson speaking.

'Look, mate, look there.'

Straightening his back, he follows the pointing finger. There in the distance somewhat to the west but not too far away a red light flickers, grows and fades then leaps up once again.

'That's a campfire, Henry. You done it, boy, you done it. Now don't forget, no talkin'. If they ask we'se just prospectors who didn't find nuthin'. Don't mention gold.'

XXIV

FAMILY

 'IT'S BETTER GOING UP, CAPUN. IT'S SAFER TOO. MEN don't fall off the way they did off ladders.'

'It'd better be, Thomas, considering the cost.'

Thomas sighs inwardly. His stepfather does not miss a chance to complain about the man engine and Wheal Emma's precarious financial state. Of course he has good reason. The combination of Kit Robin's profligacy, the falling copper price and the quality of ore they're mining has brought Cornish Consols close to bankruptcy. Although the situation is not of his making, it is his duty now as Captain to turn the mine back into profit, a duty much easier said than done. At least he and his stepfather are once more in control. They stand together at the bottom of the shaft as miner after miner steps off the little wooden platform on to the 330 fathom level while others, exhausted from a night of work, step on to disappear in one swift upward motion. Beside them the great reciprocating rods plunge up and down, driving both the man engine and the pump which sucks and heaves the water from the sump beneath them.

'We cut the North Lode again, Captain. Perhaps you should go and have a look.'

They both turn to see Kit Robin standing there in the candlelight, dressed as always in his fancy leather boots, serge trousers and fustian jacket. He look less like a man who has spent the night clambering around a mine and more like the Duke's gamekeeper ready for a pheasant shoot although his dandy's clothes are completely soaked with sweat. He has accepted his demotion back to Night Captain, if not exactly with good grace, at least without complaint. And so he should, thinks Thomas. He's lucky not to be locked up in Bodmin along with Mary Scoble awaiting the next assize. 'That's good news Capun Kit,' he says, 'We'll go see it directly. Is she rich or poor?'

'Rich, I'd say Captain. Rich and very wide. I'm sure you will be pleased. Now by your leave Captains, I must up to the counthouse. Good morning to you both.' He steps on a rising platform.

'Don't know why we kept him on, the bugger,' Mathew Clymo grumbles as they set off down the drive. 'Did he not try to poison me?'

'I don't believe he did. His part was unwitting. He was misled.'

'Misled by his nether parts, I'd say. Can't never trust a man like that.'

'If we'd dismissed him most likely he'd be out there causing trouble and blackening our name.'

'Hm, I suppose you're right.

They carry on in silence, Thomas thinking how good it is to have Captain Mathew Clymo back in charge. Even peevish as he is, he part lifts the burden from his shoulders. Three hundred yards they walk along the tramway, heads bent low until the back lifts up and away and they are in a great hollow chamber the far end of which is beyond the reach of their feeble candles.

'What did we take out here, Thomas?' Mathew asks. He unknots his neckerchief and mops the sweat that trickles down his face.

'Mostly mundic, Captain.'

They walk on, clambering over rubble waste not deemed rich enough to tram and hoist to surface. At the far end of the stope the roof drops down to nearly meet the floor and they must crawl on hands and knees between the baulks of timber holding up the back. But then it opens up again, this time on a slant, the stope sloping upwards into darkness. Finally they are at the face. They both light second candles and hold them high. They look in silence at the face then at each other. Thomas shakes his head. 'This is the North Lode. He's right in that, no question but it's not rich. This is mostly mundic mixed with pyrite and very poor in copper.'

'Useless bugger. I told you so. But we'll mine it anyway.'

'I suppose we must if we're to get the copper. Wheal Emma is a damned arsenic mine these days.

'And what of that? Arsenic's a better price than copper.'

'Arsenic is poison Capun, as you know better than most. We lost two men last month – poisoned at the works they were.'

'When's that woman up for trial?'

'The hearing's set for next month's Assize. But don't change the subject, Capun. The arsenic workers are falling sick and dying.'

'That's because they don't protect themselves the way they should.'

'You almost died yourself from less than a teaspoon every now and then. How can they be protected when they shovel it in barrows and fill up fifty barrels every day. It's a miracle we don't kill more. If we can't find copper or a tin lode, we should shut this mine for good and all.'

'Listen, boy, I'll not have my mine closed just because you're too lily-livered to mine a bit of mundic.'

'I'm not a boy Capun, if you please, nor am I lily-livered. You called me back to help you. I've done my best. I've searched and searched for weeks, on every level, used all the knowledge I once had and all I learned from my dear father. There is no more copper at Wheal Emma. It's gone, it's finished and all that's left is mundic. I'll not mine it any more.' They are shouting at each other now, their voices echoing through the dark and empty spaces.

'Then take yourself back to damned Australia and leave this mine to me.' Mathew Clymo shakes his fist dropping molten wax onto his hand. 'Damn and blast,' he shouts.

'Capuns?'

'Good Christ Jakeh James, don't creep up on me like that you villain. Where's your boys?'

'They'm right behind. You wants us to mine this here? Take it up to grass?' Like them, the stick-thin miner is pouring sweat but it seems not to bother him at all.

Mathew Clymo looks at his stepson who has stepped away and is gazing down the stope watching the glimmer of approaching candles. 'Yes, get to it Jakeh.' Mathew sniffs. 'God man, smells like you ate a ferret.'

'Sorry Capun, I were out with the Irish last night a-celebratin'. We had more than a bit o' drink – Caleb Chapman's cider.'

'Celebrating what?

'Why Capun', Michael Mc Carthy's weddin' to your daughter. Tomorrow ain't it?'

Mathew Clymo grunts. 'It is indeed. I'd not forgot, nor am I likely to . . . ever. Hah, here's the damned boy himself.'

'Mornin' Capuns.' Michael McCarthy stands before them felt hat in hand.

'You ready for tomorrow, Michael?' Thomas asks.

'I am sir, that I am. And thank you sir. And good morning to you Capun Clymo. It's good to see you well again, sir.'

'Is it now?' He turns to Thomas. 'Come. Let's get back to grass. We've much to do today,' he says and walks off through the stope.

'Ten tomorrow morning at the chapel, Michael. Don't be late,' Thomas says as he turns to follow.

'I won't, sir. You can be sure of that,' the boy calls after him.

Catching up with Mathew, Thomas falls in step behind him. He notices how his walk is slower now, not yet the tottering of old age but not the commanding stride of old. And the stoop they must adopt in the confines of the tunnel does not leave him when they reach the shaft. His stepfather stays hunched as he steps onto the man engine. As they rise near effortlessly towards the surface, he doubts that Captain Mathew Clymo could still climb the two thousand feet of ladders to the surface. But it is not his physical condition that worries him. It is not surprising, that although he has recovered from the poison, he is not the man he was. He has no patience, shouts at his family, takes umbrage at imagined slights, forgets what he has said and once or twice has not known where he is. A worried Grace confided in him, 'He may be well enough in body, Thomas, but I fear that in his mind he is not well at all.' Nonetheless, Thomas knows that someday soon, he must face his stepfather and make him understand that Wheal Emma has no future. And if that is the case, then his future, indeed that of his family, lies not here but back in South Australia. They must join the flood of Cornish miners who take families and their skills to seek new lives in far-off lands. At least he has a fortune ready made and awaiting his return to Wallaroo. His telegram received a prompt reply – *All well. Sold 1000 head while prices high. Lambing in full swing. H.H. Downe jailed drunk and disorderly. Now disappeared from district. When will you return?*

'This is some comfort,' Maisie said when he read it out to her, 'Although 'tis sad to hear that Henry's been in prison.'

'You believe him then?'

'I do. Surely he would not tell so bald a lie?'

'I think you're right. Besides a simple telegram to the magistrate will tell us all.'

'And shall we return?'

'I do not know, my love, I do not know.'

But now he does. They will go soon, whether the mine is closed or not. There is little more he can do here and with his sister married, his duty will be done. He steps off one platform, onto the next and looks upwards where daylight filters down the shaft – almost back to grass completely without effort.

'You had no right to tell that heathen boy he could marry Emily.'

Thomas shakes his head and takes another bite of pasty. 'You were at death's door and she's my sister. I had every right.' They face each other across the counthouse table taking croust.

'He's Irish, a damned Catholic and tomorrow I must entertain a popish family in my house.'

'You're happy to have the Irish mining for you at rock bottom rates. Besides if it were not for Michael's father you'd be dead. You know it was he who told me the cook was Mary Scoble.'

'Ah, don't throw that at me again,' Mathew shouts and bangs the table scattering pasty crumbs across the board.

Thomas does not answer but looks across at William George the purser who watches them from a high stool set beside the wall. His two clerks sat beside him are bent over ledgers the only sound now the scratching of their quills. With eyebrows raised Thomas nods towards the door.

'Come boys,' the purser says and all three leave.

'Captain . . . Father,' Thomas says once they are alone, 'let us not argue over what is done. Emily is happy, as is my mother and we shall

202

not have a bastard in the family. The fact that Michael is a Catholic cannot be changed. We should be glad that he and his father have agreed to a marriage in the Chapel.

'Hah, what about the child? Will it grow up a Catholic?'

'We do not know and frankly I do not care. Besides, neither you nor I are chapel goers.'

Mathew is silent. He finishes his pasty brushing crumbs from off his waistcoat, staring at his stepson.

'Let us put our differences aside for now. Tomorrow is a day of celebration. Shall we not shake hands?' Thomas leans across the table, hand outstretched.

Mathew nods and takes his hand and to his surprise and shock Thomas sees tears in his stepfather's eyes.

Grace looks around the dining room and heaves a sigh. How wonderful it looks. Broad white ribbons are looped along the picture rail with large pink bows like butterflies at all four corners. Two wedding cakes are on the sideboard, one for the guests and one for the couple.

The table is full laden with a breakfast for the guests who are gathering outside and waiting for the bride and groom. Mathew sits in an armchair in the corner studying his polished boots. She cried at the chapel service when Emily and her lover made their vows and handsome Michael placed a ring upon her daughter's finger. Her brother James, down from London just for the night, gave her away. Her husband did not even smile. Outside the chapel bal maidens in their finery and miners in their Sunday best lined a flower strewn path to the horse and carriage that now draws up at Penpillick House. She goes to the front door to watch the couple step down from the carriage. She smiles to see her Emily looking so grown up in her pale pink gown and matching cape and holding a bouquet of roses. The guests file in behind the couple and the house is filled chatter and laughter, Irish accents mingling with voices she has known all her life. In a corner of the dining room stands big Col McCarthy wearing a fine frock coat, high collar and blue bow tie. A group of miners seem to hang on his every word. How strange it is to have the Irish in the Clymo family.

'You must be happy, Grace.' Jenny Tuttle at her side is smiling as she too gazes around the room.

'I am Jenny. And thank you so much for helping me. But I'd be happier still if Mathew were his old self again. Just look at him.'

'He's a misery all right but least you still got 'im. That mundic's evil stuff. Took my Lewis from me.'

'You're right. I am so sorry and so pleased that you are my friend again.' She lays her hand on Jenny's arm.

'Well my love, what else could I do but be your cook now that wicked Mary Scoble's gone. I could scarce believe it when I heard. But enough o' that. Ain't our grandchildren a sight to see an' how they've grown since they been back.' Maisie stands at the table helping her sons and daughter to sweetmeats from the spread. 'You think they'll stay now, Grace – stay with us once and for all?'

'I don't know. I dearly hope so. Don't think I could bear to see them go so far away again. 'Twould break my heart.'

'Mine too. I'd have no one.'

'We'd have each other . . .an' I'd have him.' She nods towards her husband still seated grim-faced in his chair drinking claret. 'But Jenny, let's count our blessings while we can.'

That night she lies beside her husband wide awake, seeing again the bridal couple riding high and handsome in the Brougham off to their honeymoon. It would be but a short few days for Mathew gave them little money and neither Col McCarthy nor his son had much to spare. They would be back and settle down in a miners' cottage in the village. Her daughter, educated as she is, is now a miner's wife, just as she once was. Well, even if Thomas and his family leave her once again and return to Australia as she is dreading, she will have Emily's family for comfort and another grandchild on the way. She is content.

'Mathew, you are awake?' She knows just from his breathing that he is not sleeping.

'I am.'

She turns to him and lays her arm across his chest. 'Thank you for my daughter's wedding. I know it did not make you happy.'

He sighs, 'No, it did not. But what's done is done, my lover.'

She rests her head upon his chest, listening to the steady rhythm of his heart. How near she came to losing him and how good it is to have him still by her side. She lost one husband to the mine and would have lost a second were it not for Thomas. 'Mathew?'

'Yes my love?'

'Will Thomas stay?'

'I do not know.'

'Do you still need him now that you are well?'

'Perhaps. Now go to sleep. I must be up early.'

Grace Clymo smiles, lifts her head and kisses him. 'Good night my love.'

'Good night.'

She sits bolt upright in the bed. A grey light filters through the lace curtain. It must be dawn. There is a banging at the front door and someone shouts beneath the window.

'Capun, Capun, wake up, wake up.'

Another voice takes up the cry, 'Capun Clymo, Capun Pascoe. Come, come quick. You are needed at the mine. Help, help.'

She shakes Mathew's shoulder. 'Wake up husband, wake up.'

He stirs, rolls over. 'What is it, Grace? What is it now?'

'I don't know. There's men outside. They're calling for you.' She hears footsteps in the passage and Thomas opens the bedroom door.

'Capun, get your boots on. There's been an accident. We're needed at the mine.'

Grace goes to the window, throws it open and calls down to the two men below. 'They are coming now. What has happened?'

'The man engine, Missus, the man engine. 'Tis gone, all broke, 'tis fallen down the shaft an' taken many miners with it.'

She turns back to the bed where Mathew is pulling on his clothes. 'They say the man engine broke and is fallen down the shaft.'

'Damn, damn, I knew it. If I'd not been sick. Damn that Dandy Pants.' He rushes from the bedroom and clatters down the stairs behind his stepson.

Grace stays at the window watching as the men folk run down the road towards the mine. She knows that she should follow them but the thought of standing at the shaft brings back the images of her first husband's shattered body when they brought it up to grass so many years ago. She turns away from the window sheds her nightgown and begins to dress.

'Stand back, stand back. Get back there.' Mathew shouts, holding back the press of men and crying women gathered at the Wheal Emma shaft, watching as one by one the injured and the dead are brought to surface. 'Give us room, now.' He peers down the shaft to see the bearded, sweating face of Caleb Chapman looking up at him, the limp and broken body of a miner in his arms. 'He's live this 'un Capun,' Caleb gasps.

'How many more Caleb?'

'Lord knows Capun. This'un's from 130 fathom.' He pauses, panting hard as willing hands lift the injured man out on to the ground. 'There's many more down there. We can't get to the bottom till the ladders all be mended. That Col McCarthy's got a crew down there workin' like demons.'

'Good. And Thomas?'

'Up an' down an' everywhere Capun. He's got a man on every sollar an' another on the ladder in between. We'se passin' 'em up from man to man. 'Scuse us, Capun, I best get back down. Here comes another.'

'Take care Caleb,' Mathew shouts as Caleb disappears from view. He steps away from the shaft just as a weeping miner's wife clutches at his coat. 'Capun, Capun, my Davy's down there. He ain't come up. Oh Lord Capun, please tell me he ain't dead.'

'I don't know Martha. I'm sorry, I cannot tell you. But we're working as fast as we can to bring them all to grass.'

The woman bursts into tears and covers her face. 'Oh my poor Davy, my poor Davy.'

Mathew walks along the line of bodies laid out on the ground.

Thirty-two so far and they're not yet halfway down. And many, many injured – mangled and broken limbs, bleeding heads and bodies pierced with shards of timber. The noise is dreadful – groans from injured men, one miner with a massive splinter through his guts, held down and shrieking as Dr Crouch and his assistant gently draw it out. Blood gushes from the wound pooling in the dirt beneath him. The doctor swabs the wound and wraps a dressing round it and looks at Mathew. 'Worst I've seen since Crimea,' he says.

'Bloody man engine.' He looks up at the great iron beam, motionless and protruding skyward from the engine house, an empty hole where the bearing for the top pump rod should be. Here lies the cause of the disaster, the cause of all these injuries and the cause of men's lives lost. The bearing, ill-fitting, badly fixed, who knows, has simply snapped letting fly the pump rod, all quarter ton of it, to plunge straight down the shaft smashing men and timberwork to smithereens. They say it could be worse for only those miners who had left early from their shift were on the engine at the time. If it had been full, all hundred platforms taken on the upward stroke, God knows – he can only shake his head. And of course the pump is stopped – his mine is flooding. It will take weeks, nay months to repair the damage in the shaft, replace the many broken rods and join them one to the other. And all the while the water will be rising, day by day, drowning level after level. He wished he were down there himself so he might know first hand what's to be done. But Thomas went in first, secured with a rope around his waist as he clambered down the broken timber work. Ten minutes later he returned, calling for timber men and volunteers. He looked at Mathew, shook his head and said, 'Capun, it's bad down there. Leave it to me. We nearly lost you once. My mother would not forgive me. Besides you're needed here – they look to you for hope and comfort.' He knows that this was right, that he can't yet manage ladders, let alone climb about in the wreckage of the shaft So he keeps control of this crowd of desperate miners' wives, their children and their friends and gives comfort where he can. He's organised a buggy to take the badly wounded to their cottages and made sure the dead are laid out decently and covered. What more can he do?

A whisper passes through the crowd. 'It's Capun Kit. 'Tis Dandy Pants.'

He pushes his way back through them to the shaft and indeed it is. He looks uninjured, although his face is deathly white and his eyes stare blindly at the sky. Then as they lay him down Mathew sees the back of his head is all stove in. Perhaps he heard the timbers falling, crouched down, terrified maybe, but all to no avail. Mathew looks up once again at the naked useless engine beam. 'Kit Robin's Engine,' he mutters to himself.

XXV

ADELAIDE

'LET'S HAVE A TOAST, HENRY. TO THE FISH HILL MINE. But keep yer voice down.' Joe Watson looks around the bar of the Colonel Light Hotel and leans across the table, glass raised.

Henry grins lifts his brimming glass of beer and clinks it against his partner's. 'To the Fish Hill Mine,' he says.

Both down their beers in a single draught.

'That, Henry, was without a doubt, the best beer I ever tasted.' Joe wipes his lips. 'Another?'

'Yes, and another after that.' It seems to Henry he will never satisfy his thirst, though many days have passed since they staggered into Mingary railway camp. It is something he never will forget – his disbelief that he had done it, that he had reached the railway which in those last days, had seemed no more real than the mirages that shimmered through those fevered outback afternoons. Guided by the faint flicker of the campfire, he put one foot before the other, often stumbling, urged on by the whispering at his ear from the burden on his back. Finally he stood there before the fire, swaying, felt Joe slip down to the ground, heard the oaths and the astonishment of men gathered for their pre-dawn breakfast. The smell of wood smoke, tea boiling in the billy and eggs frying in a pan came to him like little miracles, the sight of those weather-beaten faces in the firelight, extraordinary .

'Is this . . .is this the railway?' he croaked, staggered one last time and toppled to the ground. He lay there staring at the stars.

'Here sit up, mate. You need to drink.' Someone put an arm about his shoulders and held a mug of hot sweet tea to his cracked and blistered lips.

'He carried him,' they said, 'He carried him.'

'How far?'

'Bloody miles. Four days he's carried me. This here's Henry Hopeful Down – a Cousin Jack and the best mate a man could have.'

'Strewth – four days yer say, on 'is bloody back. Some sorta hero eh?'

'From where? Where d'you boys come from then?'

Someone gently bathed his face with a wetted cloth and he heard Joe say 'Way northwest of here. We was fossickin' around east o' Teetulpa when we was flooded out. Lost all our gear, horses an' all.'

'Did yer strike it rich?'

'Nah. Bit o' gold dust in the creek. Nothin' more.'

He lay back then and slept.

They stayed three days in Mingary Camp, well looked after by the railway men. A doctor tended to them both, pronounced Henry's feat remarkable and Joe Watson's leg as on the mend. The makeshift backpack never left Joe Watson's side except at night when he used it as a pillow. The railwaymen looked at him and at the pack, noting its weighty swing and nodded to each other, muttering. Two of them packed up their gear and headed off north-westward. Once well enough, Joe and Henry rode a railcar west to Peterborough then took the train due south to Adelaide.

'That grin'll split yer face,' Joe Watson said but Henry just smiled the more. Steam engines of course were commonplace on mines but an engine pulling passengers across the plains at speeds he'd not imagined, filled him with boyish joy. The seats of buttoned leather, the clack of wheels on rail, the acrid smell of coal smoke, even the smuts on his sunburned face were a source of wonder and amusement. Much of the five hour trip he spent head out of the window gazing at the countryside and thinking to himself how much easier it was than walking. And every turn of the iron wheels, every push of the piston rods, brought him closer to Mabel, closer to the woman he now knew that he loved. At the thought of seeing her and more, of telling her that his luck had turned, that they had struck it rich, that she was richer still, made him want to laugh out loud. But he sat back in his seat and looked across at Joe with the backpack on his knees and simply grinned.

Once in Adelaide their first stop was the bank next to the station where they sold a small portion of their gold dust for one hundred pounds.

The teller took them through a padlocked inside gate to a well-lit back room where he poured the gold onto a balance scale and noted down the weight. 'Where's it from?' he asked.

'Somewhere north of here,' Joe said and the teller laughed. He took them back to the cashier's desk where their money was counted out in one pound sovereign coins, placed in two canvas money bags and passed to them through the grill.

At a nearby draper's store they bought shirts, trousers, jackets, new boots and a Gladstone bag. They changed in a curtained cubicle and put all the gold and most of their money in the bag with their filthy bush clothes on the top. 'You'd best carry it, Henry,' Joe said. 'Pretend it ain't so heavy.'

Next they visited the Lands Office in King William Street and bought a mineral lease for five sections of land of eighty acres each, forty miles north of Mingary.

Ed Scrivener the clerk said, 'You'll need to get a survey done, Joe, to make sure your title's good. I'll keep it quiet for a week or two to give you time.'

'Could you make it a month, Ed?' Joe said, 'Give me leg time to heal? We'd make it worth your while.'

The clerk looked at the office door, down at the maps spread on the table and scratched his head. 'A month it is then Joe, but no more. All right?'

Joe slapped a sovereign on the table. 'This do it?'

'Indeed it will,' Ed Scrivener said, pocketed the coin and shook their hands.

Outside in the sunshine on busy King William Street, Joe Watson did a little, one-legged jig to the amusement of passers-by. 'It's ours, Henry, the Fish Hill Mine is bloody ours,' he said.

'And Mabel's. Only half is ours. And don't forget old Mr Mole up in Wilpena. We agreed a tenth for him.'

'You're right of course. I ain't forgot. I'll go and see old Moley when I go up with the survey team. He'll be happy. And we'd best find Mabel now before the news gets out. That bank clerk will be tellin' all the world, make no mistake.'

'She said to find her at the Colonel Light Hotel here in Adelaide. You know where that is?'

Joe laughed. 'Everybody knows the Colonel Light – just down the road from here. Shall we go right now and see her. If she ain't there we can have drink or two and I could do with grub.'

So here they are at midday waiting for Mabel and already on their second beers. The Colonel Light Hotel is bustling even at this early hour. The tables all are taken and a line of drinkers is seated at the bar. The place smells of last night's booze and stale tobacco smoke, the bare wood floor has not been swept and several drunks lie fast asleep outside the door. The shouts and cheers of a game of two-up erupt from the next door taproom as a blowsy waitress puts two bowls of mutton broth before them. 'Mutton stew to follow?' she asks.

They both nod already spooning up the soup which is manna to them after months of eating little but dried kangaroo and damper.

'Barman says you're looking for Mabel.'

'Yes, Miss,' Henry says. 'She said we'd find her here.'

'Not till tonight. What would blokes like you want with her ladyship?'

'That's our business, I reckon?'

'You bushmen then?'

'Miners.' Joe says. 'You got rooms?'

'Yes mister. Fifteen bob a night at the back, pound a night at the front.'

'We'll take a front room, the best you got.'

'The best eh? You strike it rich?'

'Nah. Not really. Just done alright. We'll take the room for a week.'

'Where's yer swag?'

Joe looks up at her. 'You gotta lot of questions.'

She shrugs. 'The room'll be a fiver for the week – no extras. Pay at the bar. I'll get yer dinner.' She winks and walks away, hips swaying.'

Joe leans across the table. 'We're gonna get a lot of that. We gotta be careful. I shouldn'a asked for the best room. You got your feet on top o' that bag?'

212

'I 'ave. Couldn't we 'ave left the gold safe in the bank?'

'We could but I didn't want the teller to know how much we got. News would be round the town in no time.'

The waitress returns with two plates piled high and steaming with mutton and potatoes. 'We sent a boy to tell her ladyship she's got important gents to see her.'

'We ain't important, Joe says, 'Just hungry.'

'But that bag under big boy's feet's important, ain't it?'

Joe looks up at her and wipes his mouth. 'Listen, Miss, we just come in for dinner and a room. Who we are an' what we got is our business.'

'Mister, I seen too many miners come in here, throwin' money about – new clothes like you, stay a day or two and leave with not much more than their underwear. There's some bad folk about an' most of 'em'll be in here tonight. So watch yer step seeing as how you're friends of her ladyship. More beer?'

They nod in unison and she goes off to the bar.

'You think Mabel owns this place?' Henry asks.

'Who knows? Maybe. She weren't short of dough last time we saw her.'

'Wonder why she calls her "her ladyship"?'

Joe just shakes his head and returns to his mutton stew. But Henry doesn't have long to wait for an answer. He looks up from his meal as a sudden silence falls upon the bar. There in the open doorway stands Mabel, dressed not as he has seen her before in the frills and flounces of a working girl but in a high-collared grey silk dress and matching gown that even Henry Hopeful Down, a simple Cousin Jack, knows is the height of fashion. A small black-feathered hat is drawn low down on her brow and she carries an opened parasol.

'Look,' Henry whispers, nudging Joe beneath the table.

Joe turns towards the door and mutters, 'Blimey, Mabel.'

She sees them, smiles and folds her parasol, walks across and stands beside their table looking down. 'My oh my, just look at you two all in yer Sunday best. Big Henry from Wallaroo and Little Joe. Might a lady have a seat?'

'Of course, Mabel,' Henry gets to his feet, half stumbling as he pulls out a chair.

Holding up the ribboned bustle of her dress she perches on the seat and whispers, 'Well boys, are we rich or have you spent it all already?'

'No, Mabel, no we ain't. Mabel you look . . . beautiful.'

'Jeez, Henry,' Joe mutters.

'What's the matter Joe? Can't Henry pay me a compliment? But Henry, you mean you ain't spent it or we ain't rich?'

Henry feels her hand warm upon his knee. 'No. . . no we aint't spent it. It's under the table.'

'Ah, what's under the table?' she says running her hand up Henry's thigh.

Henry stifles a groan. 'Gold,' he whispers, 'gold.'

'You got some for me, Henry?'

'Christ, Mabel, we need to talk business, somewhere private. We gotta a tale to tell yer.' Joe looks around the barroom. Several drinkers have turned on their stools and watch them. 'Is this your place Mabel?'

'No, I just run the back rooms for Mr Boddington. He owns this and half the street. Finish up, boys. Let's go to my place. It's just a step away.'

'You're limping, Joe. What happened?' Mabel asks as they go towards the door.

'Broke me leg in a flood.'

'A flood? What flood?'

'It's a long story. Tell you when we get down to business.'

Heads turn as they walk south down Currie Street and up the steps of a double storey brick-built house. A maid opens the door and bobs a curtsey. 'If anybody calls I'm busy and not to be disturbed,' Mabel says. They walk down the shadowed hall, boots tapping on the chequered tiles and turn into a richly furnished parlour lit by a shaft of sunlight. Henry hesitates, breathing in the smell of perfume, cigars and something else he cannot quite define.

'You done all right,' Joe says, looking from the plush armchairs to the mahogany dresser, the polished table and the richly patterned carpet.

'There's plenty of men with money in Adelaide these days and plenty of girls to help them spend it,' Mabel says, shutting the parlour door. 'Talking of which that Millington cove was in town a couple of weeks ago throwing his money around again.'

'Lord, I'd forgotten all about 'im. Was she with 'im?'Henry asks.

'Believe she was.'

'Mebbe they've sold the rest of Mr Pascoe's sheep. Reckon I should go back to Wallaroo.'

'First things first, Henry. Sit down, tell me all. You found copper? In the bag is it?'

Joe laughs. 'Didn't find no copper. Found something better.' Joe says. 'Open it up, Henry.'

Henry hoists the Gladstone bag upon the table and takes out their dirty clothes and lays them aside. One by one he lifts out three screw-topped jars and two heavy leather pouches. Taking a jar in both hands he holds it up to the light, and they watch the gold dust glittering as he it turns it this way and that.

'Oh my goodness. That's gold.'

'Pretty ain't it,' Joe says. 'Now the nuggets, Henry.

Loosening the leather lace, Henry upends a pouch to leave a glowing pyramid in the middle of the table. He sighs and whispers, 'Nuggets, Mabel, gold nuggets. Did you ever see the like?' The gold glows in the shaft of sunlight filtering through lace curtains.

'Beautiful, Henry just beautiful.' She takes up a handful and lets it trickle through her fingers like tiny golden pearls. 'Is there more and is it ours?'

'Yes, there's more, much more and it's all ours,' Joe says.

'All ours but for a tenth, which belongs to Mr Mole,' Henry adds.

'And who is Mr Mole?'

'Well, listen and we'll tell yer.'

As always, Joe Watson does all the talking, slouching in an armchair his short legs in new leather boots stretched out before him. From time to time, Henry nods or adds a word or two but mostly he stays silent, his gaze moving from Mabel's face to Joe's and now and then back to the gold.

'So there it was, the bloody mother lode on top of the bloody hill,

215

six foot wide or more and we don't know how long, but at least two hundred yards.' He coughs and pauses. 'Jeez, Mabel, talkin's thirsty work. You gotta beer or two?'

Mabel smiles. 'You deserve better than beer, Joe. Would real scotch whisky do?' She rises from her couch and takes a bottle and three crystal glasses from a cupboard in the dresser. 'Bowmore,' she says, 'Gift from a grateful customer. I've been keeping it for a special occasion. I think this is it, don't you?' They nod and watch the golden liquid purling from the bottle as Mabel pours three generous tots.

'Here.' She hands them each a glass. 'That's quite a story, boys.'

'Oh it ain't done yet. The best bit, nah, maybe the worst bit, is still to come.' He swirls his whisky, takes a deep, enthusiastic sniff and looks at Henry. 'Come on Henry, you tell the rest.'

'Well, the rain come yer see an' all our got gear washed away an' I thought . . . I thought Joe here was drownded.' He stops and sips from his glass. 'Better than old Moley's grog this is.'

'C'mon Henry, get on with it. Tell Mabel what yer did.'

'Yes, come on Henry, tell me all.'

Henry looks down at his boots. 'Well like I said, I thought Joe was a goner. Thought I was all on me own out there. But I weren't cos' Joe'd just broke 'is leg . . . an' I. . . .' His voice dies down to a mutter.'

'Jeez Henry,' Joe sighs, 'Let me tell it.'

As Joe Watson finally falls silent Mabel shakes her head in wonder and turns to Henry. 'So for three nights you carried this larrikin on your back?'

'Two nights it were Mabel, not three. An' he's but a little feller.'

'Henry you're a hero.' She goes over and sits on the arm of his chair and ruffles his hair.

He shrugs. 'No I ain't. You got any more o' that whisky?'

'Of course, Henry.' She pours them all another shot and goes back to the couch. 'Right, so if I understand correctly, we own the Fish Hill Mine – that's what you call it?'

Both men nod. 'Old Moley named it Fish Hill after the bloody great nugget he showed us,' Joe says.

'And you've got a mineral lease.'

'Yeah. I'll have to go up with a survey team soon as I can. Get it on the map.'

'You're the boss, Mabel. Whatever you think's best.'

'Henry?'

'Like Joe says. Not sure about meetin' investors though. Toffs they are in my book and I is just a Cousin Jack. What they gonna think?'

'They'll like you. See you as honest. It's Cousin Jacks have made the mining business here. Just look at Captain Hancock – made more money for your English toffs than most anybody else.'

Joe heaves himself to his feet. 'Mabel, you got a dunny out the back? All them beers and now the whisky.'

'Down the hallway Joe, door at the end.'

'I've missed you Henry,' Mabel says once Joe has left the room.

'I missed you too. Couldn't think o' nuthin' else, specially at night.'

'Stay here with me tonight. We need to talk.'

'Joe won't like it.'

'Henry, he owes his life to you.' She crosses to his chair takes his hands in hers and pulls him to his feet. Looking up into his bearded face she whispers 'Kiss me Henry.'

He takes her head in both his hands bends down and presses his mouth to hers. 'I dreamed and dreamed o' doin' that.'

She smiles. 'Tell you what Henry, you go back now with Joe to the Colonel Light. I'll be there tonight till closing time. Then you can come back here with me. By then Joe will be too drunk to care.'

Henry lies back on the softest pillow he has ever known watching the way the crystals of the chandelier sparkle in the candlelight. He smiles. His life seems to have become a dream, a dream from which he never need awake. He is not drunk, he's happy. Mabel loves him. This she whispered to him earlier. They bathed together in the biggest tub he'd ever seen. She cut his beard and hair and dried him and kissed his naked body as no woman, no person even, had ever done before. And more than all of this, she is with child – his child. When she undressed, her back to him then turned, he caught his breath. The flat white belly he remembered was gently swollen now.

She laughed. 'No Henry, I've not got fat.' And coming to him naked she laid his hand below her navel. 'I'm going to have a baby – your baby, Big Henry from Wallaroo. What do you think of that?'

'Mabel, Mabel, I don't know. I don't understand – my baby? How? I never thought . . I mean you . . . did you make a mistake?'

She put her arms around him and pressed her body close. 'No mistake,' she whispered, 'I love you. Did you not know?'

'In my dreams may be. So last time we was together up there in Moonta, you?

'Yes, I let it happen, hoped it would. Are you happy, Henry?'

'I am. I ain't never been so happy.'

She looked up at him pushing him gently back towards the bed. 'Come. I have missed you.'

'Can we? Should we? With the baby an' all?'

She shook her head and chuckled. 'Of course, Henry, of course we can.'

He hears her now, bathing once again, singing quietly to herself. He smiles. What an evening he has had. First those hours in the Colonel Light, the bar jam packed with carousing men and women, he and Joe ensconced on high stools at one end of the bar, drinking less than they might have done had the place been less tumultuous. And such entertainment – first a circus strong man taking on all comers, then a woman acrobat in spangled top and stockings, twisting from a rope suspended over the drunken mob, swinging, turning, upside down with legs akimbo, and finally a tinny orchestra and couples dancing as best they could in the press of bodies all around. Amongst the mob were many well dressed men who throughout the evening came and went through a swinging door at the far end of the bar. And on the dot of eleven-o' clock a ringing bell and shouts of "Time, ladies and gents, time now please." as the clientele spilled out into the night, some singing, some still dancing and many too drunk to stand.

Joe got off his stool and said, 'You coming then?'

He shook his head.

'Mabel?'

'Yes, I'll be with her tonight.'

'Women and business – don't say I didn't warn you.'

She comes back to bed, lies down beside him and holds his hand. 'I've quit the game. Henry. Told Boddington to find someone new.'

He's silent for a while, just lying there, the feel of her against him, her perfumed body, her gentle breathing. 'You didn't have to just for me,' he says.

'I did – for you, for me and for the baby.' She leans across and kisses him. 'I've not been with another man since our last time in Moonta.'

'You didn't need the money?'

'I haven't done it for the money for quite some time. Business has been good to me. And now with a baby on the way, you back in my arms, a gold mine of our own. Lord, ain't we struck it rich, my lovely Cousin Jack.'

He laughs and holds her body close to his. 'Oh Mabel, my lovely tart.'

'Mr Charles, Mr Stanley, may I introduce Mr Joe Watson and Mr Henry Hopeful Down. These are the gentlemen I spoke to you about.'

Henry and Joe rise from their armchairs, cross the room and shake hands with the Englishmen who are both dressed in three piece suits, high stiff collars and carry bowler hats.

'Please sit down gentlemen. Coffee?'

They nod and all four take their seats around Mabel's polished table. She pours coffee from a silver jug into five china cups.

'Cigar, gents?' Mabel asks passing round a freshly opened box.

Henry shakes his head. The other three light up with elaborate ceremony, lean back and blow smoke towards the ceiling.

'Henry, would you do the honours?' Mabel says sitting down.

He looks at her. 'Honours?'

'Show them what we've found, Henry.'

'Right.' Henry lifts the Gladstone bag from beside his chair, places it on the table and takes out its contents one by one. Each jar of gold dust makes a gentle thud as he puts it down. Undoing the leather pouches he makes a single pile of gold watching the visitors' faces all the while. It dawns on him that both were amongst the many men he saw the night before sidle through the swinging door in the Colonel Light Hotel.

Mr Charles withdraws gold-rimmed pince-nez from his waistcoat pocket and perches them on the bridge of his nose. 'Very nice, very nice,' he says, leaning across the table until his long nose is only inches from the gold. 'I won't ask you where this pretty stuff is from, for I am sure you will not tell me. But, dear sirs, describe for me if you will, just how it lies – the disposition of the gold, if you get my meaning.'

Henry looks at Mabel who in turn looks at Joe, one eyebrow raised.

Joe Watson puffs on his cigar and blows a plume of smoke across the table. 'Disposition? Well, I s'pose you wanna know how much of this there is. That I can't really say 'cept that we got this lot in a few days working sand an' gravel beds along a creek that must be two or three mile long. We only worked a bit of it – maybe a coupla hundred yards. But that ain't all.' He takes another puff on his cigar and looks across at the Englishmen with a broad grin on his weathered face.

'There's more?'

'Certainly is, mate. The creek runs along the bottom of a hill and on the top we found the mother lode. Six foot wide she is and at least two hundred yards along.' He draws a rectangle in the air with his cigar and watches the smoke curling toward the ceiling.

'You have some samples?'

'Nah, 'fraid not. Yer see our camp got washed away in a flood so we had to get out. We was goin' to drill and blast it but we didn't get a chance. Bloody rain came down an' we nearly bloody drowned.'

'Then how did you know it was the mother lode, sir if you did not assay it for gold?'

'I don't need no assay. I was at Bendigo an' Ballarat. I knows gold when I sees it.'

'Yes, I suppose you do. You have a mineral lease?'

'We do.'

Mr Charles removes his pince-nez and rubs his bald head. Leaning back in his chair, he looks at his colleague who nods. He gives a little cough. 'Ah, Miss Mabel, Mr Stanley and I would like to have private chat. Is there somewhere we could go?'

'Of course. The dining room is just across the hall. Feel free.' Once they have left the room and the door is closed she turns to Joe and Henry. 'Did you see their faces when they saw the gold? They'll bite, just wait.'

And sure enough it's only minutes before the two men are back.

'Miss Mabel, gentlemen, we'd like to make you an offer,' Mr Stanley says. His voice is deep and gravelly. He pauses looks from face to face and says, 'But first, we need to know how long will it take for us to travel to your diggings and see them for ourselves – at our expense of course. Would it be a week or more perhaps?'

Joe and Henry look at each other and Joe holds up his unmaimed hand and counts off on his fingers, 'One, two, three, hmm, maybe four days. Yeah, four to get there, coupla days there and four to get back here. So ten days altogether if we take the train up north. Then we'd need a buggy for me and a cart for our gear. I can't ride. I broke me leg – see.' He stretches out his leg beside the table.

'Of course – whatever's needed. The trip will be entirely at our expense. We sail for London in a month so that will give us time. Now, we can offer you five hundred pounds in exchange for fourteen days to visit your diggings and decide whether or not we wish to buy your property. During that time you will not offer it to anybody else, nor even speak of it. Does that sound fair?'

Joe rubs his chin and looks at Mabel who smiles and shakes her head. 'No Mr Stanley, it does not. I know how these things are done. Joe and Henry are honest men. You can rely on what they say. They nearly lost their lives on this venture and they deserve your trust. You'll have to name your price today or we shall seek out other buyers. They are not in short supply as I'm sure you both must know. And do not forget, as I told you from the start, only half of our interest is up for sale.'

'Indeed Miss Mabel, indeed, quite.' He pauses puts both hands upon the table and looks at Mr Charles who nods. 'In that case we will pay one hundred thousand pounds for fifty one percent. That is our best offer. What say you?'

Mabel nods. 'Thank you, gentlemen. We shall talk it over and give you our reply tomorrow.'

'Thank you Miss Mabel. We shall take our leave. Until tomorrow then?'

'Luncheon at the Colonel Light?' Mabel says.

The Englishmen nod and get up from the table. They all shake hands.

As he is about to leave Mr Charles turns to Henry. 'I surmise you are from Cornwall, Mr Down.'

'I is. I is what they call a Cousin Jack in these parts.'

'You were a miner?'

'I is a miner still.'

'That gives me much reassurance, sir. Might I enquire where did you work?'

'At Penpillick, sir, the Wheal Emma Mine. With Capun Clymo.'

'Oh dear. A tragic tale, was it not?'

'What? What you sayin' sir?'

'Oh, I am sorry. Had you not heard? A dreadful accident. A shaft collapse or so I read in the London Mining Journal. Many miners lost and the mine closed down three months ago.'

'No, no. I doan believe it. Wheal Emma gone?'

'I am afraid so. I am truly sorry to be the bearer of such dreadful news.'

'An' Capun Clymo, Thomas Pascoe? What of them?'

'I heard that Captain Clymo is with us still although he has been ill for many months. Thomas Pascoe? I cannot say for sure. I don't recall his name amongst the dead. What I do know is that many miners and their families are leaving Cornwall. Perhaps they are amongst them.'

'Capun Clymo? Leave Cornwall? I doan see that.'

'Well, that's as maybe. What is more than certain is that things in Cornwall have gone from bad to worse. The price of copper is much fallen, not least because of the riches discovered here in South Australia and in the Americas. And tin from the Malays and Dutch East Indies swamps the market. These are the places we invest today, not poor Cornwall. Well, I wish you all good day.'

'Wheal Emma closed. I can't believe it. 'Twere the richest mine in all of Cornwall. And Capun Clymo – he'll be heartbroke.' Henry shakes his head and collapses in an armchair, head in his hands. 'That means that Thomas an' the family they'll be comin' back to Wallaroo. Maybe on the way already. Three month ago – how long do it take on one o' they steamships across the ocean then? Oh Lord what's Thomas goin' to say when he finds all his sheep are gone. I must go up there. I must go tomorrer.'

Mabel sits on the arm of Henry's chair and puts a hand on his shoulder. 'Henry love, tomorrow we must give our answer to the offer. Once that is settled we can decide what we can do about your Mr Pascoe and his station.'

He looks up at her. 'I doan know Mabel. I cain't think straight right now.'

Mabel goes to the dresser and once again pours out tots of whisky. 'Here Henry, this'll calm you down.'

Henry knocks it back in a single gulp and holds out his glass for more.

Mabel smiles. 'That's better eh?'

Joe sitting in the other chair rolls his eyes and says, 'Mabel, why didn't ya just say yes? We'll not get a better deal. An' they might change their minds before tomorrer.'

'They won't I'm sure of that. Did you not see their faces when they clapped eyes on all that gold? They want it Joe and they want it bad. I did not say yes there and then for two reasons. You and Henry own almost half and you must make your own decisions. Secondly if we had agreed today they would have thought they'd paid too much. Better leave them wondering, if only for a day.'

'But you're gonna say yes?'

'I am. Will you?'

'How much each we gonna get? I ain't that good at numbers.'

Mabel takes a sheet of paper and pen and ink from the dresser and sits once more at the table and begins to calculate. Looking up she says. 'If Mr Mole keeps his tenth and we three sell in proportion to our holdings, you will each get twenty four and half thousand pounds. My share will be fifty-one thousand pounds.'

'Lord,' Henry says.

'And being owners of a tenth each you will get one tenth of all the profits. Now what do you say?'

'Sounds okay to me. What d'ye say Henry?'

Henry scratches his head. 'If it's good enough for you and Mabel it's good enough for me.'

'So we're agreed?'

Joe nods. 'But tell us Mabel, how is it a lady like you knows how these things work?'

'"A lady like me?" Why don't you just say it, Joe – a madam, a keeper of a bawdy house?'

Joe shifts in his chair. 'Yeah well, I just wondered is all.'

'I'll tell you how. There's a lot of men in this town and more in Moonta and Wallaroo have got awful rich from mining. And rich men like nothing better than to tell a woman just how rich they are and just how cleverly they done it – you could call it pillow talk. And if a woman like me ever wants to leave the life, she's gotta be sharp and listen. I listened – that's how.'

'Yeah, it was pretty sharp of you to take half at the beginning.'

Mabel pours herself a tot of whisky and sips it looking at Joe over the rim of the glass. 'Joe, are you trying to pick a quarrel?'

'No, Mabel, no I ain't. It's just that . . . oh bloody 'ell. Henry, mate, are you all right with this?'

'I am. Why wouldn't I be?'

'No reason, mate. Right then, we say yes tomorrow and I'll take 'em up to Fish Hill on me own. You can go to Wallaroo an' sort out the Pascoe Station. Whatd'ya say I bring 'em back there an' we all meet up in a coupla weeks?'

'Good idea,' Mabel says. 'So we'll see you tomorrow at noon?'

'Er, yeah, right okay.' Joe gets up from his chair, hesitates before going to stand beside Henry and clapping him on the shoulder. 'Don't worry, mate. It'll all work out.'

Henry looks up at him and nods.

'I think Joe is a little jealous, Henry,' Mabel says as they hear the front door slam.

'Ee doan't need to be do ee?'

Mabel smiles as the unlikely trio of two bowler-hatted Englishmen and little, limping Joe leave the Colonel Light Hotel. 'I wish we could have gone with them Henry. It will be quite a trip. And I'd love to see the gold – to see your Fish Hill Mine with my own two eyes.'

'We coulda' gone with 'em if it weren't for that bugger Millington. Mind you if it weren't for him I wouldn't be with you. Nor would I 'ave gone a fossickin' for gold with Joe. Strange ain't it how good things come outa bad.'

'It is. My life was mostly bad till I met you.' She leans across the table and lays her hand on his. 'You do understand Henry, that between us, you and me will own a third even after those English coves buy in.'

Henry nods and sips his beer. 'Mabel I ain't thought too much about it since I heard about Wheal Emma. Me mind's stuck on Thomas Pascoe, his family an' maybe old Capun Clymo all goin to the Pascoe Station when there ain't nuthin there.'

She sits silent for a while, holding his hand and studying his face. 'Henry, we can fix that. We're going to be very rich and I've found that money fixes most things. I need a week or so here in Adelaide and then we'll take the train up north and see what's to be done. 'She gives a sudden start. 'Don't look now, Millington and your wife just walked in.'

'God, I should kill the bugger,' Henry growls.

'They're coming over. Stay calm now Henry.'

'Well well, won't you just look what the cat drug in.' Millington stands at their table, 'Ain't they a pretty pair?' he turns to Jane a step behind him.

She looks down at her feet and mutters 'Come on, Bob, let's get a drink.'

'What you done with Mr Pascoe's sheep?' Henry says.

'Oh hark at him. "Mr Pascoe's sheep." Oh dear, where have they gone? Little Bo Peep has lost his sheep. How would I know, you great oaf?'

'You thieving bastard,' Henry shouts, jumping to his feet and towering over them. He grabs Millington by the scruff of his neck and draws back his fist.

'Henry, Henry, no. Put him down.' Mabel grabs Henry's arm and pulls him away. 'Get out of here you two before I have you thrown out. You ain't welcome here.'

'Yes, Madam, whatever Madam wants.' Millington says and walks out, Henry's wife trailing behind him.

'Whyn't you let me hit 'im?'

'Violence never solved anything, Henry. Listen now. Lewis Madley is a friend of mine. I'll talk to him and get those two arrested. Sheep stealing's a serious crime and he could swing.'

'Who is Lewis Madley?'

'Police Commissioner.'

Henry looks at her and shakes his head. 'Seems like there ain't nobody who matters in this city you don't know is there?'

'No, Henry, not if they wear trousers. Now listen, if we're going to fix up your Mr Pascoe's station, we're going to have to buy some sheep. So I reckon we need to get down to the sale yards. You know enough about sheep to know what you're buying?'

'I do. We'd have to take on drovers to get 'em up there. But what we goin to pay for 'em with?'

'Henry love, we are rich and going to be even richer if what you and Joe said about Fish Hill is true.'

'Tis true all right.' He sighs. 'Well let's get to it then. Where be these sale yards?'

XXVI

HOMECOMING

ON A LATE SUMMER EVENING FOUR WEEKS AFTER the Wheal Emma mine disaster the families sit around the table in the dining room of Penpillick House. Plates are cleared away and the children are all abed. Mathew sits at one end, Thomas at the other with Grace and Maisie on his left and Emma and Michael on his right. A single candle burns in the middle of the table.

'So Thomas, what sentence did she get?' Grace Clymo asks.

'Ten years for attempted murder.'

'Judge was soft on her – taken in by all that weeping and wailing in the dock pretending repentance. She should've got life and been transported,' Mathew grumbles. He and Thomas are back from the assize where they were both called as witnesses at Mary Scoble's trial.

'Well, it's all over now, Capun. Besides there's no more convict ships to Australia these days.'

There is silence round the table at the word "Australia". Grace looks at Thomas and he stares down the table at his stepfather who stares back without a word. It is Maisie who finally speaks. 'I've told the children we are going back.'

'When?' Grace asks.

'As soon as I can book our passage.'

'Oh Thomas, must you go so soon?'

'There is nothing left for me to do here, Mother. I must get back to Wallaroo. Why don't you and the Captain come with us.' Thomas sighs as his stepfather leans back in his chair and folds his arms.

'Now tell me, why would I want to do that? Go the other side of the world, leave all this, this life I've made, my mine, my home, my family?'

'You know why Capun. We are your family, us and Emily and Michael here.'

'He's right, Papa. Now the mine is gone there's nothing for us here.

And Wheal Emma's not the only mine that's closed – they're shutting down all over.'

'Wheal Emma is not gone, not gone at all. She's right here under our very feet and when I've pumped her dry she'll be makin' our fortunes once again. Go back to Australia and your sheep, Thomas, if you must, but don't ask me to come with you. I'm staying right here in Penpillick.'

'Capun, Cornish Consols was losing money before the man engine collapsed, even with the arsenic. There's no point in opening her up again just to dig out mundic. We both know that.'

'Don't tell me what I know, boy. An' I'm sick of you carping on about the arsenic. Price today is better than it ever was. If we don't mine it others will, be sure of that.'

Thomas shakes his head and turns to Grace. 'Mother, what do you say? Would you not like to come with us and see Australia?'

Grace looks from her husband to her son and back again. She folds her arms. 'Mathew, it near broke my heart last time Thomas left. If Emily and Michael leave us too – it don't bear thinkin' about.' She shakes her head and lays her hand on Thomas's arm. 'We will come with you Thomas, all of us.'

Mathew Clymo bangs both fists upon the table and stands, 'Damn and blast. You all defy me. I'll not have it.' He turns away stamps from the room and slams the door behind him.

For a minute or two there is silence around the table. It's Michael McCarthy who breaks it. 'Ah, me father would be just the same. These old bulls they always want their way. Think they know the best.'

'He's a stubborn man is he not?' Thomas says shaking his head.

'That's always been his way,' Grace says. 'But I will talk with him.' She rises from her chair. 'Do not fear, he will come with us to Australia. Good night my children.'

As she closes the door behind her, Thomas looks around the table. 'Well,' he says, 'Tomorrow I shall go to Plymouth and book our passage on one of the new steamships. They are much faster than the clippers even – sixty days or less I'm told.'

'Oh Thomas, I am so excited. Are we come and live with you on your sheep farm?' Emily says.

'If you wish, Emma. There is work enough especially with Henry gone. But if Michael still wants to be a miner, they are crying out for men.'

'Could we ask me Da to come too? Bring the whole family. Times are hard with so many mines round Camborne and Redruth all shuttin' down.'

'I do not see why not, Michael. There's room for all in Australia and passages are cheap.'

'Ah that would be wonderful, sir. Just imagine – all of us together in Australia. Who woulda' thought it?'

'Thomas,' Maisie says, 'What about Henry? Do you really think he would have abandoned Wallaroo as Middleton has said?'

'I do not know, Maisie. It could well be if he has taken to the drink. He always liked a glass of cider. But I will send telegrams to Adelaide and Wallaroo poste restante telling him we are coming back. Who knows perhaps he'll meet us off the ship.'

She lies beside him staring at the ceiling. 'Mathew my lover, I know you are not sleeping. Come now, we must talk.'

Mathew grunts and turns his back to her.

'Husband, do not be foolish. Thomas is right. You know he is.'

'I know no such thing.'

'You said yourself if he cannot find more riches underground then no one can.'

'I do not need more riches underground. There is plenty left. I just need to pump the water out and repair the damage in the shaft.' Rolling out of bed, he crosses to the window and watches the setting sun. 'Then get back to mining.'

Grace sighs and shakes her head. He is not yet his former self, perhaps he never will be. Shadowed against the sunlit window she sees the outline of his emaciated body through the thin stuff of his nightgown. 'Mathew, you nearly died. If it were not for Thomas I would have lost you. Will you not heed his advice? And how can you think of mining mundic? That awful stuff was near the death of you.'

He comes and stands beside the bed and takes her hand. 'Grace, what shall I do out there in Australia? Grow old in a rocking chair?' And

229

what of James, our son? Shall he come too?'

'James has made his life in London. We barely see him as it is but perhaps he will want to come.' She draws him down to sit beside her on the bed. 'Please come with us Mathew, for if you do not I shall go without you. I could not bear to lose Thomas and his family once again. Nor can I bear to lose you.'

He lays his head on her shoulder. 'I will come Grace. I will come.'

She rests her head against the glass of the half open window watching the countryside flash by. How strange it is, how different. On board ship and listening to her son's exuberant depictions of life in South Australia, she tried to imagine how it would be – hot he said and sunshine every day and endless pastures and blue hills in the distance and animals stranger than anything in a childhood bestiary. And so it is but more so – the distances so great it seems to her that this land is but a continuance of the endless ocean they have taken weeks to cross. Leaving home for the first and only time in her life, she did her best to hide not just her terror at the thought of life at sea, but a deep and constant apprehension of the unknown she would face once here in South Australia. But she need not have been concerned – life on board the SS Orient was comfortable to a degree even though Thomas thought it wise that being so large a family they would travel second class. In fact she enjoyed five weeks at sea as, for the first time in her life, having neither work nor duties to occupy her time, she entertained herself with socialising and enjoyment of the recreations and amusements the ship provided. And after but three days on Australian soil she feels at ease – the people look and sound familiar, food and drink is much the same although she wonders if there's any other meat than mutton. But she is so far, so very far from home – the home she will never see again. She watches the passing of wide and treeless pastures and vast grey-green plains of bushes she knows not how to name, all under a cloudless sky, the bluest she has ever seen. Yet she hears her home, surrounded as she is by the voices of her family, her son her daughter, Maisie and her grandchildren mingling with the Irish accents of the

McCarthy family. And by her side sits Jenny Tuttle, her lifelong friend. Even Mathew begins to take an interest . For days and days across the grey Atlantic, he sat on deck glum and silent gazing at the waves. She recalls the sight of him leaning on the stern rail, staring at the green receding hills of Cornwall, his shoulders hunched. She recalls too her sense of his deep sorrow, her knowledge of what he had lost and what he mourned. And of course the children – their excitement knows no bounds and that gives her joy, 'Look look,' they cry, standing on the seats, heads hanging out the window, eyes red with streaming smut.

They change trains at a place called Balaklava all piling out of the carriage along with their trunks and boxes and leather suitcases and this is less than half their baggage the rest to follow on a goods train. Grace remembers watching the cart piled high with crates of crockery and linen, and household goods, her home entire, trundle down the track from Penpillick House on the start of its journey to this, the far side of the world. And now they are nearly there, or so Thomas says – their destination Wallaroo is now but two hours away. They sit on wooden benches in a stifling waiting room then all decide it's cooler on the platform or outside in the street, where a fitful breeze stirs up the dusty. Perspiring in her pleated travelling dress she thinks that on the morrow in the hope of keeping cooler she will not wear her woollen undergarments. But Thomas says it cools at night on the Pascoe Station.

It is dusk by the time the little train huffs and puffs its way into the crowded station at Wallaroo.

'We have rooms at the Globe Hotel,' Thomas tells a porter as they all alight, 'Could you see to it that all our luggage is delivered.'

'I will indeed, sir. Welcome back.'

Thomas nods and smiles at being recognised. Heads turn as the Pascoe, Clymo and McCarthy families walk down the main street in a gaggle towards the smelter and the docks where the sun sets deep red through the smelter smoke. Suddenly, in spite of the evening's warmth and the warbling calls of unfamiliar birds, Grace feels echoes of her home. The smoke has that old familiar sulphurous stink and the accents of many of the townsfolk are Cornish. The buildings are half-familiar too, stone built miners' cottages but with verandas and corrugated iron roofs instead of slate, a great stone church whose shape and gothic windows echo a Cornish chapel and miners and smelter workers homeward bound dressed in shirtsleeves just as they would be on a hot summer's day at home.

'Here we are,' Thomas says and ushers them through the wide front doors of the Globe Hotel where they take four rooms just for the night.

Next morning excitement is at fever pitch when a cavalcade of carts and buggies line up at dawn outside the Globe and the families take their places, Thomas, Mathew and the two McCarthy men in the leading buggy, the women folk in an open carriage and all the children perched on the luggage carts, following up behind.

'Thomas, why did they seemed surprised in the bar last night when we said we were going to the Pascoe Station?' Mathew Clymo asks as Thomas flicks his whip and they set off northward out of Wallaroo.

'I don't know. Struck me as odd that they were all so close mouthed when I asked about my foreman Millington. The landlady said he hadn't been in town for quite some while, which I think is somewhat strange. She gave me the telegram I sent to Henry still unopened so it must be true that he has left the district. But anyway an hour or two and we'll be home.' Thomas is much more concerned than he appears. People he knew from two years back would not meet his eye and changed the subject when he enquired after the price of wool or how the grazing was, or in fact anything to do with sheep. He is worried too that Millington has not seen fit to meet them in the town as he requested in the telegram he sent from Plymouth. What is worse, it seems that many days have passed since any traffic came this way. The dusty track ahead is unmarked by wheel, or hoof or footprint. He shrugs and takes a deep breath – the air is sweet, clean and warm and he is happy to be back here – happy to have left so far behind the chaos and the misery, the dispossession of Penpillick and Wheal Emma, the loss of life and the knowledge of the water rising in the shaft. He cocks his head listening for the sound of sheep but all he hears is the creaking of wheels and the shouts and laughter of the children. It is not until they reach the boundary of the Pascoe lands that a dawning sense of dread takes full possession of his mind. The wooden gate hangs open, fence wires sag and rattle in the breeze and he knows that something serious is amiss. He does not, dare not, speak, cannot admit to what he already knows – the Pascoe Station is abandoned. Riding on in silence, he gazes across his empty lands. There are no sheep. As the homestead hoves into view, a sombre silence descends upon the company as even the children cease their chatter and their laughter. Thomas draws the buggy to a stop outside the homestead, steps down and looks around. No smoke rises from the kitchen chimney, doors and windows stand ajar and the place is silent save for the rustle of the breeze in the eucalyptus trees behind the house.

'What now Thomas?' Mathew Clymo says still seated in the buggy. 'Where are the sheep?'

Thomas fights back the tears, he cannot answer, he is close to throwing up.

'Thomas, Thomas, what has happened? Where is Mr Millington and Jane?' Maisie is at his side clutching at his arm.

'I do not, I do not know,' he stutters looking down at her. 'What are we to do? I have brought you all so far to this.' He puts both hands to his head pushing back his hat. 'We have been robbed, all our sheep, all gone. How, why? Oh Lord, I do not know.'

The company sits silent staring at the desolation until big Col McCarthy gets down from the buggy and stands at Thomas's and Maisie's side. 'This land we've crossed – 'tis all yours still, is it not?'

Thomas nods. 'Yes,' he whispers. 'Yes it must be.'

'And the houses and the barns?'

Thomas nods again.

'Then I suggest we get to work. There's plenty of us, children too. Won't be the first time I've started with next to nothin'. Come on folks, get down now, start unloadin' We'll all be needin' food and drink and beds to sleep in before this day is out.'

XXVII

REUNION

'HOW MANY SHEEP TO GET YOU STARTED UP AGAIN, Thomas?' Mathew Clymo asks.

'A hundred ewes is all I can afford.' He sniffs in disgust. 'We had ten thousand when we left. I cannot believe what Millington has done. The constable says he left some months ago on my instructions – the lying dog. 'Twill take us years to build up the flock again. I'll have to go back to Adelaide. There's no sheep for sale here in Wallaroo.'

Thomas Pascoe, Mathew Clymo and the McCarthys father and son take their dinner at the Globe Hotel. After a week of work repairing houses, barns and fences, hanging gates and settling their families at the Pascoe Station, they have come to town for more supplies and in the hope of buying sheep.

'I could send for funds from home,' Mathew says. 'The funds I would have spent on bringing Wheal Emma back to life – if I'd stayed, if I weren't here.' He looks around the bar. 'Most o' these are mining folk are they not?'

'Mostly, though some are Welshmen from the smelter. The mine is closed for now but they say that Moonta still cuts it rich.'

'Michael and meself thought we might go down there this afternoon, get ourselves some work. You say it's but ten mile away.' Col McCarthy forks a potato into his mouth.

'It is. Look for Capun Hancock. He's a Devon man. He'll see you right. And thank you both for all you've done for me. Without you, I don't know what I'd have done.'

'Thomas, I am glad to be out of England. There was nuthin' for us there.'

They look across the bar as a great shout of laughter comes from the table in the corner where two well dressed gentlemen are carousing with a stumpy little bushman. One of the gentlemen shouts out, 'Barman, more champagne over here, if you please.'

'London toffs,' Mathew mutters and turns back to his mutton stew.

They finish their meal in silence and are about to get up and leave when Col McCarthy nods towards the door and says, 'Well there's money in this town for sure. Just look at them two. Ain't she just a picture? Did yer ever see the like? Such a beauty wid' a great big fellah like him?'

They all turn to look at the couple standing in the doorway silhouetted against the midday sunshine. She is dressed in the height of fashion – a lilac dress and matching ribboned bonnet, and has her arm on his. He wears a smart black morning coat and well tailored trousers and collar and tie.

'By God, that's Henry Hopeful Down or I'm a Dutchman,' Mathew says. 'Ain't it Thomas? Ain't it? What have they done to him?'

Thomas spins round in his chair, jumps to his feet and strides across the bar. 'Henry, Henry, is it really you?'

A slow smile lights up Henry's face. 'Thomas,' he says 'Thomas Pascoe,' and steps forward hand outstretched.

They are silent looking at each other, shaking hands. Thomas is the first to speak. 'My, my Henry, that villain Millington wrote that you were down and out but it looks like you found a gold mine.'

Henry laughs out loud. 'I did, I did, or we did, Thomas. This here's my friend Mabel. She grubstaked us and over there is my mate and partner Joe Watson. Mabel this is Mr Thomas Pascoe and there behind is Capun Clymo all the way from Penpillick. Capun how many years, how many years.' The tears are running freely down his face. 'Oh Lord Thomas, we been through such times you won't believe. I lost all your sheep. I'm so sorry. But Thomas they're a comin' back – five hundred on the train tomorrer. An' many more as soon as we can get 'em up here. Ah, Thomas, I'm so pleased to see you though I were dreading it before.' He stands there pumping Thomas Pascoe's hand.

'Henry love shall we not sit down – look here is Joe. And Mr Charles and Mr Stanley over there – looks like they're celebrating.' Mabel ushers him into the middle of the bar where Henry does not know which way to turn.

'Damned right we celebratin' Mabel. Henry, Henry, I got such news.'

Joe Watson grabs his arm and stands there looking up at him. 'Fish Hill – it's bigger, much bigger than we thought.' He nods towards the Londoners and with lowered voice says, 'They love it, mate. They'll do the deal. Mabel, Henry, we is rich, we is richer than we ever thought – the Fish Hill Mine, Jeez Henry.' The little man is almost skipping.

Henry wipes his eyes. 'Thomas, Capun Clymo, this is my mate, my partner Joe Watson. Me an' him went a fossickin' an' found a gold mine.'

'My word Henry Hopeful Down, did you now? So that's why you're dressed up to the nines.' Mathew Clymo shakes Joe Watson's hand.

'Miss Mabel, gentlemen, if I might interrupt?' Mr Charles stands before them pince nez perched on his nose, sweat beading on his hairless pate. 'I could not help but overhear. Captain Clymo of Cornish Consols fame? And Mr Thomas Pascoe, finder of the Pascoe Lode if I'm not mistaken. My friend James Sanderson in London often speaks of both of you and fulsomely. I was so sorry to hear of the tragedy at Wheal Emma, my profoundest sympathies. But how well met to find two such famous Cornish miners here in this outpost of Empire. And these gentlemen?' He looks at the McCarthys who have joined the group standing in the middle of the bar.

'Col McCarthy at your service, sir. Well you might say me an' Michael are Cornish miners too though in fact we're Irish and proud to be so.'

'Excellent, excellent. And something of a happy reunion here is it not? Might I be so bold as to suggest we join our forces?' He does not wait for their assent but shouts, 'I say, barman bring up chairs and tables over here and more champagne.' Once everyone is seated, leaning forward in his chair he looks around them all and says, 'Miss Mabel, Joe, Mr Down and Captain Clymo, gentlemen.' He pauses, sips his champagne and they too all lean forward, for he speaks just loud enough for only them to hear. 'My colleague Mr Stanley and I, we came to South Australia to invest in mining. We are delighted with what we found, or should I say what gallant Joe and Henry found on the far side of the Flinders – a gold mine which we believe could prove far richer even than our present expectations. But, Miss Mabel, gentlemen, we